REA

TO LOVE AND LET GO

by

Grace Morrison

Pillar Press
636 Tarryton Isle
Alameda, CA 94501

The author gratefully acknowledges permission to quote from the following: "On Children," from **The Prophet**, by Kahlil Gibran; copyright 1923 and renewed 1951 by Administrator C.T.A. of Kahlil Gibran estate and Mary G. Gibran; published by Alfred A. Knopf, Inc. "I Wish You Were Here," words and music by Malvina Reynolds; copyright 1962 by Schroder Music Co., Berkeley, California.

Cover design by Carolyn L. Ryan

Library of Congress Catalog Number:
83-061412

International Standard Book Number:
09611190-1-2

FOR caring men and women anywhere who might, just might, consider offering love to children whom they will one day have to let go.

FOREWORD

This book had to be written. I kept hoping someone else might do it, but no one did. That bothered me.

Our national press does offer beginnings of the story. In 1981, *US News and World Report* writes of a 21% rise nationwide in child abuse. The following year, Senator Daniel Patrick Moynihan of New York quotes a study in his *New Republic* feature article. That study found that one-third of America's children are undernourished. *Newsweek,* October, 1982, and *Life,* July, 1983, both report that every year more than one million American children between the ages of ten and seventeen run away, many fleeing not only neglect, but physical, often sexual, assault. The neglect and the abuse often both derive from their parents' economic problems.

Such suffering is unconscionable in a country as wealthy as yours and mine.

Where are these children? Some are left on the streets hiding and growing irretrievably hardened. A few, rescued from abusive homes or from the streets, are kept out of sight, usually in some protective institution. A tiny percentage, the luckiest, go to foster homes.

O.K. So, what can *I* do about these things? What can any single person, or couple, or family do?

No big thing. We might make a beginning by opening up our minds a little. Our hearts a little. Our homes a lot more.

I often meet people who tell me how much they wish they had children in their homes, but they can't afford them. Or, they're not sure they were cut out for parenthood. Or, they are too old or too young to cope with children.

We hadn't any money in the bank when we began foster parenting. And I don't know if anyone is "cut out for parenthood" no matter how old he or she might be. Like most parents, you just do the best you can.

I do know, though, that the happiest, most productive and growth-filled years for me and for my family were the years in which we "borrowed" other people's children. Many foster parents tell me that the same was true for them.

Nevertheless, the concept of foster parenting is strange to most people. Maybe it could help if I told it just like it was for us. I think we're typical foster parents, whatever "typical" means. We made mistakes. We did poorly and well. Like anybody.

Events described in this book derive from actual happenings. Scenes have been reconstructed as I remember them, or as they were described to me. Correspondence included is essentially as it was written. Of course, names have been changed, and, in some cases, the story has been simplified by having two or three adults written as a single persona. Many people helped make our family happen — too many to include them all.

And many people helped this book happen: Clarence Cunningham, retired Superintendent at Contra Costa County Juvenile Hall; Martina Jussel, Supervisor of Foster Home Licensing, Alameda County, California; Dr. Marianne Leppmann, Department of Pediatrics, Kaiser Foundation Hospital, Oakland; Violet Smith, Director of Contra Costa County Crisis and Suicide Intervention; and Claire Barry, Alameda Unified School District. Each of these read all or parts of the manuscript-in-process and offered much appreciated suggestions and criticisms.

Most of all, I would be extremely remiss if I did not thank my husband. Without his abundance of love, steadying intelligence, and natural generosity, neither this book nor what is recorded in it *could* have happened.

-G.M.

"They are the sons and daughters of Life's longing for itself. . . ."

1

RENA

Sunlight entering the room gave it a warm and almost cheery atmosphere. On the long horseshoe shaped table, flowers had been placed for decoration. Food was set, smorgasbord fashion, on a side table so all the children could help themselves to any of the steaming dishes that had been prepared for lunch. It could have been the employees' cafeteria of a small business. Or, perhaps the dining room of a boarding school. My place at the table had been set next to the assistant superintendent, Ted McKay, and across from the child I had come to see — although she had no knowledge of my purpose.

Ted McKay and I seated ourselves. Immediately we could hear children moving down the hall. They seemed quieter than most children their age, but not silent. On they came; walking, skipping, or jumping down the hall in an easy fashion, occasionally calling to others further ahead or behind them in line.

They stepped to their places without wasting time.

Two things marred the scene of carefree adolescence: the locking of each door by the juvenile hall wardens after the line of children had passed through, and the children's uniforms.

The youngsters from each table took turns helping themselves to lunch, but the adults present were served. Rena had been assigned to serve me. I tried not to stare at her.

She could have been beautiful. Her skin was unusually pale and unblemished. Her hair, "stacked" in the unflattering style of her sub-culture, was a shining light blonde. She was quite tall for her fourteen years, and her body was so well developed that she could easily have passed for three or four years older. What most struck me were her eyes. They were large and a very light blue. They had the look of eyes accustomed to tears. She kept them down when she didn't need them for her tasks. It was the sadness of her eyes which brought out everything maternal in me.

But her voice! That almost broke the spell. It was hard and loud, and the rural Arkansas accent made her words practically unintelligible to me.

Seeing her then, it was difficult to believe that this girl could have been as violently destructive as Ted McKay had told me she was.

"Why don't you take our guest on a tour of the hall, Rena?" Ted was saying. "I'm sure you could show her things and tell her much better than I about what we do here."

"Ain't y' comin'?" she asked him with mild surprise.

"No," he replied. "I'm sorry, I can't. I have to get back to my office. But you go on ahead."

The girl seemed pleased to have this break from her usual routine and energetically led me to the door where she waited for the assistant superintendent to unlock and open it. He locked it behind him, then walked with us down the long hall to the Girls' Division where again the unlocking, passing through and locking ritual was observed. Rena smiled with the good nature of a real estate agent showing an overpriced mansion. "Come on," she said. "Over here they'll be folk dancin' in a few minutes."

We didn't wait for the folk dancing. When I told her that my husband and I taught school, she took me directly to the classroom where she showed me the frog she recently had dissected. Next, Rena hurried me to the recreation area and the television room. These still were decorated for Christmas, although the holiday was two months past. The girls were so proud of their gaudy handiwork that they could not bear to take it down. Huge bells and loops of silver paper hung over three cots that were temporarily stationed in the television room to alleviate overcrowded conditions at the hall.

Rena's bright hostess performance slipped only once — when I asked to see her bedroom.

"I can't," she said, suddenly becoming sullen.

Later I told Ted McKay, "You were right. Absolutely right. I can't explain why, but I am just crazy about her."

"What about that little boy you wanted for Steve to play with?" His tone was teasing. I had been insistent that a teenaged delinquent girl was the last thing we had in mind for our first foster home experience. My friend, Ted, had told me, "Just come and meet her. She won't have to know why you're there. I've been meaning to invite you over to the hall anyway."

So I had come — with misgivings. And I fell in love with Rena.

I asked Ted, "Why couldn't she show me her room? She showed me the other girls' bedrooms."

"She was embarrassed. Her room is absolutely bare. If we give her a cot, she unscrews all the hardware. If we give her curtains, a mattress, or even a blanket, she rips them to shreds."

"You mean she sleeps on the bare floor?"

"What else can we do? Some nights when it's been especially cold, I've worried about her. Once I drove all the way back to the hall from home, got her a blanket from the linen supplies, and brought it in to where she was shivering on the floor. She didn't even wait until I began to talk to her before she was tearing it apart."

I thought about my own blankets and furniture. They were old. We called them "hand-me-down modern." There was nothing in our house that we would mind losing except our very precious Steven, our only child, now almost eight years old. We liked to tell ourselves we were getting a companion for him; but a companion like Rena?

"I'll have to convince my husband, of course," I told Ted. "And frankly, there is one thing I'm worried about."

"What's that?" The growing tension on his face betrayed the deep concern he felt for Rena. She had been at the hall for more than three hundred days, but as yet, there was little they could do for her.

"I'm worried about Stevie's safety."

The lines on his face grew perceptibly deeper. "You're right. Of course you have to consider him. Would you like to talk to Rena's psychiatrist? I think I can arrange it while you are still in town."

Ted explained that Rena's violence had been so irrational, so apparently unrelated to the facts of her environment, that her probation officer had arranged for visits to a psychiatrist once a week.

The psychiatrist was an ethical man. He refused to say anything about his patient to anyone before first securing Rena's permission. I had to wait for another day.

I found Bill, my husband, easier to convince than I expected. True, he had been thinking in terms of a little boy just a year or two younger than Steve. But I seemed so positive, he felt it must be right. His only hesitation was, like mine, concern for our son's safety.

It was fortunate that Bill tentatively agreed to take Rena. Ted told me that that night, one of the counselors at Juvenile Hall let our secret slip.

"Well, Rena, how did you like your new foster mother?" she asked.

"My *what?*"

"They tell me your new foster mother came to see you today."

"Nobody came to see me. Nobody's allowed to."

"But Mr. McKay told me . . . ."

"*Her?* Her! You mean that lady? She wants me? Really?"

The counselor laughed and assured Rena that of course I wanted her. Anyone would once she had gotten to know her.

Rena's joy was unbounded. She ran into the television room to tell the other girls.

"Did you hear that? I've got a foster home! I met the lady. She's real nice, even if she did used to teach school. And she's not old at all. I bet she's got a real big place. Remember? She was at lunch today!"

The girls shared Rena's joy. A magnanimous mood swept over her, and that night Rena could not do enough for the counselors, the girls, or even for Juvenile Hall, itself. When the time came to go to her "bed," Rena could not sleep. She sat down on her floor, pulled her legs up tight to her chest, and stared out the high, barred window for several hours.

Rena willingly gave her permission to her psychiatrist to tell us anything he wished. She especially asked that he tell us she smoked — cigarettes. (Thank God, nothing stronger.)

Our visit to the psychiatrist was reassuring. Dr. Blake's young, serious face gazed directly at us, giving the uncomfortable impression that he was studying and analyzing us as we talked. He seemed relieved that our first question dealt with a concrete interest in the future rather than value judgments about the past.

"No," he assured us without hesitation. "Your son is in no danger. Rena has been violent, that is true, but her violence has always been directed toward things — never toward people."

"But, how can you be sure that won't change?" Bill prodded.

"I can't, of course. But I have rarely met any young person who so sincerely loved people, especially children. Her main frustration now is that the authorities will not permit her to go back home and take over the care of her younger siblings. Your son should be showered with her transfer of this affection."

"Then, why won't they permit her to go home?"

"Well, as I understand it, it's primarily because she would most likely run away again. For some children, running away becomes a habit — a way of dealing with any kind of difficult situation."

We felt that we were prying, but if we were going to be able to help Rena, we needed to know as much as we could about her. Bill asked, "What kind of difficult situation did she run away from? We were told that she only ran away to keep a girlfriend company."

"That's the story Rena tells, but of course there's more to it than that. Actually, she has run away twice. The first time was just over two years ago when she was only twelve. Her family decided it was time for her to get married. They picked out a local farm worker for Rena and managed to get her as far as the altar. But no sooner had the minister asked the usual question, than Rena replied, 'I won't!' and ran out of the church, not stopping until she was well out of the county. It took them weeks to find her."

I told myself I had better expect theatrics if I were going to live with this girl.

"Was the second runaway that dramatic?" I asked.

"No, although she probably felt somewhat heroic going along to help her friend. My own opinion is that within herself she realized the hopelessness of her situation. Rena had complete charge of her house, her younger brother and sisters, the cooking -- everything. When a note arrived from one of the children's teachers, Rena went to talk to the teacher. She paid the electric and water bills each month. She literally had little time left for school or for herself."

"I thought she lived with her mother."

The psychiatrist smiled one of his rare smiles. "Yes."

He didn't elaborate, but I gathered he thought me naive for thinking that parents naturally manage all households.

"But why is she so violent? Mr. McKay tells us that Rena removes doors from their hinges and plumbing from its installation."

"Rena ran away to be free. The result, both times, was that she was locked up. Since her hands are unusually strong, violence is the way she demonstrates her frustration. I don't think you'll find her destructive once she is living with you."

I felt even more concerned now than I had before. "It seems to me that a foster home may be just another kind of prison."

"No, I don't think so. I believe that in a real home Rena will be free for the first time in her life."

Dr. Blake volunteered little information, although he answered fully all the questions we asked. He seemed to be as anxious as Ted McKay to get Rena out of "Juvie" and into a home. He waited until we were completely reassured to warn us, however, that her ignorance of men might lead her to a "crush" on my husband, Bill. But as he probably knew, by the time he told us that nothing would deter us.

Rena arrived at our home around dinner time one day late in February. Her few belongings were in a cardboard grocery carton. Ordinarily, the county moved more slowly in placing a child in a foster home, allowing her first to come for dinner, later for a weekend, and then encouraging all parties concerned to reconsider for about a week. But we were all so sure that this arrangement was what we wanted that the usual trial period was by-passed. Rena had waited long enough.

Her room was ten by ten feet, and furnished with unmatching single bed, desk, chair, nightstand, and a chest of drawers. The room needed painting, but we felt that the colors ought to be of Rena's choosing. To her, the room seemed large and beautiful, as was the rest of our house which was officially described on our tax bill as a "cottage." She marveled at our many books and did not seem disappointed at our lack of a television set. She told us that she did not like television.

Dinner was a stiff affair. I tried to keep the conversation flowing.

"Did you know we have a hundred dollar money order to spend on clothes for you, Rena?"

"A hundred dollars! But they gave me clothes before I left the hall."

"Sure. But now we can buy you some more things. What do you need?"

"Nothin'."

"Nothing? Don't you like new clothes?"

"Yeah, but not yet. Didn't you notice how fat I am? We don't do too much at Juvie 'cept eat and sleep. So, everybody gets fat. It'll go 'way now, though."

Miss West, Dena's probation officer, recommended waiting a week or two before registering her at the local junior high school so that Rena might settle in. That meant that Rena would be with me wherever I went. I determined to try to do some things that might interest her. Remembering the Christmas decorations in the Juvenile Hall television room, I suggested that we plan a party for Stevie's coming birthday. Delighted, Rena said, "I know; we'll make it a cowboy party! C'n I make the decorations?"

It proved an ideal way for Rena to break into her new family. With black and gray construction paper, she made each guest a cowboy hat. She made candy cups that looked like tiny boots. On the walls she pinned replicas of ropes, six-shooters and carefully drawn horses. On the front door she pinned large letters spelling HOWdy PArdNEr. She invented several games with western themes, making sure that every young guest would go home with some small prize.

It was Rena's party, although given in Steve's honor,

and it was a complete success. Enchanted and proud, Steven introduced the tall, pale teenager as "my new sister" to his wide-eyed friends.

Two young neighbors, a brother and sister, went home to ask their mother, "Why don't you get *us* a teenager like Steve's mother got for him?"

Whenever possible, we took Steven with us wherever we went. Naturally, we expected to do the same with this girl who so quickly called us Mom and Dad.

"Rena, how would you like to go to a play?"

"A what?"

"A play. You've heard of a play, haven't you?"

"Is that a kind of game?"

"Well, in a way, I guess." I had never tried to define a play before. I assumed everyone knew what the word meant. "It's a story," I explained, "like on television or in the movies. The difference is that it has real people in it."

"Aren't they real people on television?"

"Well, yes. They are actors — or rather, pictures of actors."

She frowned.

"Try it this way, honey. Some university students will get on a stage and pretend to be different people in order to tell you a story. Why, what's the matter, Rena?"

"I don't know what you mean." Her tone was desperate. "I know what 'students' are, but not the kind you said. And what are they doin' in a rocket?"

"University students go to a university. That's where you go when you finish high school."

"*After* you finish high school! What f'r?"

"To learn more. There's always more to learn."

"So these kids is learnin' about rockets?"

Neither of us liked the shape the conversation was taking. It was as important to me as to Rena that she should not appear foolish.

"I seen rockets on TV before. They was flyin' around the world real high. And they had things they called stages. I seen it!"

It was also not clear to her that the people on some television shows were real people being themselves and some were actors pretending to be someone they were not. I understand that many adults maintain this confusion, sending birthday cakes to soap opera heroines and lavishing other attentions on actors they confuse with their fictional portrayals; but until then I had never personally encountered so many confusions in one human being.

Many of our conversations dealt with things I thought "everyone knew." I tried to keep such discussions matter-of-fact, and Rena tried her best not to appear "too stupid." She was interested in everything and determined to fit into her new family.

The trip across San Francisco Bay was a thrill for Rena. She had never been in a car going across a long bridge before. She bombarded us with questions such as how the bridge was held up, how long it was, what would happen if it fell down, and how ships dared sail under it. To her it was excitingly dangerous. She held her head out of the car window, holding onto her hair with both hands to keep it from blowing out of shape. Steven watched her with awe.

The sight of the university auditorium caused her face to freeze again. Rena was afraid of crowds. That danger was not the roller-coaster kind she felt on a bridge, but a more intangible threat that she could not deal with. We got to our seats as quickly as possible, seating Rena between Bill and myself. We tried to focus her attention on the printed program.

The play was Lorca's grim *House of Bernarda Alba*. Rena watched in growing fascination as the character-sisters were stifled together in their forced eight years of mourning under the watchful eye of a domineering and dehumanized mother. They all wore black. There were a few light touches, but no comedy relief.

During the intermission Bill whispered to me, "What a terrible choice for a first play!"

But Rena loved it. Lorca might have been writing about her: how it felt to be locked up, forced to wear a uniform, and never go anywhere or do anything that was fun. The society that crushed the life out of the characters on the stage was, for Rena, the same society that tried to crush the life out of her.

In the play, one of Bernarda Alba's daughters rebels. She dares to put on a red petticoat and run away to a life of forbidden freedom. Rena understood that girl very well. True, the rebel died. O.K. She was still right. One has to fight and fight and continue fighting when she is in a prison — or Juvenile Hall — or a house like Bernarda Alba's. It's better to be dead than not to fight for life.

During the intermissions, there was no point in talking to Rena. She was in a trance. Even after the show she seemed unwilling or unable to move out into the crush of humanity leaving the university theater.

In the car she was quiet for a long time, then she said, "Mom, those people on the stage. They was goin' to school?"

"That's right, honey. I don't think any of them is more than twenty-two years old or so."

"An' y' hafta finish up high school before y' c'n go to that school?"

"That's right."

"Mom, I'm ready to go back to school now. Take me there on Monday."

The local junior high school prided itself on being college preparatory and was unprepared for a girl like Rena. We enrolled her in the ninth grade, but there were few courses she was prepared to take. Rena could only read at about third grade level, and her other academic skills were not much better.

The counselor assigned to Rena had been a juvenile probation officer for several years before becoming a school counselor, so he understood the needs of a girl from Juvenile Hall. He carefully chose her teachers for their patience, insight, and probable willingness to launch a major remedial program for one student. He made it a point to talk to each one privately about her as soon as possible.

The first day in school, Rena was extremely tense. She knew it was against the school rules to smoke, so she took along several packages of chewing gum to compensate. She did not know that chewing gum was also not allowed in most classes. In her art class, the teacher told Rena to take the gum out of her mouth, put it on her nose, and sit on a stool facing the other students. She walked out, and spent the remainder of the period in her counselor's office.

The next day she was back in her art class with everything explained and forgiven.

One of the most difficult things for Rena to face was the surge of young bodies in the halls between periods. Even at Juvenile Hall she rarely had been in a situation for very long in which so many people were together under such crowded conditions. She did everything she could to leave each class late. Her teachers understood this fear, and one of them gave her a permanent "tardy pass."

Disagreements with teachers occurred regularly, but her counselor knew when to let her talk it out, when to discuss the matter at some length with the teacher involved, and when to tell Rena that she, herself, was the problem and why.

Rena precipitated problems when she knew an exam was due. Tests frightened her more than the crowds in the halls. One math teacher told me she once watched in horror as Rena took the sharp end of a compass and jabbed it deep into her own right hand so that her painful condition would excuse her from the dreaded ordeal of an exam.

Rena's English teacher quickly diagnosed her problems in reading as primarily optometric. The county, that pays all foster children's medical bills, supplied her with the needed glasses. Rena hated the way she looked in them, but wore the glasses with good grace to school and for study.

Since she was allowed to smoke only at home, and not allowed chewing gum at school, Rena began to chew her fingernails. She bit them down so far that the tips of her fingers were sore. This interfered with her typing class. We decided not to make an issue of the fingernail biting yet. She was dealing with enough problems and challenges.

Our city had a Children's Theater Guild that presented four inexpensive plays a year on Saturdays for children of elementary school age. When Steven brought home the announcement of the year's offerings, Rena's interest caught fire at once.

"But, you can't go there by yourself," she insisted to Steve. "Who will take you?"

"Nobody. What for? It's only in the daytime," Steven told her, "and I can go with my friends, David and Laurie."

"But I think you ought to have someone with you. Someone older."

"Like who?"

So Rena indulged herself in four more plays a year, enjoyed them immensely in spite of their juvenile themes, and saved face by pretending that she was merely looking after the children. Crowds still bothered her, but she felt safer in her "mother" role. She watched the actors on the stage with great concentration, sometimes later explaining to Bill and me how she would have played one or several parts better herself.

When Rena came to live with us, her visits to the psychiatrist continued. It meant a forty mile drive for me once a week, but I didn't mind as it afforded me two concentrated hours additionally each Wednesday to become acquainted with this stranger who had so suddenly become our daughter.

Driving, like doing the dishes, invites confidences -- perhaps because the chattering driver and passenger need not overcome any embarrassment that might occur in face to face discussions. Rena enjoyed these drives for another reason. They took her out of school and along familiar roads. She loved pointing out trees, houses, or other landmarks that brought forth some memory of importance to her.

On the first of these drives, Rena started talking about men. She said she had known very few men since the death of her father when she was seven. ("An' he was usually drunk!") But these few men had made an indelible impression. She began by telling me about the psychiatrist whom she was seeing.

"Oh, the shrink's all right, I guess, but I don't really get what he's talkin' about half the time. He talks funny -- like a teacher or somethin'. Keeps bringin' up sex. Hell, I don't wanna tell him about things like that. He'd blab it all to my p.o. (probation officer) for sure!"

"What could he tell her that she doesn't already know?" I asked, rather transparently encouraging Rena to go on.

"Nothin', I guess. It's all on my record anyhow. Like the time my mother kicked out my step-dad."

"Oh, she kicked him out? I thought he just disappeared."

"Oh, no. She kicked him out. She was real mad at him for what he done."

"What was that?"

"Oh, one night when she was over to church and all the

kids was with her, I didn't feel so hot, and I went to bed early. Then I woke up and there was my step-dad tryin' to kiss me. I was mad an' I hit him right off, but he kept talkin' and tellin' me how pretty I was and all that kind of stuff. He hadn't even been drinkin', either!"

I held my breath anticipating a grim end to this tale, but I had underestimated my girl. She said she blackened his eye, left him with more bruises, and managed to push him out the door and lock it so that she could get her sleep in peace. The next morning she told her mother the whole story, and he was never seen by anyone around there again.

When Rena first ran away, she "hitched" a ride, but she said she had to jump from the truck because of the sexual insistence of the driver.

Once, she said, when she was picked up by a member of the local sheriff's department, he drove her to a lonely spot and offered her freedom in exchange for sex. Rena then opened her mouth and screamed loudly, like a horn out of control on a car. She kept right on screaming until she got to the relative safety of Juvenile Hall.

At "Juvie" Rena met very few men. They were, after all, her jailers, and aside from Ted McKay and one teacher, usually appeared only when they had to forcefully restrain her from injuring herself or the building during one of her rages.

In short, Rena feared and distrusted them all — especially "cops."

The second time I drove Rena to the hospital where she was to visit her "shrink," we became so involved in talk that I missed the freeway turnoff I should have taken. When I finally realized it, we had almost reached the toll gate.

"Good grief, Rena. I think I left my wallet in my jeans. I don't have a cent to pay the toll — or even my driver's license. Did you bring any money?"

"Hell, no. I never thought of it." There was a note of panic in Rena's voice. It touched me that she should take my situation so to heart. She grew tense and her face became old and pale. I thought the problem over quietly.

Suddenly she said, "There's a cop! Will he arrest us?"

Of course. Rena had sized up the situation in the light of her own experiences. Cops are out to get you. One now had a wonderful opportunity to "get us" both.

I swung my Plymouth into the least used of the toll gates and quietly rehearsed what I hoped would sound like an appealing, helpless little speech. The policeman I approached was quite young. Oh, please, I inwardly beseeched him. Be kind.

"Sir, I feel like such an idiot. I don't know how it happened, but I missed the county seat cutoff. Was it marked back there?"

The young man looked mildly aghast. "Lady, you've come an awful long way outa your way. You've got to go back about seven or eight miles. Here. There's no use your paying a toll."

I had not even mentioned my missing wallet, but he stepped out of his little booth, walked onto the freeway, and with some effort directed traffic away so that I could back up, cross the freeway, and turn around without getting smashed or having to pay a needless toll.

When I was finally headed back in the right direction, I happened to glance at Rena. On her face was an expression of utter shock.

"Did you see what that cop done? Did you see it? He didn't even know you. He didn't ask for your name er nothin'. You couldn't have given him no money with him out there on the street like that. God! What did he go and do that for? He might of got himself killed!"

Rena met a number of other kind men outside our family. A policeman came to the house once to see if Rena had news of a runaway girl she had known in her home town. During his visit he noticed Rena's carefully arranged and decorated sea shell display. He returned later to bring her a large shell in which he had planted a miniature cactus garden.

A friend of Bill's who was the local men's tennis champion gave Rena tennis lessons. She worked hard at this, and her figure soon regained its natural slimness.

In a short time, the psychiatrist dropped Rena's case. He told us that all she did was talk about us and about her wonderful new life. As he had correctly predicted, there were no more violent outbreaks. Her immediate and future development was in our hands.

As Dr. Blake had further predicted, Rena became

fascinated with Bill. Her interest was essentially academic, but it made Bill uncomfortable. He was aware of her staring at him during meals. Frequently she would ask him, "Why did you say that?" or "What did you do that for?"

Rena was most at home in the company of housewives. She would join eagerly in discussions of food and children, and she would often swing the topic around to her current favorite, men. She would amuse or bore them with endless accounts of what Daddy did this morning and her own analysis of why he did it.

We made good use of Rena's interest in Bill and his company to help her catch up in arithmetic. Bill taught her to play two of our favorite card games, casino and cribbage. Both are dependent not only on luck, but on the instant ability to add together simple sums. Rena showed a natural aptitude for cards. In a short time she was counting her points quickly, "Fifteen-two, fifteen-four, fifteen-six, and a run of three, that's nine." Then she would let out her Woody Woodpecker laugh, "Ha ha ha HAAH ha!"

We developed a "family championship" to stimulate interest. Anyone who "skunked" the other players became the champion and remained so until someone else "skunked" him. Rena was often champion, and if she ever lost the honor, she would not rest until she won it back.

Her arithmetic improved. Her teacher told us that she might be ready for algebra the next semester.

But Rena had problems outside of school.

Her older sister, Carol, had not run away from the altar, as Rena had done, when she was twelve. She was now sixteen and had four children in whom she showed little interest. She was bitter, and spent much of her time in the bars located near her home. Like Rena, she looked much older than she actually was. Rena's letters to her caused a latent jealousy to mushroom in Carol to such an extent that, ultimately, it would destroy all the dreams we were to develop for this girl we called our daughter.

Rena wrote Carol of her beautiful new clothes, of her "large" private bedroom, of the exciting things she did.

Carol wrote back that Rena's "desertion" of her family had caused nothing but disaster. The children were all sick. The school authorities were threatening her mother. It was Rena's fault. How could she be so unfeeling when her selfish running away had caused so many family problems? Her place was back at home taking charge of the family's affairs.

Carol's letters came almost daily. Rena would withdraw into her room to read them, and then withdraw even further into sullenness.

"What's the matter, Renie? Can't I help?"

"No. There's nothin' you c'n do."

"Maybe if we talked about it."

"There's nothin' anybody c'n do now. It's all too late."

"Something wrong at home?"

Rena could not cry easily. Instead, she usually said what hurt her in loud, sharp words.

"They're gonna take away all the kids! I know it! Mom don't take care of them like the school wants her to, and it'll just kill her to lose them. Them people don't understand her. She's a good mother; really she is!"

"Are you sure they're going to take the children away?"

"No. But it'll happen. Carol says things are a mess, and it's my fault. I shoulda stayed and helped out. I like to do all those things that Mom can't do."

"Rena, if she's as good a mother as you say, they won't take the children away from her; I'm sure."

"But they don't understand her. Mom don't care about washin' the kids or their clothes, and she don't send 'em to school half the time. But that's only because she loves 'em so much. She likes havin' em home. She just sits and watches 'em play. Everything they say is great with her. My mom loves everybody, most specially the kids. But she don't show it the way the cops and the school and the social workers think she should. She needs me to do that!"

"Why can't Carol?"

"Carol has her own kids. They's too much f'r her. She don't care nothin' f'r kids, least of all Mom's."

"Then why does she keep writing you about them?"

"She says I gotta come home."

"You know that's not possible, Rena."

"I shoulda never left."

Without telling Rena, I wrote to the probation officer and asked her to forbid Carol's letters. She did, yet the nagging sense of guilt never quite left Rena. The letters stopped, but Carol's influence as the older sister did not.

Possibly to expiate the guilt Rena felt, as well as to demonstrate fidelity to her own family, Rena decided to attend the local Pentecostal Church. In her close-knit home community, the church played a major role: a social meeting place, an educational center for the children, recreation, a way to give meaning to otherwise dull, meaningless lives. The members felt like a large family, and took an active interest in the affairs of one another.

Rena only attended our city's Pentecostal Church once. She came home upset.

"It was just awful. All the ladies wailin' and cryin' and tryin' to git me to go up to the altar and confess my sins. Everybody kept lookin' at me. I felt stupid. I used to go up to the altar sometimes at home, but they was my friends. I didn't even know this preacher or the ladies er nobody. How can you confess to people you don't know?"

"I should think it might be easier."

"Hell, no! It's embarrassin', that's what."

We would never have insisted, but Rena decided on her own to try our "church." A quiet Friends Meeting is about as different from the excitement of the church Rena grew up in as it can possibly be. Friends, or "Quakers," sometimes spend an entire hour together without any sound at all other than, perhaps, the crackling of a wood fire. Yet, Rena loved it. She was surprised and pleased to find Ted McKay from Juvenile Hall there. She felt, but had never been able to acknowledge, the interest he had taken in her -- an interest which led her to our family.

If anything caused us to miss Meeting, Rena was disappointed. If there should be any reason for an extra Meeting during the week, Rena wanted to go. The idea of a "Meeting for Worship on the occasion of marriage," as Quakers call a wedding, appealed to her so much that when Ted's daughter was to be married, Rena could hardly wait.

The usually austere meeting house had been warmed by the placement of ivy and home grown flowers in every possible corner. White candles stood on each window ledge. People sat in folding chairs around the fireplace, but the fireplace, itself, was hidden by a long table covered with a lace tablecloth. Behind the table sat the bride, the groom, and two of their friends. There was no music.

A reverent, peaceful silence was maintained while participants basked in the joyful awareness of being drawn close together. A few guests, unaccustomed to the extended hush, squirmed uneasily, embarrassed by the resultant squeaks of their uncomfortable chairs.

After about twenty minutes, a message flashed between the eyes of the bride and groom. The couple stood up and faced each other. She was wearing a long flowered dress; he a dark business suit. Folding their hands together, they said their carefully memorized promises. "In the presence of God and these our friends, I take thee, Marianne . . ."

When each had said his own pledge to the other, the groom placed a ring on his bride's finger. They stood for a second or two longer before sitting down in their new reality as husband and wife.

The brother of the groom brought them the marriage certificate, which the groom signed first, followed by his bride using her new surname. The certificate was then read aloud to those who had witnessed the last solemn few minutes.

There was another period of silence, and then a woman who had been bursting to do so stood up and said with a rush, "I have known Marianne since she was only three years old and I have watched her grow into a fine young woman. Her kindness to the children in the Meeting, her patience with the elderly, her developing artistic ability; all these have been a source of pride for her entire family. I have the deepest confidence that the years ahead will be rich in the work and experiences that make life more meaningful when shared."

A happy sigh went around the room. At last! Someone had broken the silence. Now others spoke of the young couple, of the meaning of marriage, of their joy in the occasion.

Too soon, the Meeting for Worship was closed by hand shakes all around. Rena was in that trance I had not seen since *The House of Bernarda Alba.*

At the reception, a relaxed and happy Ted McKay made his way over to Rena. He was studying her as he asked, "How did you like the wedding, Rena?"

The still transfixed girl said, "Oh, it was nice. Real nice. Y' know, when I git married, it's gonna be exactly like that."

"Fine," Ted said warmly. "I hope I'll be there."

"You will. I promise I'll invite you."

"Fine," he repeated. "Let's seal that promise. How would you like to have one of the candles that decorated the Meeting House for the wedding?"

He could not have offered her any gift she would have treasured more at that moment. Her strong hands held the white piece of wax with the gentlest care, despite its thickness.

At home, the candle was permanently stationed on the night stand next to her radio.

But Rena wasn't ready to think about marriage seriously yet. There was too much she wanted to do. And there were things that had slipped past when she was younger — things that had to be caught up.

Rena loved fairy tales, and delighted in reading them aloud to Steven. Her reading was imroving, but the fact was that Steve could probably have read them better to her. He enjoyed the attention, and, as if it were a perfectly natural thing to do, he helped his big sister with the difficult words.

Rena shyly told me that she never owned a doll. "I won one once in a baking contest down to church, but the bills was so much then that Mom had to sell it. She wouldn't-a done it if she didn't really have to."

We bought Rena the loveliest doll we could find. The fourteen year old played with her doll constantly for about two weeks, talking to it, dressing it, sleeping with it. Then she was through with it. The doll decorated her bed, but lost the humanity that a child can breathe into an inanimate object.

She enjoyed clothes, but had had very few of her own in the past. She usually wore Carol's outgrown things. The money the county gave us to purchase clothing for her was quickly spent, and the monthly allowances we received from the county for her care was needed for ongoing expenses. Anxious to find something for those large, strong hands to do, I taught Rena to sew. It did not take long. After a few weeks she was a better seamstress than I. She had far more patience with matters like fitting, basting, marking or remarking details. Her handmade dresses, pants and pant tops gave her great pride.

Since country music was an important part of her background, I suggested Rena take the guitar lessons offered at a nearby community center. They cost little, and an inexpensive guitar had long stood as little more than a decoration over the fireplace. Rena leaped at the opportunity. As with anything that really interested her, she concentrated intently on learning the instrument and soon graduated from "Skip to My Lou" to the country and rock music she listened to for hours daily on the radio.

But Rena's greatest talent was her ready understanding and sympathy for those who needed them.

While Steven played, she would watch him with the fond glow she once tried to describe to me as habitual to her mother. She loved Steve's little dog, Kelly, but reasoned that it was Steven's dog and should get most of its attention from him. Steven was outside playing when Kelly was crushed under the wheels of a bus. Screaming hysterically, Steve came running home with the little form lying limply in his arms. Rena and I flew to him, but she was there first, taking charge.

"Oh, Steve, how awful! How did it happen?"

Steven was too frenzied to talk. Rena took the lifeless form from him in spite of his screamed, "No! No! No! He's not dead. He's not!"

Rena said, "I bet he was havin' a real good time when it happened, wasn't he, Steve?"

He quieted down a little. "Mmm. He was chasin' the bus . . . and he thought he was so big . . . and he was making so much noise. But I don't think the driver even heard him." Steve's eyes were darting wildly again.

"Well, Kelly didn't know that," she said gently. "He was like a big hero in a war. He wasn't afraid of nothin'. I bet he thought the bus attacked him because it was scared."

A little laugh, more like a snort, escaped from Steven, replacing the sobs.

Rena soothed him for a while longer, then gently moved Steven away from the strangely quiet little dog, and interested him in something else.

She suggested to Bill later that they should give Kelly a nice burial, but not where Steven could see it. Together, Rena and Bill went down to the bay, dug a deep pit, and put the crushed creature into it. When they got home,

Rena found Steve and told him, "We found a real nice place to bury Kelly. Right by the waves. Remember how he used to like chasin' the waves? When we put him in, we laid him down on his side, and he looked just like he was takin' a nap."

We all felt that it was important to get another dog as soon as possible, but it should not look or be at all like Kelly. We found Tippy, a half Shetland Sheep Dog and half German Shepherd, at the local S.P.C.A. Tippy, too, soon had his run-in with a bus, but his size saved him. He escaped with a broken leg.

The veterinarian told us to keep Tippy very inactive so that his leg could heal. Rena went out to the garage and pulled down Steven's old play pen. She scrubbed it out, placed newspapers on the bottom, and imprisoned the mournful Tippy inside, explaining to him that this would only be for a little while so that he could grow big and strong again. She saw to it that he rarely lacked for company, and whenever she was at home, she listened for the whimpered warning that meant Tippy would have to be lifted up and taken outdoors for a few minutes to attend to urgent necessities. The veterinarian told us that he had never seen his advice taken so seriously. Tippy's recovery was swift and complete.

I began to think my girl should be a nurse.

A nearby hospital had a junior volunteer program for girls fourteen years or older. The hospital was several miles away, but I thought this might provide exactly the incentive she needed to consider the vocation I thought so suited to her. Rena's enthusiasm was characteristically immediate. These two hours a week became the time she looked forward to most.

The girls were trained by adult volunteers in the history, philosophy, and methods of the hospital. Each girl was responsible for her uniform, a pink pinafore with a white blouse, white socks and shoes. After twenty-five hours of service, the uniform included a pink hairbow, and after fifty hours, a matching cap. The girls helped in the laboratory, in the medical records department, and on the ward floors. Offices and laboratories bored Rena, but she had a quick empathy with patients. The nurses recognized her talent, and asked to have her assigned to work with them during all of her volunteer hours.

When patients were despondent or lonely, Rena would be sent to cheer them or to sympathize. She seemed to know which approach was called for. She could joke, tease, interest the patient in something new, or simply sit by quietly. She was entrusted with delicate glass instruments, narcotics, and once with a corpse that had to be taken down to the morgue. Rena was unshockable, a useful companion trait for empathy. She was matter-of-fact about less attractive human functions and malfunctions. She never gossiped on duty or off.

Since it was dark by the time Rena was through at the hospital, I picked her up. One night when I arrived at the neat brown shingle house in which the volunteers dressed, I found Rena sitting on the steps, her face set in hard, angry sullenness. I parked the car and walked over to her.

"What now, Rena?"

"My supervisor wants to see you." Rena's lips were set in a thin line.

She made no move to follow me.

The supervisor was tense, as if at the end of a particularly trying day. "You have quite an unmannerly girl there," she began without ceremony.

Her bluntness took me by surprise. "Rena?" I asked foolishly.

"She has no respect for authority."

"Very little," I agreed, regaining my composure, "unless she feels it's justified authority." The supervisor's face showed me I was on a wrong tack. "Would you care to tell me what happened?"

She would. She could hardly wait to tell me. "One of the girls came to work today without the required white socks."

"Was it Rena?"

"No. It was another girl. She claimed she lost them on her way over here. So, I told her she could not work today. She was to go home."

Knowing Rena's highly developed sense of what-was-right and what-was-wrong, I could imagine what was coming.

"That girl, Rena, had the nerve to tell me that I was being 'arbitrary' — that's what she said — 'arbitrary.' She knew the rules, but she was telling me that I ought to make an exception."

I was feeling rather proud of Rena and hoping it didn't show. I wondered where she had picked up that four syllabled, appropriate word, "arbitrary."

The supervisor was still talking. "Well, that other girl was perfectly willing to go home, but when she heard that she resorted to crying. And do you know what Rena did? She took off her own socks and gave them to that girl saying something like if that's the way I felt about it, she wouldn't work today, herself."

I was privately cheering, but since I was expected to keep up my end of the conversation, I said, "So what happened? Who got to go on the floor?"

"Neither one. I couldn't let one girl give another her socks. It's not sanitary. So, as a result, we were shorthanded today."

I tried to think of something appropriate to say, but I found it difficult to get as excited over this small challenge to authority as was the authority who felt so challenged.

The supervisor was not through. "There's one other thing I have to tell you. I'm sorry to have to do this. I know it will come as a shock."

Oh, no, I thought. It would kill Rena if this woman had decided that she must be dismissed.

Sighing, the supervisor told me, "Your daughter smokes! I caught her doing it today."

I had to control myself not to burst out laughing. I hate that habit myself. I'm one of those unfortunate people made physically ill by cigarette smoke in close quarters; but other things I find far more shocking than cigarettes, cancer statistics notwithstanding.

I explained that Rena was a foster child. Unlike all of the other volunteers at that time, she came from an economically poor background. (I skipped the part about Juvenile Hall. If smoking shocked her, Juvenile Hall would probably be more than she could take.) I asked her to try to understand if Rena seemed a bit odd at times, because I knew how much the volunteer program meant to her. Like most others I explained these things to, the supervisor became instantly sympathetic toward "my poor waif."

Ultimately, a kind of warm tolerance grew between them. Rena never again smoked in her supervisor's presence, and somehow, rules did not come up between them again.

A neighborhood dramatic group was starting, and to Rena's joy, I agreed to become its first director. We planned a gay nineties revue as the initial presentation, reasoning that an old fashioned melodrama could mask limited acting skills and that bright costumes might hold interest when musical offerings left something to be desired. Then, too, the usual community sing at the end could be counted on to leave an audience in a happy frame of mind. We called our new group The Jefferson Players.

Rena offered to help with costume construction. She made elaborate hats of colored paper, scraps of material and paper salad plates. She invented "high button shoes" that were simply high heeled pumps and long matching socks with contrasting ribbon sewn on as "lacing."

Shyly, Rena asked if she could sing in our revue.

She was quite pretty. There was no question that Rena would look attractive in a chorus line, but what she really wanted was a solo. Her singing voice was strong and far more musical than her speaking voice, but I was concerned about the many deep fears that still might surface easily. If she became terrified at the last minute, it could be a disaster. I talked it over with the Players. They encouraged me to give Rena a chance.

She enjoyed any song she could "belt out" raucously. No gentle "Bird in a Gilded Cage" type was she. The song for Rena was obviously "Frankie and Johnny."

With actors, we worked out a pantomime to the absurd lyrics. Rena was costumed entirely in black and bright Kelly green.

As I had feared, on the first night of the show, Rena shook with stage fright. Her face was pale; she stood apart, chewing her nails viciously, saying nothing.

"Should I sing it for you, Renie?" I asked.

She shook her head, but I began mentally rehearsing the words of her song.

The time for "Frankie and Johnny" finally arrived. I was still feeling uncomfortable when I saw Rena take her place on one side of the stage. After working my way around behind the black curtain beside her, I asked in a low voice, "Are you all right?"

She shook her head. Then, in a frightened whisper, "I can't remember the words! I'm gonna fergit. How does it start?"

Before I could answer, the house lights went off and a green spotlight bathed Rena. The girl began to writhe and shout the song. Her voice got louder; her motions more exaggerated.

Our 1890 go-go girl was a smash hit, and her flushed face after the number showed she knew it.

Later, Bill and I talked over Rena's future. Perhaps she should consider a career in entertainment. I had been through that in a small way myself and had rejected it with relief. But Rena did have much in the way of natural beauty and talent. I knew I could train her.

No, we decided. Theater is a great hobby, but a terrible profession. A nursing career was best for Rena.

Tuesday was Rena's busy day. She worked at the hospital from four to six, then I picked her up for a hasty dinner and hastier homework. She had to be at the community center by eight p.m. for her guitar lessons. She would come home to finish her homework and, usually, get to bed late. Rena liked days like this. Since she had no friends of her own age, such activity allowed her little time to feel lonely.

One night, Mr. Epstein, the director of the community center, happened to stay late and wandered in to watch the advanced guitar class. Rena caught his attention. He was struck with the earnestness with which she listened to the teacher and applied herself to the techniques demonstrated. Others in the class socialized or let their eyes and thoughts wander, but Rena spent the entire hour frowning over the problems at hand.

Mr. Epstein knew nothing about Rena or her background, but he offered her a job immediately after the class session. Would she consider becoming a junior counselor at the center's summer day camp?

Would she! It was an answer to her unuttered prayers, although something of a scheduling problem for Bill and myself. We had agreed to teach for six weekends at a Friends summer high school in a distant city. Later, we planned to visit Bill's mother who lived some five hundred miles away.

I went to see Mr. Epstein. I felt that it was important for him to know something about Rena's past; but to my surprise, he seemed concerned neither about her Juvenile Hall experience nor her continuing supervision by a probation officer. Her serious application to her job was of more significance to him than any past history. As to our scheduling problem, he offered to let Rena work at the day camp for just the first five weeks. He would find a replacement for the second half of the summer.

We took Rena with us during our weekends at the summer school. The teenagers there treated her politely, but as an outsider. It seemed to us that it would be a long time before Rena would fit into our culture and that probably she would never again fit into the culture from which she had come. Until she reached an age when differences were admired, or at least accepted, we feared that Rena would continue to be a lonely person.

We were wrong about Rena's appeal for people her own age. True, most of them ignored her and some, particularly boys, disliked her openly. But there was one young man, two years older than Rena, who felt just as lonely as she did. Inevitably, they found each other.

2

LOVE

Although he was a professor's son, Jim did poorly in his studies. The professor and his wife found this difficult to accept. To make matters worse, Jim had a younger brother who turned anything he touched academically into "A's." As president of Rena's junior high school he received all the attention that Jim longed for.

Jim retreated into himself, soothing his loneliness by daydreaming and by teaching himself to play the guitar. In all his sixteen years the only successes he knew had been with children. His quick grin and sense of fun made him an easy leader of youngsters. It was this quality that was noticed by Mr. Epstein, and Jim, too, was invited to become a junior counselor at the Community Center Day Camp.

After camp hours, Rena and Jim became inseparable. Each grew noticeably happier in the company of the other. Rena mothered Jim. He took her to those places that teen-agers with no ingroup enjoy going: swimming, roller skating, dancing. Rena did not have any of the skills for these things, but for Jim's sake, she learned. She preferred to go to the movies, but she allowed Jim to make most decisions. In his company, crowds did not seem to disturb her.

Day Camp ended a week before the Friends Summer School closed. The following Wednesday night, Rena woke up screaming.

She had had some pain all day but assumed it only heralded the oncoming of a menstrual period. Menstruation was usually painful for her, but the nurse at Summer School told her, "Don't baby yourself. A woman's life is one pain after another, and you might as well accept it without complaining."

This struck Rena as sensible, so she did not tell us about the pain that was intensifying in her abdomen. Now it could no longer be ignored. Her face mirrored agony and panic.

A little probing indicated the possibility of appendicitis, so in the middle of the night we got her into our car as quickly as possible and rushed her to the emergency room of the local hospital.

"Are you her mother?" the woman at the admitting desk asked.

"Yes. Well, no, not exactly. I'm her foster mother."

"We'll have to have her parent's signature before we can do anything."

"Why? We've never had any problem before. I have her county aid card right here."

"But this is different. She'll probably have to be hospitalized. We can't do that without her parent's signature."

"What can we do?"

"You better take her to the county hospital. And from the looks of her, you'd better hurry."

Bill drove as smoothly as he could, but every stop and start was another stab for Rena. She was crying hysterically now, holding onto me tightly.

The county hospital was about fifteen miles away. Bill drove into the entrance marked "emergency." A man dressed in a white hospital uniform was waving his arms. "Hey, Mister, you can't come in here. Reserved for ambulances!"

Bill continued to drive to the door.

The man kept calling, "Hey, Mister! Mister!"

Bill ignored him until Rena and I were out of the car.

While Bill drove toward home to be with Steven, I led the trembling girl through the emergency door and into a room full of serious faced men and women. I found a chair for Rena and went up to the desk.

"The city hospital sent us over here. She has abdominal pain. I think it could be her appendix."

No expression crossed the middle aged face of the woman who reached for a form. "You on welfare?" she asked me.

"Well, no, I'm not. But she's on Aid to Needy Children. Here's her card."

The woman studied the card. "This says B.H.I. That's Boarding Home Insurance, isn't it?"

"Yes."

"Then you're not her mother."

"No, I'm her foster mother -- but this is an emergency, isn't it?"

"Might be. Can't tell. I'd better talk to the doctor about this. Has her real mother been notified?"

Being referred to as an unreal mother was beginning to bother me. I felt very real.

"She can't be reached," I replied. "She lives in a little place behind a fish packing plant, and there's no telephone anywhere around there."

"You better wait."

It seemed to me that the guard-receptionist was gone for a terribly long time. While I waited, I sat next to Rena who was leaning over her own lap. She knew I was there, but said nothing. Her pale, drawn face showed the effort she was under not to cry in public.

A number of other people came into the already crowded waiting room. Some came with their relatives; some with policemen. Several were crying loudly, but most sat quietly, keeping their eyes averted from the many other private tragedies.

The woman from behind the desk came over to us at last. "This the girl?"

I was beginning to feel like saying something angry or sarcastic, but restraining myself, I nodded.

The woman said, "I'll have to take her to the examining room. You wait here."

"Can't I go with her?"

"No. It's against the rules. No one's allowed in the examining room but the patient and the doctors."

I was about to protest, but glancing at Rena, I saw her face beginning to relax. She seemed anxious to go. It was as though the adventure of investigating the procedures of a new hospital was beginning to distract my Hospital Volunteer.

"Can you make it?" the woman asked her.

Rena nodded and followed -- the drooping of her shoulders the only sign of the pain she felt. They disappeared down a hallway.

There were no magazines or newspapers in the stark white admitting room. I became aware of a growing sense of fear that gnawed like physical pain.

I felt alone; isolated. I wished that I hadn't sent Bill home to be with Steven. I needed him much more than our sleeping son did. I had nothing to do but pray a little and examine my own feelings. I felt afraid to do even that.

Why was I so frightened? Rena was not even related to me. It had been made very clear to me this night that no matter how I felt, I was not her "real mother." Rena and I had only been acquainted for six months. Would my life be substantially changed if anything happened to Rena?

I watched other people in the waiting room. Most of them were quiet and tense. Some were holding each other. In one corner, a policeman was telling a blank-faced man that his wife would die if he did not immediately get her the required pints of blood. As far as that husband was concerned, the problem was happening on a screen or to someone else. He kept nodding. Occasionally he said, "Yes, yes," but he did nothing about getting the blood.

The scene seemed nightmarish. Couldn't that policeman see the man was in shock? Could it possibly be that they would do nothing for the woman until they had those pints of blood? Suppose Rena needed blood. Could I get it for her?

I remembered that the woman at the desk had told me nothing could be done unless we had Rena's mother's signature. I went back to the desk.

When I caught the attention of the being who had led Rena away, I asked, "What happens now — about the girl, I mean?"

"It's up to you to find her mother. Otherwise, we can't do anything."

"Up to *me?*"

"That's right."

"You mean you'd let her appendix rupture rather than take a chance of getting sued or something?"

"Look, we have to protect the hospital, you know. We don't even know what she's got, yet. The doctors are all busy."

"You mean she hasn't even seen a doctor? We've been

here almost an hour!"

"There's not much point in an examination until we get that signature. Don't worry about it. If the doctor says her life is really in danger, we'll go ahead and operate. But there's not that much rush. We'd really rather wait for her mother."

Panic began to take the place of fear. How could I find Rena's mother? She lived more than fifty miles away. I was not sure I could even find her little home, especially at night. I went to the pay phone and called Bill. The semi-privacy of the booth encouraged the tears I had been holding back. I was sobbing, close to hysteria.

My husband knows when to sympathize, and when to tell me to "come off it." This time he verbally slappped me in the face. I felt much calmer when I went back to the sterile, overlit room to wait out the night.

Rena's probation officer had given us her own home telephone number. Bill called her. She called the hospital, assuring them of the county's full cooperation and approval of whatever steps might prove necessary. The hospital repeated its request for a "real" mother's signature. The probation officer then called the sheriff's department that had jurisdiction over the rural area where Rena's mother lived. The man who answered promised to send someone out for the required signature, but not until morning. They were short handed that night.

At six o'clock in the morning, an intern removed Rena's badly inflamed appendix.

The signature arrived two and a half hours later by special messenger from the sheriff's office.

We were not permitted to see Rena until she was moved from the recovery room to a ward. She looked far better than I felt.

The floor where Rena was placed had only one nurse on duty, and several overworked nurses' aides. In a matter of hours Rena was out of bed and helping. With a professional manner she answered lights, emptied bedpans (something she was never allowed to do in her Hospital Volunteer capacity), and made beds. We brought her beloved guitar to her. She became the clown of the floor, banging out guitar accompaniments to popular songs wherever they would have her, or singing "Frankie and Johnny" in her loud, throaty, female baritone. Rena was useful and appreciated. I had rarely seen her so happy. She may have broken a few hospital rules, but it bothered no one — least of all Rena. She never assumed that rules were automatically self-justifying. If they made sense to her, she obeyed rules. If not, Rena was a natural rebel.

Everyone at the hospital — patients, nurses and nurses' aides — seemed sorry when Rena was dismissed. In spite of her large scar, to Rena the experience seemed more like a satisfying vacation. Returning home, she became the standard bore, chattering incessantly about her operation.

After that surgical adventure, the trip to see Bill's mother seemed like an anti-climax for Rena. She soon missed her volunteer hospital work, the day camp children, and most of all, she missed Jim.

Once, when Bill's mother and I were alone, she said, "I don't know why you want to have a stranger around. You're a young couple. You have all kinds of things on your minds, and Steven takes plenty of your time. He might even get jealous."

"Steven, jealous?" I asked incredulously. "Why, Mom, haven't you noticed how much he adores her?"

"Of course he likes her. She gives him attention. What I mean is that girl takes your time away from him. And there's Bill's time, too."

I wondered if Mom might be concerned about the kind of attention Bill gave to this young, blonde beauty. Surely Mom knew him better than that.

Her dark eyes were steady, searching. "What do people think about this thing you're doing?" she asked. "Do you know anyone else who has foster children?"

I had to admit that none of our friends was a foster parent. It is definitely not an "in thing" in circles familiar to us.

"But, Mom," I argued. "The job has to be done. Why, Rena's probation officer told us that just to keep up with the current need for places for kids who need them, there would have to be three new foster homes made available every single day. Who's going to do it if we don't?"

"Older people," Mom replied firmly. "That's who. Older people have more time. And the experience. Older people are much more patient." Then, warming to her point of view, "This is a job the senior citizens ought to take over. Young people don't know enough."

I don't believe that Mom disapproved of Rena. Foster parenting was something totally outside of her experience, and Mom needed time to get used to it.

Rena's sullenness, brought about by her boredom in an unknown small town, did not help matters. Finally, when our car broke down, her interest ignited at the auto shop. She watched the mechanic's every move. Machines fascinated her. For the rest of the visit, she spent most of her days at the mechanic's, watching and asking questions. At night, she played the guitar and sang. Mom's neighbors began to come in, to make requests, and occasionally, to sing along.

One evening, a couple in their late sixties came to hear her. They brought with them a pair of large, mongrel dogs that they addressed affectionately and watched over with tender alertness.

Mom, sitting close to me on the other side of the room, said in a low voice, "Do you see what I mean? Look at those two. They're retired, and all they have to think about is those dogs. The money they spend on meat and vet bills you wouldn't believe."

I took another look at the now sleeping canines. There was nothing special about them.

Mom continued, "Those people have never been healthier or had more time on their hands. They should be spending all that attention on children like Rena; not on dogs. Children are more important."

Her words brought to mind a pair of retired teachers I once met. They had made new careers for themselves taking entire families of children into their lives. The children called them "Grandma" and "Grandpa," and the former teachers seemed to be having a wonderful time making cookies and treehouses for their appreciative wards.

Bill, Steven and I were so obviously proud of Rena that Bill's mother gradually accepted her. Although she was pleased to be called "Grandma" herself, it took her more time to approve of anyone other than Steven calling Bill and me "Dad" and "Mom."

Rena was happy and relieved to get home again. The first thing she did was to telephone Jim. He was at our front door before we had the first suitcase unpacked. He had put off his birthday celebration until Rena came back so that they might enjoy it together. Rena appeared to be touched by this gesture of devotion.

Her world was expanding fast. Jim enjoyed Rena's company most when he could take her somewhere she had never been before. For his birthday, he took her to a lovely restaurant with a Hawaiian decor. Rena took it all in, making mental notes so that later she could copy some of the ideas for her bedroom or a party.

Jim helped Rena plan her own fifteenth birthday party at an outdoor swimming pool that had an area for dancing and barbecuing. Rena invited some of the boys and girls she had met at the summer school where Bill and I taught. It was Rena's first birthday party, and completely successful.

Jim's family invited Rena to accompany them to see *Aida* performed by the Metropolitan Opera's road company. The invitation pleased her, but the old fear of appearing "stupid" plagued her again. This time Rena was willing to meet the fear head-on. She asked Bill and me to teach her all we could about *Aida*.

We found the story of the opera for her and a short summary of the composer's life. After she had read these, we played recordings of several of the principal arias, explaining who was singing and approximately what he was saying in the aria. We drilled her in the correct pronunciation of the main characters' strange sounding names. She was ready for the professor's family, but instinctively included the good sense not to be too obvious about it.

Rena surprised herself by enjoying the opera very much. ("And do you know what? They had real elephants on the stage!") She was also more than a little smug about the knowledgeable impression she had made. We began to feel a little uneasy about the importance Rena attached to impressing Jim's family.

Summer was almost over, and Rena was growing quiet and withdrawn again. She had graduated from junior high school with a respectable record, but the imminence of attending a new high school with an enrollment of nearly three thousand students had Rena biting her nails and smoking with renewed frenzy. I tried to change her agitation to something like anticipation.

"Renie, I think you're going to need some new clothes for high school, don't you?"

"I don't need anything."

"Sure you do. You've grown about two inches this summer, and you're much slimmer. Wouldn't you like to try making some new things?"

"Well . . . I would like to have a plaid skirt like yours. I think I could make one of those. And a print dress like the one you wore the other night. And I'd like to have a long sleeved blouse like the one you wear with your suit and . . . ."

Like mine. She wanted to dress as much like me as possible. I looked closely at Rena. Gone was the sprayed, stacked hair style she had worn, and in its place was a pageboy like mine. She no longer wore high pumps on her feet as she once had, but instead, sandals such as I preferred. They did little for her size ten feet. Like me, her only makeup was light lipstick. My friends had commented that they could no longer tell us apart on the telephone, as Rena had picked up my speaking voice and telephone manners.

The girl was, consciously or nonconsciously, copying me. I was not flattered, but worried. Such a responsibility! I made a mental note to take a long, critical look at myself since someone was going to use me as a blueprint.

In further preparation for the possibly traumatic experience of high school, I made a special trip to see Rena's new counselor and the Dean of Girls. I told the story of Rena's past problems and future potentials to them both, and received quite different reactions.

The counselor listened intently, and then made an appointment to have Rena come in advance to meet him and take a tour of the school. He reasoned that if she knew where every room, every lavatory, and every other facility were located, she might have an advantage over the other incoming sophomores. This could mean confidence gained earlier. He promised that he would choose Rena's first group of teachers with special consideration.

The beautifully groomed Dean of Girls, after hearing the same story, remarked, "Well, as I've always said, blood will tell. If she comes from that kind of background, sooner or later she'll come to no good. By the way, be sure to tell her that friends of mine do *not* smoke."

Switching the subject to herself, she told me how much she liked her work. "I'm paid to be a witch," she said, "so I'm a witch, all right."

I wish I could have kept up my side of the conversation, but her words left me dumbfounded.

I did not tell Rena exactly what the Dean of Girls had said, but, in honesty, I felt Rena should know that the Dean impressed me as "extremely firm about school rules and regulations."

In later months, when Rena was challenged to a fist fight by two girls who spotted her as "a tough one," Rena had the good judgment to take the matter directly to "the witch." If anything were going to come of it, Rena did not want the blame. The two challengers were transferred from all of Rena's classes without being made aware of the reason for the change. Rena never saw them again.

Although Jim was two years ahead of Rena academically, he looked forward eagerly to having her in the same school with himself. He suggested that she enroll in a pottery class for an elective — the only one which they might take together. She did, and once again surprised us by displaying marked ability. Her strong hands, once used for tearing apart plumbing and bedclothes, now expressed themselves in forming clay into attractive, functional creations. For an entire hour she had no need to bring the comfort of cigarettes or fingernails to her mouth. Her feet on the potter's wheel and her hands on the clay danced together in a joy of new rhythms.

Her pottery captured some of that joy. The plates, bowls and vases were of professional caliber and several civic art exhibits displayed them.

Seeing Jim daily also did much to help Rena through that first high school year. He continued to be her only teenaged friend. Jim often came home with her to sample some of her cooking or to practice guitar pieces with her.

I believed that Rena felt secure in our family. We all loved her as a real daughter or sister. But the expression on her face when she sat alone or in Friends' meeting betrayed that there was still much to be accomplished before she could attain anything like serenity. Her deepest anxieties were hardly below the surface, but she could not, or would not talk about them.

My father died.

I had everything and nothing in common with my father. Like him, I read at every opportunity. I enjoyed a good argument. I had strong religious leanings. I "dreamed big." My father encouraged these traits in his offspring.

But ironically, these very traits that he encouraged pulled us apart. I read different things than he did. My arguments were too often with him. I chose a different religion. And my dreams usually led me to do something.

Dad's dreams were reality enough for him. For years before my mother's death, his real life was a tiresome cycle of going to and from a job he hated. He didn't go to church because he disagreed too often with the sermons. Evenings and weekends he read, watched television, or dreamed of a business he would start "some day."

At sixty-five, my father retired from the company he had worked in for twenty-five years. Dad looked around and found he had no friends and nothing to do. He did not understand or agree with his grown children. He grew lonely and bitter. He was found by neighbors several days after his heart stopped beating -- just short of his sixty-sixth birthday.

The news came by telephone. Within two hours I was on a flight to the city where he had lived. It was up to me to help my brother and sister with the multitude of details that inevitably crop up when one's parent dies. I did not look forward to the trip, but I had no worries about leaving my family. Rena, as usual, took immediate command.

"Now, Mom, don't worry about a thing. You know I'm a good cook, and I'll take real good care of Steven."

These things were true. Her Mexican dinners were events that we invited our friends to. Steven spent much time with her, during which Rena would play him her growing collection of popular records or read him her assignments in English literature. Steven admired Rena, but he felt perfectly free to criticize her smoking and nail biting. Rena would bristle when he brought these things up, but nevertheless, she continued to welcome his company.

Rena, Bill and Steven saw me off on the plane. I watched

them from the window with a growing sense of self-satisfaction. I was pretty smart, I told myself, finding a girl like Rena to join my family. If she hadn't been there, I probably could not have left Bill and Steven to take this trip. I had no idea how long I would be gone, but it didn't matter. Steven would not be alone after school. Bill would not have to eat his meals in restaurants. I knew the house would be neater when I got home than when I had left. Pretty clever woman, I, having a Rena in the house.

When the plane reached its destination the landing gear refused to come down. My euphoria dissolved. I looked down on the landing strip and saw it surrounded by fire trucks and ambulances. The stewardess was saying the exact words she had been taught to say to avert panic. I did not feel panicky, but I suddenly knew for certain that I was not ready to leave my family to anyone — not even during a relatively short stay in a hospital. I was as mortal as my father, and I knew I had a lot more I needed to do before I left this world. I quietly apologized to my Maker for my little fling with vanity.

The landing was bumpy, but no one was hurt. My brother and sister who had come to meet me looked as if they had had a much worse scare than I.

After two days, my father's affairs were in order. On the third day, we had the funeral. No one came except his three children, a friend of my mother's, and one man representing the company where my father had worked. Since Dad could never find a minister he agreed with, the mortuary supplied an ordained stranger for the occasion. He made polite sounds about general things like the importance of being a father and a man who worked hard all his life. It was a depressing affair.

I was glad to get back home.

The Jefferson Players were back at work on two new shows: a one-act serious "message" play about becoming well informed before voting, and a full, three-act musical comedy called *Pussyfoot.* Rena, predictably, wanted to be in both.

The one-act play featured, among its leading characters, a pair of teenaged twins. The parts were dramatically demanding, but I felt that Rena could handle the girl's role. She wanted short, dark Jim to play her twin brother, although he did not resemble her at all. When no other teenaged boys read for the part, I, of necessity, relented.

Jim and Rena made an excellent team. Each seemed to inspire the other to exceptional levels of acting. Both took direction well. With a dark color rinse on her blonde hair, Rena was able to pass for someone at least related to Jim. Our one-act performances were well received.

Casting her in *Pussyfoot* was more difficult. She was muscular, but not graceful, and the choreographer found her difficult to work with. Nevertheless, she was so noticeably pretty that it seemed natural for her to have at least one solo number. The choreographer created a comic dance for her as a cannibal queen. The movements were wildly vigorous and grotesque. Rena took her small role seriously. She screeched as she gesticulated around the stage wearing a leopard printed leotard and a turkey bone in her hair. Her large feet pounded a frantic accompaniment. Characteristically, she virtually "stole the show."

Rena seemed happy on a stage. As the anticipated moments grew closer, she exhibited all the symptoms of "galloping butterflies," but her stage fright vanished as soon as the curtain parted. She threw herself totally into whatever role she happened to be playing. Any anxieties that troubled her, whether those that had to do with her portrayal or those that had to do with her own life, vanished while Rena was on stage. It served her as both release and creative satisfaction.

Her first year in high school brought Rena her first all "A" and "B" report card. Her counselor beamed as he told me that next year Rena would move into the university preparatory classes. Bill and I were proud, but Rena, herself, seemed curiously unconcerned.

The following summer, she was hired to work full time at the Community Center Day Camp. At her request, she was assigned to the pre-school group. Every night she came home grimy, beat, and completely happy. She had not yet reached sixteen when one day she came home shouting with unusual excitement, "Mom! Guess what! I'm not a junior counselor anymore. I'm a real counselor!"

The camp had run into financial difficulties. Some of

the paid staff had to be laid off if the endeavor were to pay its own expenses. In the pre-school department, the older counselor was deemed more expendable than Rena. In spite of her youth and relative lack of training and experience, Rena was trusted to handle the entire program alone, with a raise in salary in spite of the camp's financial problems. Like a new part in a play, Rena took her real life role seriously.

Rena saw more and more of Jim. It came as no surprise to us when she announced one day that she and Jim were engaged. I pointed out to her that she was still a ward of the court, and I did not think that the court would look too favorably upon a marriage in the very near future. This did not worry Rena. Apparently, being engaged was quite enough. Marriage could wait.

Not everyone took the announcement so casually. The next night Jim's father telephoned to say he was coming right over to talk to us. Would we be home? He did not ask if this were convenient; he just arrived ten minutes later.

Without preliminaries, he began, "Have you any idea what those crazy kids are up to now?"

"Up to? Why, what do you mean?" I asked mechanically.

"Jim tells me they're engaged!"

"Yes, so we hear."

"You hear! And do you mean to tell me you approve?"

"It's not up to us to approve or disapprove," Bill pointed out calmly. "Rena is a ward of the court of this state. Neither she nor we have any real say over decisions of this kind. Only the court does."

The not-quite-legal status Bill and I held could be trying at times, but there were situations when we were happy to pass the responsibility on to the obscure powers of a faceless state court. This was one of those.

Jim's father was obviously not impressed by the loftiness of Rena's legal guardians. To him, Jim's entire family was faced with the imminent prospect of disaster.

"Have you any idea just how young Jim is? I mean really, he's just a kid. He still has to ask his mother for money for a haircut. And last week he was angry with his brother, so he kicked a hole in his brother's bedroom door. The idea that he could possibly be old enough to get married is just plain ridiculous! Besides, boys and girls of fifteen and seventeen just don't get married!"

Where had this man been, I was wondering. Was the university such an "ivory tower" that he could not read newspaper statistics? But then, no one can learn what he will not allow life to teach him.

Jim's father was saying, "I want it clearly understood that I will not allow such a thing to happen — ever."

I began to get the drift of his real concern. "Why?" I asked. "Why not *ever?*"

"Because it is completely unsuitable."

I could feel my body growing as rigid as his attitude. But I would not let him get away with this glossing over of his prejudices. "Just why would it be so unsuitable — ever?" I repeated.

"You know what I mean."

"No," I lied. "Tell me."

To speak forthrightly seemed hard for Jim's father. He indulged in a long sigh while he carefully chose his words. "I am referring to that girl's background. It is not her fault — or yours — that she comes from such poor stock. You've done your best, I know. But see what it has brought her to."

Now Bill looked steely eyed. He said, "Go on."

"You have given her completely unrealistic expectancies and goals. She is overreaching when she seriously believes that Jim's family could ever become her own."

There it was. The old "blood will tell" philosophy dressed up in neater words. With restraint I kept myself from saying that this beautiful, expanding human being whom we considered our daughter; this almost straight "A" student; talented actress and artist; warm and compassionate camp counselor and hospital volunteer was probably too good for his family. I was trembling with anger.

Bill came to my rescue. "I don't think you have any real concern. As we explained, the court would have to agree to any marriage, and I feel quite sure that none would be sanctioned for at least two years."

I suppose that to the professor we appeared to be dangerous social climbers. He left our home as soon as he could.

I did not try to explain our discussion or my discomposure to Rena. I did not think that I could do so with impartiality.

That night I lay awake a long time wondering at the warmth that permeated me whenever I thought of Rena. I tried to explain it to Bill beside me. Such a joy as I felt needed sharing.

"Honey," he said, "this is not good. You're heading for a terrible letdown."

"Letdown? I love that girl. Love is not something that I learned from my own family like you and most other people did. It makes me feel wonderful and complete when it happens. I feel that I'm growing when I can love anyone besides you and Steven."

"It may be something other than love. And even if it is, it could cause you terrible hurt."

"Rena won't hurt me. I know her."

"But you don't know the future. Be careful, honey. Don't get carried away."

New things began to take up the minds of all of us. School started. Steven discovered science fiction and was reading books that were way beyond him.

Rena's fine record the previous school year had led her to be placed with the academic preparatory group. We began to think that perhaps Rena should think of kindergarten teaching rather than nursing as a future vocation.

Bill and I were extremely pleased with Rena's new academic level. We didn't notice the sudden silences into which she retreated at the mention of school or studies.

"Rena, don't you have any homework tonight?"

"I suppose so."

"You *suppose* so? What on earth does that mean?"

Rena's face hardened. "I don't want to do it tonight."

"What are you talking about?" Sometimes I found Rena's conversation terribly exasperating.

She said, "I'm bored with that stuff."

"How can you be bored? It's only September!"

"Mom, do I have to go to school?"

"Of course you do, Rena. Where would you be if you didn't finish high school?"

"Lots of people don't finish high school. My mother only went through fifth grade. My uncle got all the way through tenth grade, and then he could only get a janitor's job."

"Rena, you have to get through high school so you can

become a nurse or a teacher. Don't you want an interesting job like that some day?"

"I suppose so," she responded in a tone that belied her words.

More and more it seemed that there was a wall growing up between us when I tried to talk to her. It took hammering to be heard through that wall, and sometimes I just didn't feel like hammering.

While playing basketball with his junior high school students, Bill tore a muscle in his leg. Rena brightened at the prospect of being able to nurse a sick man, but Bill had no inclination to play invalid. He continued with his normal activities, but with a new silence borne of pain whenever he tried to walk. He became irritable, and consequently, so did I. I was particularly short with Rena.

A letter arrived from her sister, Carol. Rena had not heard from Carol for more than a year. Eagerly she took the letter into her room. Later, at dinner, Rena was quiet and pale. However, so as not to trouble Bill further, I waited until after dinner to talk to her about it.

Rena did not want to tell me about her letter at first, but eventually her pain broke through. "They did it, Mom. They did! They took all the kids away from Mom!"

It took me a minute to digest the meaning of her words. The two "Moms" confused me. Rena rarely spoke of her mother as "Mom." That was my name, and my thoughts hung on this confusion rather than on the significance of Rena's news.

She was continuing with an unusual rush of tears. "Carol says they left her only the baby. The other kids are all going to be placed in foster homes. That's going to kill Mom!"

"But, why would they do that, honey?"

"Carol says Mom didn't take right care of them. They didn't hardly ever go to school. Mom never could handle getting them all out of the house every morning. I knew it! I knew it!"

Rena was clearly blaming herself. Carol, apparently, had placed all the guilt on Rena either by word or by implication.

I did not feel that I could convince Rena of her innocence

in this matter. Some early thinking or training, deeply rooted in the personality that made her the individual she was, could never be moved by my words -- no matter how well I chose them. A different approach was called for.

"Well, honey, if they are all going to be placed in foster homes, why not here?"

Her blue, swelling eyes looked up at me with surprise. "All of them?"

"Well, no, dear. We don't have room for five more. But we might take one of your sisters. Or, Steven might enjoy the company of your little brother."

Her eyes retreated again. She said, "Yes. One of them. Please try."

The energy and sparkle drained out of Rena. She went through her days mechanically, saying little. Daily she asked me about our progress in securing one of her young siblings for our family. The welfare department did not answer my written request.

Finally, in response to Rena's gentle but insistent prodding, I telephoned the welfare department in Rena's county. I talked to the social worker in charge of the case and was told that since Rena's brother and sisters were non-delinquents, they would automatically be placed within their own county. Only delinquent children were ever placed out of the county. The answer to our request was an emphatic and final no.

The strain was serious for Rena. She no longer spoke pleasantly to anyone. She broke up her longstanding romance with Jim, who, deeply hurt, blamed his father's visit. I was too concerned over Bill's slowly healing leg and temper to be able to give Rena the sympathy and understanding she needed. My words to her were too often more short or judgmental than I meant them to be.

One morning early in October, Rena was late leaving for school. Without preamble, I said, "You're going to be late, you know."

She did not respond.

"I said you're going to be late."

"Dad'll give me a lift."

"He's already gone."

Rena's sullen face showed hurt surprise. Usually, Bill waited to drive her, even when it put him under pressure to be on time himself.

"Have you done your homework?" I continued.

"No. I better go."

"Why didn't you get it done? You had plenty of time."

"Can I go now?" Her face bore that defiant expression that I could not stand when it was directed towards me.

"Not until you tell me why you didn't do your homework."

"I don't know. My mind wasn't on it."

"Rena, this is the last time that is to happen; do you understand?" The words came out high and sharp.

She stood looking at me for a moment, clutching and unclutching her school books. I was silently berating myself, but didn't know how to retreat in the face of her quiet fury. Rena turned and went back into her room.

She was going to make herself late. I decided not to say any more. Maybe the tardiness would be a good lesson for her. I would let her do as she pleased for now.

Rena came out of her room wearing the dress we had purchased a few weeks before for a father-daughter banquet she and Bill attended at the high school. It was light blue with white embroidery on the yoke. I noticed that the blue exactly matched her eyes. Rena picked up her books without a word and left.

We never saw her again.

We waited dinner until 6:30, then ate without appetite. At first we were put out about her thoughtlessness in not letting us know that she would be so late. Gradually our apprehension turned to fear. We exchanged a series of anxious what-ifs.

After dinner, I reluctantly phoned Jim. He told me Rena had not been in pottery class that morning. He promised to let us know if he heard from her.

I was growing numb with fear.

At about eight o'clock, Bill told me gently, "I think it's time we called Rena's probation officer."

Bill believed that Rena had run away. I felt it was my fault. I had been so unreasonable that morning.

"Well, honey," Bill said, "shall I call Miss West?"

I nodded.

Miss West told us to notify the local police right away. Meanwhile, she would call the sheriff's office in Rena's home town and have someone go immediately to the house where Rena's mother lived.

"Please let us know the minute you hear anything," I pleaded, my voice already close to tears.

"Of course," Miss West promised. "But, frankly, I wouldn't get my hopes too high."

The policeman who answered my frantic call sounded bored with our report of a missing girl. "You say she's run away before?"

"Yes," I admitted. "Twice. But that was a long time ago, before she lived here."

"How long ago?"

I tried to get my brain back into gear. "Just over two years ago was the last time."

Two years. Was that all it had been? Yes. Then, actually, I had been Rena's mother for *less* than two years. Why, then, was the pain so deep?

"Don't worry about it, Ma'am," the policeman said. "We have lots of cases like this. They all turn up sooner or later."

I was beginning to feel my face getting set like Rena's when she felt quiet, repressed anger. How could that man sound so unconcerned?

"Aren't you going to send someone over?" I demanded.

"That shouldn't be necessary. At least let's wait until tomorrow."

"Tomorrow! Now look here. Rena is too young and too attractive to be out wandering around heaven-knows-where late at night. She might be hurt or raped somewhere. Or she might even get picked up by some police officer!"

"All right. Of course. If you feel it's as serious as all that, we'll send a man over right away."

As I hung up the phone, I began to wonder if perhaps I might be taking this matter too seriously. "Bill, I think the sheriff's department will find her at her mother's place. She was probably just worried about the way her mother was taking the loss of the children."

"Sure," he replied. "That makes sense." But his face was as tense as mine.

The police officer who arrived seemed more interested in the disappearance than had the man on the phone. His relevant questions about her activities and friends gave us confidence. He promised to telephone us by the next day whether he had any news or not.

The phone was silent for the rest of the night.

Steven wept, but I could not think of any words to make him feel better. Steve loved Rena too, and like me, he seemed to take Rena's disappearance as something said directly to him.

It was well after midnight before any of us could go to bed.

Bill and Steve were both reluctant to go to school the next morning. I promised that I would let them know if anything came up.

Miss West, Rena's probation officer, arrived early. Her thin, sharp face showed her deep concern. "How did it happen?" she asked, as if we were discussing an automobile accident.

"I don't exactly know. She seemed to be worried about her mother having all the children taken away. Did you know about that?"

"No! I hadn't heard. Are you sure?"

"Yes, all but the baby. I called the welfare department and asked if we might have one of them placed in our home. But they wouldn't hear of it."

"You should have called me," Miss West said. "I think I might have been able to arrange it."

"You could? But those children were with the welfare department!" The drained feeling I had gave way to anger with myself. Why hadn't I thought of calling Miss West?

"Well," she continued briskly, "I guess there's no point going over all that now. The important thing is to find Rena before anything happens to her."

"Like what?" I asked.

"Well, the longer she stays away, the more serious it becomes. This will be her third runaway. I'm going to have a hard time keeping her out of the State Youth Authority."

"What's that?"

"That's where we send the youngsters who are considered incorrigible."

"Incorrigible! You know Rena better than that."

Miss West was not looking at me. Her thin eyebrows were drawn together, separated by two deep vertical lines. Her mouth seemed thinner than usual. "I can only do so much. I recommend things. I make reports. But it doesn't always work out. I'm not God. I'm not even the Juvenile Court!"

Miss West's cool, efficient manner was falling away. Her words were no longer the usual polite responses and leading questions needed for her reports.

"You have no idea how proud I was of Rena," she continued. "The children who come to our attention so often do so too late. And *then* try to find them a home! Nobody wants a teenager with a delinquency record. We keep them at The Hall and try to do what we can. But Juvenile Hall is just no substitute for a home, and we know it!"

"And neither is the State Youth Authority," I added, catching her mood.

"No. Neither is the Youth Authority. But, as I said, it's not entirely up to me."

The beautifully dressed woman before me was about to break into childlike tears. That would have been all I needed to do the same.

Sitting up rigidly, I asked, "Well, what do we do now?"

"I thought there might be some value in just driving all over her home town. We might see something."

"But shouldn't someone be here in case a phone call comes in?"

"We can call and check when we get back. Come on."

All day we drove around the area in which Rena had grown up. We stopped at the home of her uncle, her pastor, her sister, her friends; all of them expressed surprise at Rena's disappearance. She was not at her mother's house, either, but I felt that her mother knew more than she would say. She kept changing the subject to trivialities. Each person we questioned promised to let us know if he heard anything from Rena. We did not believe them, but there was nothing more we could do.

We drove home without speaking. Miss West and I were both going through our own little hells of self-blame, blaming others, and what'ifs.

Our telephone calls to the sheriff's department and to the local police station developed nothing new. Worn out, I went to bed as soon as Miss West left.

The energy was completely drained from my body. I could not manage the simplest of my responsibilities. At first I stared blankly at the ceiling, but eventually the tears came. I missed Rena. I felt injured by her. I cursed myself for not understanding the intensity of her feelings, especially about her mother and the rest of her family. I feared for Rena's future.

For about two weeks, the only thing that got me out of bed was one of the false clues that kept coming up.

Ted McKay heard a guitarist singing in the house next to his. The voice sounded like Rena's deep, warm, sometimes raucous contralto. He phoned us. When we rushed over, we found a young couple enjoying their stereo.

Someone from the sheriff's department thought he recognized Rena as a passenger in a car that drove into and quickly out of a gas station while he was having his car serviced. Bill drove Steve and me back to Rena's town to look, the way Miss West and I had done earlier. We found no one who looked like our daughter.

Bill was not willing to let the long trip be for nothing. He decided to try to talk to some of Rena's family himself. The responses he received were those of innocent concern that Miss West and I had heard before.

At last we reached Carol's house. Bill got out of the car alone. Rena's sister was sitting on the porch. When she saw Bill, she came down the steps to meet him. I stayed in the car and watched her. I noticed that her fine features were set in the same hard lines that Rena's face took on when she was angry or worried; but for Carol, that expression had become her usual one. It made her look ten years older than her eighteen years.

From where I sat I could clearly see my husband and Carol standing in the unweeded yard. Children were playing behind the house, and their voices made it impossible for me to hear what was being said near the car. Bill did most of the talking at first. Carol listened intently, glancing occasionally in the direction of her youngsters. Suddenly she turned to Bill with a rush of words that caused him to move back as if he had been physically pushed. He listened, then leaned forward, shaking his head as he talked. Carol said no more. She walked into the small, unpainted wooden house and shut the door.

Bill came back slowly to the car. I waited for him to tell me what he had learned. His hands took the steering wheel as soon as he got into the car. First his fingers gripped, then he began tapping with one finger in a slow, monotonous rhythm.

"She's left the state," he said. "Carol says she's married."

It wasn't until months later that we were able to piece together from several sources the details of what had happened.

When Rena walked out of our lives, she walked first to her high school, then past it. She continued walking until the books she was carrying became a burden for her. Then she decided to abandon all the school supplies she had recently come to hate. She walked with resolution into the ladies' room of a gas station and, as if by accident, she left them all on the mirror shelf.

It took her most of the day to walk to Carol's house. Questions along the way might prove dangerous. She had to find the direction by forcing her mind to remember the way I drove her on the days when we had visited the psychiatrist.

Carol was not surprised to see her weary sister. Her letters had been written with the hope of just such an outcome.

"You gotta hide," Carol told her sister. "The cops will be here to get you any minute now."

"I don't care about that," Rena replied. "How can I get to see Mom?"

"In time. In time. Don't you know that's the first place they'll look? Renie, you may not know it, but now that you've gone and run away for a third time, y're gonna have to go to jail."

"Jail! You mean Juvie. I can stand that. And they'll have to catch me first."

"How can I make you understand? Carol insisted. "When a person runs away three times that's a big law they broke. They don't give you no more chances. They just put you in jail until you're eighteen or so."

Rena's only thought as she walked the long way home was to see her mother. Now Carol was forcing her to look at her situation practically. Was it possible that Carol was right?

The doubt flickering across Rena's face was encouragement

enough for Carol. She hurried on.

"Look. I'll take you over there now, but only f'r a few minutes. Then I'll hide you out at the house of a friend of mine."

Rena found her mother in much better spirits than she had anticipated. Actually, the woman seemed rather relieved to be responsible for only one baby. The other children had all been placed within an easy bus ride of where she lived, and the mother was allowed liberal visiting privileges. Rena's brother was with an uncle and still attended the family's church regularly.

Seeing her mother so relaxed about the situation freed Rena's mind to consider more seriously the position in which she now found herself.

"I better go home now," she told Carol. "My foster parents will think of somethin' to do."

"It's too late," Carol told her. "They already musta told the cops. Now the cops is in it, nobody else c'n do a thing. Don't you remember how cops are?"

Rena's weariness overcame her judgment. She allowed herself to be hidden in the home of her sister's friend.

The next day Rena had difficulty deciding what to do. The confines of the stranger's house were like a prison to her. Contrary to the advice of her hostess, Rena walked back to her sister's place.

"Carol, I just don't feel right about stayin' there. I came here to see Mom. You told me she was real sick about losin' the kids, and I was worried."

"She is upset. She's just hidin' it."

"Well, now that I'm here, I don't see what good I can do. I think I wanna phone home, anyway ."

"Can't I get it into y'r head that y're in trouble? Real trouble!"

"Well, what can I do about it? Just hang around at your friend's place? I sure can't stay with Mom."

"There's only one way you c'n make the cops stop lookin' for you. You gotta get married."

"Married! I don't wanna get married."

"It's either that or go to jail. Listen to me! Ain't I y're big sister? I had lotsa experience with cops. If y're married you can go see Mom whenever you want and the cops can't do nothin' about it. If you don't do it, you'll go to jail f'r sure!"

"But I don't know anybody I want to marry, now," Rena told her.

"Don't worry about that," Carol said. "I got it all worked out."

That evening, Carol introduced her sister to the man she had picked "to help Rena out of a jam." Sam Jones was more educated than anyone in Rena's family. He had a high school diploma. He was thirty-two years old. Somewhat like Rena, Sam was on probation from a state prison, and he adored his guitar. During the day he worked as an auto mechanic. At night he strummed and sang, for fun or for drinks, in the local bars.

Forty-eight hours after they met, Rena and Sam Jones were married by a Baptist minister in one of the hasty marriage chapels in Reno. Rena was still wearing the light blue dress she had worn when she left our house.

Rena was not told until after the marriage had taken place that Sam had broken parole in at least three ways by marrying her. The terms of his parole included staying single. He was not permitted to cross state lines. And he was contributing to the delinquency of a minor by aiding a sixteen year old ward of the court to run away.

Rena and Sam had to keep moving and hiding for about seven months before they were finally found and arrested. Sam was sent back to the state prison to complete his sentence for forgery. Rena was sent to the State Youth Authority, now branded an incorrigible delinquent.

Miss West came to see Bill and me as soon as we told her that Carol's story had been verified by the city police. The door of Rena's strangely quiet room which faced the living room where we sat, had been closed for about two weeks. Miss West sat on the couch, her fingers alternately clutching and releasing the handbag in her lap.

"Sometimes I think we do these kids an injustice," she told us.

"In what way?"

"Who are we to say what's best for children? We decide that all children should be warmly clothed, well fed and in school. But that's *our* idea of what's right. Did it ever occur to you that we might be wrong?"

Miss West's voice hardened as she continued to let out the flood of disappointment and bitterness. "They let us know in every way possible that they don't want what we want for them. They act up at school. They destroy the property we give them. They run away. Just as soon as you think you're getting somewhere with them, wham!"

"I don't think you mean what you're saying," I told her gently. "You're just upset about Rena."

"Rena? This is my fifth runaway this month! You know something? I wasn't even worried about Rena. Perhaps it would have been better if we had just let her stay away the first time she ran years ago. and all those other kids we think we know what's best for, too."

"Including the ones with drunken or sadistic parents?" Bill asked.

"Yes, them too. I can't imagine why I ever got into this business!"

The telephone rang with a call for Miss West. Her face relaxed as she took the receiver. In her usual professional tone she said, "Yes? Miss West here."

Her expression gradually moved from cool detachment to heavy strain as she listened to the problems that had arisen in another of her cases.

"You mean both of those children are going to have to be moved again? But this will be the third time this year! . . . Mm hm . . . Mm hm . . . But can't I possibly . . . Mm hm . . . I know. But they're so little. How are we going to explain it to them? . . . Mm hm . . ."

She turned her head away so that we might not see her eyes overflowing unprofessionally.

3

ANN

On the evening of the day that Rena walked away, another sixteen year old sat in a police station. Her back was rigid; her hands folded. Long dark lashes veiled her eyes.

The man in charge of the police station that night had never run into this kind of situation before. He wasn't sure what he should say or do.

"Now look here, young lady. This is silly. You can't just sit there all night. Why don't you let one of the men here drive you home?"

"I'm not going home," she said in a soft, firm voice.

"If you don't go home, we'll just have to lock you up, you know."

"That's up to you."

The man at the desk called other officers more experienced in handling difficult teenagers. But the quiet, tiny redhead, who seemed welded to the chair, did not fit any of the patterns they were familiar with.

Another officer said, "I know how it is, kid. You had a fight with your dad and decided to teach him a lesson. Well, you've made your point. If you drive up in a police car now, you'll show him you mean business. Now, just tell us where you live . . . "

"I have no home."

Reason, threats, persuasion, promises: Nothing worked. Defeated after several hours, the officers took her to Juvenile Hall.

Miss West was assigned to the case.

Several weeks later, Miss West was again sitting in our living room, this time describing her new case to me.

"Well, we investigated," she said crisply, "and all I can say is, this girl should have left that so-called home of hers years ago. How she stood it this long is more than I can understand."

"Miss West, I'm sorry you insisted on coming over here. You see, what we want now is a little boy just a bit younger than Steven whom he can play with."

She went on as if she had not heard me. "Ann has practically reared herself. Her mother died when she was small, and her father is rarely in the home. When he does come home, he is drunk and looking for someone to beat up."

"And of course, Ann is usually the victim."

"That's right. Her body was covered with black and blue marks when she was brought to the Hall."

"Then why does she have a probation officer?"

"Well, she did run away. That's still against the law, you know. Most wards of the court are not actually delinquents. They have a probation officer for their own protection. Ann needs protection, although she doesn't exactly realize it."

"She must realize it, since she went straight to a police station when she ran away." I began to feel annoyed with myself for the curiosity I was displaying.

"No, Ann has been her own mother and father for years. She 'comes on' like a little old lady. She reasons everything through. The parent inside her told Ann that it was time she learned to live in a real family. It wasn't protection she was looking for. It was a kind of education."

"Sounds a bit schizophrenic to me," I said, mildly impressed with my own astuteness.

"Who's normal?" Miss West asked, not waiting for a reply. "We all make what adjustments we can. Ann's ways of adjusting and her school record suggest a high level of intelligence. I wouldn't want just anyone to have her. That intelligence needs careful channeling. I think you're the people to do it."

Miss West's voice sounded firm and positive, but her eyes pleaded. I was beginning to have that trapped feeling I get with door to door salesmen. It made me a little angry.

"Oh, come on. You have lots of reliable foster families."

"But none with a college education. Do you know that yours is the only home that our county uses in which even one adult has a college degree?"

"That's impossible. Your county has many well educated families."

"Yes, but they don't take foster children. With all the talk about the population explosion — not to mention the current costs of having your own — we thought that foster care should catch on. But it hasn't."

"Look," she continued. "This girl is really unusual. She writes stories and absolutely beautiful poetry. She is an all 'A' and 'B' student in spite of her lack of a home life. Long ago she reasoned that an education was her passport to a better life, so she studies hard."

Admittedly, academic ability was one of our biases. I was weakening. "All right," I told her. "Let me talk it over with Bill. But I'm not making any promises!"

When Ann came for her preliminary dinner in our home, we all had the feeling that we were bugs on a microscope slide. She was studying us as intently as we were studying her.

Ann's tiny size and grownup face did not seem to go together. She was not more than five feet tall, and very light in weight. She had dark red, curly hair which she wore long. Her freckled face retained a serious expression. Ann's sharp eyes seemed to take in every detail. They were steady eyes — either carefully focused or guardedly down. She kept her back straight as if to add every possible inch to her stature. As a result, she looked stiff, robot-like.

Ann ate little, but enough so as not to appear rude. Her manners were studied, impeccable; her language literate. Ann's conversation consisted primarily of polite answers to our polite questions. She did seem intelligent, but it was clear that the veneer of propriety would be hard to penetrate in any meaningful way.

Ann never smiled.

The evening struck me as a scene from a motion picture in which eveyone says the lines that someone else has written for him. Each of us privately welcomed Miss West's reappearance to take Ann back to Juvenile Hall.

Steve, Bill and I sat together in the living room to evaluate what had happened at dinner. No one was quite sure exactly what that was.

Steven said, "I like her. But she's sure not like Renie."

"Then what is it about her you like?" I asked.

"I don't know."

Bill said, "There's an air of unreality about her. It's as if she had just stepped off a stage and was still in character. I wonder what she's really like."

I guess it was the air of mystery that intrigued us. We decided to accept the challenge as much for curiosity as for any other reason.

The door to Rena's room had been closed since she left. There was no more avoiding it now; I had to pack her things.

The room, itself, had taken on Rena's personality. Rena had painted the walls pink, the ceiling pale blue, and the wood trim white. The windows were covered with lacy curtains. On the walls were several Jefferson Players programs and pictures of baby animals and children. On her old brown chest of drawers were framed pictures of her brother and sisters, and an award she had won for her work as a hospital volunteer. Pottery and ceramic samples decorated her desk in such profusion as to make it unusable for writing purposes. South Seas decorations from a day camp luau she once planned hung around the headboard of her bed.

As I packed the clothes that she had made, or that we shopped for together, I felt as if Rena had died. I welcomed a growing numb feeling that made it possible for me to finish my work with diminished pain.

The last thing I packed away was the large white candle that Ted McKay had given to her "to seal a promise" at his daughter's wedding -- not two years ago.

Ann arrived with a grocery carton of clothes that she was given at Juvenile Hall. A smaller box contained books of poetry and oriental philosophy. These books were the only belongings she had asked the investigating social worker to pick up from her father's house.

Ann put her things into "her" room and came out almost immediately. She gravely handed me a gift -- two bracelets of raffia she made while at Juvenile Hall. Each was beautifully designed. One was blue and white; the other, two shades of green. She also had candy for Steven. He looked at us with pleading eyes.

"All right, Steve. Just this once you may have the candy."

He was delighted.

I explained to Ann that we did not allow Steven to have candy for fear of cavities, except on special occasions.

Ann looked smitten.

"Oh, but it's all right this time, dear," I added hastily. "This is a very special occasion, of course."

Ann pulled her lips into the form of a slight smile, but her eyes showed her disappointment. I mentally kicked myself for sounding so parental.

Ann returned to her room to unpack her few belongings.

The next morning she was up and dressed early. She could hardly wait to register at our local high school. We arrived at the school before first period had begun, and were referred to the Dean of Girls.

"The Witch" remembered me and asked about Rena. I told her as briefly as possible that Rena was no longer with us. She nodded, showing no emotion. I winced inwardly, recalling her philosophy of "Blood Will Tell."

The Dean looked at the transcript from Juvenile Hall where Ann had done her most recent school work. I don't believe that the Dean saw beyond those words "Juvenile Hall."

"I'm sorry, " she said, not sounding sorry in the least. "We can't accept her here."

Ann's face registered shock momentarily, then grew hard and set.

I was stunned. "What do you mean you can't accept her?" I asked. "Is there anything wrong with her transcript?"

"No, of course not. But you see, we're terribly crowded here this year. And the semester is already well along. It would be very hard for . . . what's your name? . . . er, yes, Ann, to fit in. She would have so much catching up to do, you know."

"Ann can catch up. My husband and I are both credentialed teachers. We'll help her."

"I'm sorry. Maybe next semester. Meanwhile, I'm referring her to Continuation High School."

I shuddered at the thought of Ann's probable reaction to Continuation High School. The building mirrored the attitude of the community toward all of the non-conforming boys and girls who attended it — the truants, the misbehavers, the unmarried pregnant girls, the retarded. Our city preferred to ignore such problems insofar as possible. The taxpayers' money was not to be wasted on poor social material. So the school, like the children's hopes, decayed a little more each year. The fire department reportedly had already condemned the old wooden structure, but classes continued there "temporarily" until "something could be worked out about the students."

As Ann and I left the Dean of Girls' office I was quietly promising myself, we'll show that Witch. Ann will make such a record at Continuation High that she'll be back here before the year is out.

Ann had not said a word from the time she had been introduced to the Dean of Girls. Now she was walking beside me, still silent. Suddenly she said loudly, "That mean old lady doesn't want me in her school!" She began sobbing with the rush of emotions she had so long been damming up within herself.

For the first time I put my arms around the trembling girl. "Ann. Ann." Then I said with more conviction than I felt, "Don't you worry about it, Ann. You are not going to any Continuation School — that I promise you! Do you believe me?"

"But she said . . ."

"Never mind what she said! She's not the last word in this matter. You are not going to any Continuation School; I promise!"

I felt like a mother tiger protecting her threatened cub. I didn't know exactly where or how to take my roar, but no one was going to hurt this little girl while I was around.

I thought hard while I drove Ann home. Her tears had ceased, but I felt that it would be unbearably grim for her to sit around the house all day. "Ann, I have an idea. Let's stop by the house just long enough to drop your notebook and pack a sandwich. Then I'll take you on a tour of the city."

I silently checked my daily "have-to list" and renamed it the "should list."

Ann did not answer me.

The house seemed empty and cold when we arrived. I

felt that I should keep her busy while I did the thing that I first planned to try. I gave Ann the lunchmaking detail while I phoned Bill's school and left word for him to call home as soon as possible. The secretary must have understood this to mean an emergency. Bill called me back within a few minutes.

Briefly I told him of Ann's rejection at the high school, and as I expected, Bill was as indignant as Ann had been. He promised that he would do something.

I told him, "I thought I'd take this to the Superintendent of Schools, and if that didn't work, to the Board of Education."

"Wait a little on that. I want to think about it," he told me. "You go ahead and take Ann for that drive."

The tour did nothing to cheer Ann up. She was quiet as we drove. The nearest thing to a reaction I received from her throughout the rest of that tense day was a deep sigh as I pointed out the peeling, brown, wooden structure that was Continuation High School. Just in case we were stuck with it, I tried to say some positive things about the school, but Ann was not deceived.

When we arrived back home, Bill was already there.

"Well, Ann," he told her cheerfully, "it's all arranged. You'll go to high school in the city where I teach."

"Is it a good high school?" she asked, with characteristic practicality.

Bill's face showed he did not expect that response. "Yes, it is," he said. "It has a fine, college preparatory reputation. I talked to the head counselor there, and he was astounded by the attitude of that Dean of Girls. He said you were more than welcome in his school."

"Good," I said, with more enthusiasm than I felt. I was concerned about Ann's making friends in a city so far away that she probably couldn't socialize after school.

"You can ride there and back every day with me," Bill told her.

We were not yet through with dinner when Bill's friend, the high school counselor, telephoned.

"Say, Bill, I got thinking about what you told me, and the more I thought about it, the madder I got. So I did something, and I hope you don't mind."

"Is there any problem about . . . well, you know." Bill

did not dare to say the words while Ann was nearby.

"No, of course not. But I just phoned the principal of the high school in your city. He was sure surprised. He told me he had no idea that the Dean of Girls had such a policy — that the school wasn't so overcrowded that it couldn't take one more student. Anyway, he promised me that if Ann will go to school first thing tomorrow, she'll be admitted as a regular student right away."

"Great!" Bill fairly boomed. "Should they go see the principal, himself?"

"No. By the time your wife and Ann get there, I'm sure the Dean will have heard from the principal. And I don't think she'll seem very happy, either. Not about Ann, I mean, but about what the principal had to say to her. By the time I hung up, he sure sounded angry."

When Bill told us the good news, Ann's face, full of relief and anticipation, showed me that parents should act like tigers more often.

"Don't worry about it," she assured us unnecessarily. "I'll make a good record there, I promise."

Ann was placed, rather obviously, with the non-college preparatory students, but that did not seem to make a difference to her. True to her word, she did more than was expected of her in every class.

Unlike many other foster children, Ann's problems did not include academic ones. The theoretical, the imaginative, the retrospective and introspective subjects were not difficult for her. It was the skill of living with other human beings that she lacked. She felt this lack and tried earnestly to correct it.

She helped me in the kitchen at every opportunity, but there was no spontaneity to it. She simply felt that she should.

She helped Bill with the endless job of correcting class papers. She took the work seriously, often perceptively diagnosing students' difficulties. Bill was impressed. We decided that Ann ought to consider becoming a teacher.

Unlike Rena, who shared easily and naturally with children, Ann had nothing in common with Steve. To make up for this, she bought him endless gifts of candy. She always gave them to him with the warning, "Don't tell your parents, now, or we'll both be in trouble." This bothered Steven who loved both candy and his parents.

Ann felt most at home in her customary solitude. She read and wrote poetry. She occasionally listened with deep concentration to classical music. She wrote long, involved letters to her father, many of them describing her "bad treatment" at our home. The letters caused no reaction, positive or negative, from her father. He never came to see her; never communicated with her social worker. He never answered any of her letters, no matter how long nor how sorrowful.

Ann made no friends that we knew of in school.

Her real world lay inside herself. The world outside she saw as from within a space capsule. She made noises and gestures toward the beings that moved on the strange planet, but the walls were too thick between her and the willing earthlings to make contact in any meaningful way.

Once Bill tried to reach her through a language she seemed to understand, poetry. He wrote:

For Ann

A shadow can't tag me just because it moves,
But, that light is shining,
it certainly proves
Yesterdays I ran from now run from me.
Today the past is "it," and now I am free.

Ann was pleased by his gesture, but remained as locked within herself as ever.

The Jefferson Players were working on a new Gay Nineties Revue to be presented as a benefit for the Nursery School for Retarded Children. Ted McKay, hearing of the plan, suggested we bring the entire show to the children at Juvenile Hall. We readily agreed.

It occurred to me that this show might offer Ann a chance to bridge the gap between her imaginary world and the real one. I suggested that she take part in it. The prospect delighted her.

Casting Ann proved to be a problem. She was shorter by almost one foot than any man in the company, and had a tiny voice to match. She was, however, able to stay on pitch. One would hardly have called her pretty, although youth has its own way of being attractive.

At first, I put her into the Floradora Sextette. Their main song was "Tell me Pretty Maiden" — a naive bit of mutual seduction-plus-innocence. Ann worked on it with characteristic concentration and made up for her lack of voice by complete reliability and a surprising charm that had, until then, been indiscernible. The Jefferson Players were captivated by her adult, dedicated attitude toward her work.

I decided she deserved to have a number of her own. We worked out a pantomime version of "No, No! A Thousand Times No!" The first lines fit Ann perfectly:

She was a child of the valley;
An innocent maiden was she . . .

When Ann was costumed in a lamb chop sleeved blouse, a pinafore, and a huge bow perched atop her dark red curls, she was the picture of "Little Orphan Annie." The part was literally written for her.

When the show was just about ready, Ann ran away.

I could not believe this had happened. All the pain and bewilderment that followed the loss of Rena swept over me again, opening wounds I thought had healed. The strength gone from me, I mostly sat, or lay in bed, struggling through problems of love, expectations, and confusion of the two incidents: the loss of Rena and the rejection by Ann. There had been warnings and reasons when Rena ran away. But Ann's leaving us seemed totally unrelated to the joys and excitements that I felt were beginning to lead her to that fine career in teaching.

What we did not understand was that it was exactly the joys and excitements that caused Ann to go. She did not run away from us. She ran *to* someone else.

Ann took a bus and walked straight back to Juvenile Hall. She pounded on the door at 2 a.m. until someone finally heard her and let her in. She demanded incarceration. She had come back to tell the girls of her good fortune — one girl in particular: Lee.

Miss West had not told us about Lee. Like many people, Miss West believed that there were some problems that would just go away if one ignored them long enough. But Lee was a serious reality, and now Miss West was forced to tell us about her.

Lee had every quality Ann did not. She was tall, strong, self-assured, the undisputed leader of the girls' section at Juvenile Hall. She could, and did, play the roles of parent, confidante, champion, teacher, and on occasion, even boyfriend when it suited her purposes. Minute by minute supervision precluded any physical relationships, but Lee still posed at least a potential control problem for the Juvenile Hall counselors. Hers was a forceful, seductive power, one recognizable and fascinating to all the girls. Had she wanted to, she could have created chaos with a word. But so far, she had chosen, instead, to consolidate her influence on an individual by individual basis.

Ann left our home because she needed someone to rejoice with her. She believed that Lee would smile, listen, and understand. Ann found pain and loneliness easier to dam up inside herself than joy. She was "making it on the outside." Who might better appreciate that miracle?

Some days later, at Juvenile Hall, Ann, Miss West, Bill and I had a conference. Tears, pleadings, promises from Ann. Still pale and weak from my painful emotional reaction, I made a promise too. If Ann ever ran away again, for any reason whatsoever, it would be the last time so far as we were concerned.

Ann promised it would never happen again. Then she promised Miss West that she would never see or contact Lee again. She meant both promises, I believe, but it was the second one that appeared to trouble her.

The experience did not bring us any closer together. Ann continued to act mechanically, doing whatever she felt was proper. Bill and I were willing to accept her that way. We believed she had a fine future ahead, and we longed to guide her into it. She should go to a college that had a good course in creative writing. When she emerged, she should get a teaching credential. I began writing letters to colleges.

Christmas approached, but any mention of the holiday caused a slight frown and further withdrawal on Ann's part. We assumed she had some unhappy memories from past Christmases. Bill and I decided to make this Christmas unforgettable for her in every way we could.

A California city Christmas is different from Christmases as celebrated on greeting cards or in nostalgic tales. Snow is rare; we have little carol singing; and Grandmother's house is not "over the meadow and through the woods" -- it's apt to be hundreds of miles away. A California Christmas is plastic and tinsel. Trees are often painted or artificial, and they are often trimmed in only one or two colors. Little robots go through meaningless non-human movements in the windows of crowded department stores. Jeweled and painted Christmas trees are worn as pins or earrings. It's a day to be shiny, glittery, and just a bit phony. A day to play the twin roles of bargain hunter and magnanimous friend and relative. It's a play in which everyone may act the role he likes best.

I love it.

The first of the Christmas ordeals for Ann was Family Day, one week early at my brother's home. Ann was so tense when we arrived that I suggested she go upstairs and lie down -- a suggestion Ann readily accepted. She slept during all of the preliminary family small talk, but came downstairs for dinner. When the time came to open presents, I began to guess what it was that troubled Ann so deeply.

She had never had a gift, and did not know the correct procedure for accepting one. She kept the packages with her name on them in her lap while she carefully watched me for some clues. Self-consciously, I studied each present I received as though very curious about it. Finally, I ripped off the paper of one, examined the contents, and registered pleasure. Then I said something enthusiastic to the donor of the gift. I went through my little ritual several times before Ann was willing to try it.

Watching her was painful. The gratitude part at the end gave her the most difficulty until the last package. My sister had bought Ann a beautiful purse of real suede. Ann's eyes widened and her shoulders dropped forward as if she had been hit on the back. Her expression, no longer acting, went from astonishment to pure joy. She neglected the thanks, but it was forgiven when she substituted the more honest, "Oh . . . oh . . . oh." My sister later told me she could not have had her gift more memorably acknowledged.

On the drive home, Ann opened up just a little. "Mom, I didn't have anything to give them."

"That's all right, honey. The kids never buy presents for the adults in these big family affairs. Or for each other. It could get to be just too much."

"But that's not right."

"Why not, Ann?"

"Mom, people don't just give people things without expecting something back. Everyone expects something back."

"Not at Christmas, Ann. That's part of the fun."

But I could see that this was no fun for Ann. I thought back to our Christmas tree at home. We rarely got one, but this year we had bought a huge one, expecting it to please Ann. It was already surrounded with several packages bearing her name. I guessed we might have overdone it.

As if Ann could see the picture I was imagining, she said, "May I buy presents for you?"

"Of course! For your own family is O.K."

"For Dad and Steven too?"

"If you like. But don't feel that you have to do it."

Ann sighed deeply. I hoped that signified relief.

Our custom was that the adults opened all of their presents on Christmas Eve. That left Christmas morning entirely for the children.

Ann spent the day before Christmas in her room. She never took off her pajamas, and in answer to my inquiries, simply murmured something about not feeling well. I wished there were some way that I could say, Ann! For heaven's sake relax and enjoy it! But Ann had gone into more than her room. She was back in her space capsule with its soundproof walls.

Dinner was quiet, with only Steven chattering excitedly. Bill and I were at a loss about how to cheer up Ann. After dinner, Steven wanted us to open our gifts at once, and I thought it was probably a good idea. Perhaps Ann could enjoy someone else's enjoyment.

We went through the same routine as at my brother's house: Curiosity — hasty unwrapping — pleasure — expressions of gratitude.

Ann watched us carefully as we unwrapped the things she had chosen for us. Game-loving Bill received a Parcheesi game that he ultimately learned to enjoy as much as cards.

He smiled his gratitude to Ann.

For me, Ann had selected an oversized coffee cup with the word "MOTHER" gilded prominently within a circle of roses. Assuming that Ann was kidding my everlasting tea drinking, we all laughed.

Her face told us we were wrong. She really meant to please me — probably by the word that still gave her trouble, "Mother." Her eyes dropped from my face to the faded rug on the living room floor. The corners of her mouth pulled into her chin.

"Ann! It's really lovely! I believe it's hand painted, isn't it?" I said.

"Did you paint it?" Bill asked, knowing better.

She shook her head.

"Well, I didn't realize it before, but it's exactly what I need," I told her. "Thank you so much, dear."

But, although she smiled a small, polite smile, it was clear that Ann was unconvinced by our dramatic effort.

Steven asked, "Mommy, can we open up just one present tonight? Please!"

I glanced at Ann. Her face had lost its strained look, but her apparent calm looked like a theatrical mask.

Accepting gifts graciously is a skill. Ann had to learn how to do it. Perhaps if we allowed Steven and her to open one now, carefully keeping the whole thing low-keyed, Ann could begin to relax about the ordeal she would have to face in the morning.

The only presents Steven really enjoyed at this age were phonograph records and books. Ann's gift was the one he chose to open. It was a shirt. Steven's face fell. He recovered his composure quickly, but Ann had been studying him.

Ann opened a pair of slippers from us. She smiled and thanked us with a bit too much formality. Then she went back into her room, slipped out of her window, and ran away.

Christmas day passed bleakly for us. Steven cried a little. None of us felt like going to the meeting house for the usual Christmas Meeting for Worship. I did my best to keep up at least some front of "holiday cheer." In the early afternoon, when Steve finally left the house to look for his friends, I went back into my room, lay on top of the unmade bed, and stared at the graying paint on the ceiling. The old pain was back.

Two weeks later the *Gay Nineties Revue* went to Juvenile Hall. The boys who lived there had constructed a special stage for us in the dining hall. It was to be the first co-ed function the Hall had enjoyed for some months.

I welcomed the thought and time that the Players' preparations for our "road show" entailed. I was determined to make it an exceptional performance, even though I was afraid Ann might be in the audience.

If the Players knew how many conflicting memories and emotions struggled inside me that night, they never showed it.

"Is this the stage? It's too small!"

"Will it hold us?"

"How can we ever dance on a thing that size?"

"Hey, look at the ingenious design for the curtains! And where do you suppose they dug up a spotlight?"

"Spotlight nothing! Will you look at these wild footlights they made with juice cans? Now that's invention! Be careful not to trip over the cord!"

The prop manager came running over to me. "The bars! We forgot to bring the prison bars for 'Frankie and Johnny!' Can somebody go back?"

"It's almost thirty miles!"

"Richard, can you improvise something, quick? We've got to have bars for Frankie's prison scene."

We hurried to dress and make up in adjoining conference rooms, leaving the doors ajar when everyone was decent so that the occasional boy or girl who found an excuse to walk by could look in. The teenagers at the Hall were obviously spending as much time on their appearance that evening as we were.

Our leading man, Richard, opened the show by explaining the gay nineties format to the flower decorated girls and long-haired boys.

"Now, you'll have no trouble at all in the first part telling the good guys from the bad guys. You see, in the plays that were written in those days, everybody was some special type — a hero, or a heroine, or a villain or villainess. And part of the fun is for the audience to let the players know how much you like the good guys and hate the bad ones. Now, let me hear you cheer like you're going to do when I arrive. I'm the hero, naturally."

It was new, sparkling, and exciting to the youngsters. At first the cheers and booing were embarrassed, tentative. Eventually, they were participating energetically. When, in the play, the villain, sneeringly played by Bill, chased Jo-Anne, the heroine, out into the audience, the girls screamed and cringed in their seats.

We kept the musical section, the olio, short and lively. First came the Floradora Sextette. I took Ann's part, looking at my singing partner all through the number. I dared not look into the audience. Since this was not the kind of music they were familiar with, we exaggerated the flirting details and tried to look politely sexy. The kids loved it. They applauded loudly, whistling and stamping their feet.

The Jefferson Players' enthusiasm for their audience was growing by the minute.

"Frankie and Johnny" brought cheers. The audience especially enjoyed poor Frankie, in her huge feathered hat, trying to look tragic behind green construction-paper prison bars.

Then followed the nostalgic tragedy of the young man who lost his love to "The Man on the Flying Trapeze." The couple on stage stared intently at the spotlight floating back and forth on the ceiling symbolizing the movements of that daring young man. Soon every face in the room followed the light in as rapt attention as if it did, indeed, focus its beam on the girl-stealing gymnast.

We did not do Ann's "No, No, A Thousand Times No." None of the Jefferson Players could replace Ann's Little Orphan Annie appeal.

Richard stepped out in front of the curtain, carefully avoiding the extension cord on the improvised footlights, and coaxed the audience to join him in a community sing. He began with songs some of them knew like "I've Been Working on the Railroad" and "Bicycle Built for Two." Then, with the help of the pianist, who was banging away with more noise than usual, he led them into songs they had never heard before. We all felt warm and pleased with the way the show was going, and the actors, singers, and the backstage crew drifted onto the stage informally seating themselves on it or in front of it, joining in the singing. Finally, Richard got to the finale song, "Tavern in the Town." As the cast faced the audience they sang the ending:

Fare thee well, for we must leave thee.
Do not let our parting grieve thee.
And remember that the best of friends must part;
Must part!
Adieu! Adieu, kind friends, adieu. Yes, adieu! . . .

Bill and I with the rest of the Players moved out into the dining room and straight to each boy and girl. Every delighted child's hand was seized and vigorously pumped as we worked our way to the back of the room.

Too late to retreat, I saw Ann sobbing pitifully with her arms around a counselor. She saw me at the same time.

"Please take me back! Please! Please!" she screamed, breaking the joyous atmosphere completely.

I stood frozen, not knowing what to say or do. I don't know where Bill was then. Ted McKay flew to my rescue.

"Ann!" he said, in a low, firm voice. "You promised me!"

But Ann pretended not to hear him and kept up her "Please! Please!" while I ran, upset and embarrassed, from the room. Ted and the counselor strained to keep Ann from running after me.

Bill and I went to our car alone. We drove the near-empty freeways to our home silently. There was no point in ruining the fun of reliving the performance that the Players usually enjoyed after a show.

Once home, I went straight to bed. I can only guess how Bill felt, but he knew that this was something I needed to work out for myself. He left me alone so I could.

Lying in the dark, I felt sure about only one thing: after sixteen years of living without a family, it was probably too late to learn to live with one. At least this was true for Ann, who tried so hard.

If only Ann had come to us sooner, I thought. We could have made so much of her. She could have been a writer, a teacher -- perhaps a poet. We would gladly have seen her through any college that could have helped her to meet these goals. Ann could have been such a wonderful daughter.

We would have been so proud of her.

But, as with Rena, I would burn the bridges. I would avoid the pain of seeing her again. Even when Ann was older, if she tried to get in touch with us, I would refuse as I had done when Rena wrote to us some weeks earlier.

I rose from my bed and went into Ann's room. I caught sight of my face in the mirror. It gave me a shock.

My face, for a moment, looked exactly like my mother's.

4

SHADOWS

Your children are not your children.
They are the sons and daughters of Life's longing for itself.

They come through you but not from you,
And though they are with you yet they belong not to you.

You may give them your love, but not your thoughts,
For they have their own thoughts.
You may house their bodies but not their souls,
For their souls dwell in the house of tomorrow
which you cannot visit, not even in your dreams.
You may strive to be like them, but seek not
to make them like you.
For life goes not backward nor tarries with yesterday.

You are bows from which your children
as living arrows are sent forth.
The Archer sees the mark upon the path of the infinite,
and He bends you with His might
that His arrows may go swift and far.

Let your bending in the Archer's hand be for gladness;
For even as He loves the arrow that flies
so He loves also the bow that is stable.

--Kahlil Gibran

My mother's life was one defeated hope after another.

A beautiful girl, the adored youngest daughter of a plantation owner near Montgomery, Alabama; her development was carefully watched by parents and family servants. The words she heard most often were, "No, Baby."

After a year away at school, she was no longer permitted to play with, or even to speak to, the black children who lived on or near the plantation.

Lonely at home, she wrote poetry, but was told, "No, Baby. Ladies don't write poetry."

She enjoyed singing lessons, and secretly dreamed of an operatic career. When her dream was discovered, it was ridiculed. "Baby, you're too little to sing opera. You have to be big and fat to make your voice heard all over an auditorium. You're too little, Baby."

She enjoyed arithmetic, but was taught French.

It was understood that she was to marry her cousin.

But catastrophe struck. The plantation was completely destroyed by fire while the family was away berry picking in a neighboring countryside. They lost everything and moved to Philadelphia where no one knew them. With newly found anonymity, my mother's world suddenly unfolded.

She opened a dancing school with her sister and proved to be an excellent businesswoman. When she met and married my father, she sold her half of the business and, with him, moved to California where all kinds of opportunities were said to be waiting.

Their first daughter was born soon after they arrived; later, my brother and I.

My father lost all his and Mother's money starting a business he knew nothing about. Since there was a war on, he found work to do, and Mother turned from dreaming for herself or for my father and began dreaming for her children.

There was a demand for children in films, particularly in war movies. Los Angeles was smaller then, and opportunities were plentiful. My sister, my brother and I became movie "extras," and spent many of our afternoons taking dancing, singing and acting lessons. My sister loved the work, but grew tall and wiry early in her adolescence. There was little work for her after that. My brother and I added modeling, stage, and radio work to our lives like most kids mow the lawn or do dishes -- because it was expected of us. It pleased us to please Mother. And pleased she was!

Her face usually showed no emotion at all. But she did not appear calm; rather more like a sleepwalker. The only thing that made her face awaken was a new job for one of the children. Then her marvelous sense of humor would burst forth. She began to call us nicknames like "Skidamarink" or "Buzz Wuzz." She would suddenly, and without warning, burst into a song like "It Ain't No Sin to Take Off Your Skin and Dance Around in Your Bones!" When we worked, she came to the studio or radio station with us. When we weren't working, she did hated housework, napped quite a bit, and had "sick headaches."

In our teens, my brother and I turned our adolescent rebellions naturally against the careers, (if one could call them that), which Mother had chosen for us.

I wanted to go to college. The only way I could get my mother's support for this "interruption of my career" was to major in music. When she discovered that I had changed my major to sociology, she was stunned. She went to bed. Her half-sleep life developed into an actual illness. She died right after my sophomore year.

I stared at my mother's face looking back at me from the mirror and spoke to myself as if to her. "Woman, there is no more do-it-yourself job in the world than living. You would have known that if you could only have seen me as I was rather than as an extension of yourself."

But I was doing no better. I tried to live the lives of Rena and of Ann, seeing only what I wanted to see, not what actually went on within them. My goals were only *my* goals, not their own. But they were different people — exactly as they were meant to be.

The pain I felt when I lost each of "my" girls was not for them. I was feeling sorry for my own lost daydreams; sorry for myself.

It was time I grew up.

5

JUVIE

The Jefferson Players loved their audience at Juvenile Hall. They could not keep those young people out of their conversations, even during the rehearsals of our new documentary.

"Are you sure all those kids broke the law?"

"But they look so nice! Did you notice how the girls wore real flowers in their hair?"

"Are all those kids waiting for foster homes?"

The Players' enthusiasm spread like pollen throughout the community, and I was besieged with requests to take a group on a visit to Juvenile Hall so that they could find answers to their questions for themselves.

I did not like the idea. Children are not zoo animals. I thought uneasily of descriptions of 18th century Europeans touring madhouses for entertainment.

I telephoned my friend, Ted McKay. To my surprise, he was encouraging. "By all means bring your Players and their friends," he told me. "We have tours here just about every day."

"Good grief, why?" I asked.

"So that our students will feel they are still part of the community," he replied. "Do you know our motto? 'The community cares.' And it does! From these tours we've developed an Auxiliary and we've had fantastic offers of piano lessons, judo exhibitions, grooming classes -- all kinds of things. Maybe your Players have some talents other than those they demonstrated the other night."

"Ted," I said, "we're not even members of your community. All of us live about thirty or forty miles away. The whole idea of coming out there again seems to me to be just one step removed from Peeping Tomism."

"Well, if you really feel like that, I have a suggestion. Our tour takes only slightly more than an hour. Why don't you first go see the juvenile hall in your own county? The comparison may surprise you."

A clean, white, sprawling building sits high on a hill overlooking a freeway in our county. It blends pleasantly into the residential landscape. Outwardly, no one would recognize it as a prison for youngsters.

We were met there by a boys' counselor, Mr. Barnwell, who was to serve as our guide. His eyes seemed to stare past us through his thick glasses. He was tall and balding. His tight brown trousers and tan blazer trimmed with gold buttons did not lessen his angularity.

During the initial orientation lecture, delivered in a small, overheated room, our guide's face remained inexpressive, and his voice droned so that some of his audience fell asleep.

Mr. Barnwell explained to those who managed to stay attentive that the children were sent to Juvenile Hall for treatment. Physical restraint was rarely used unless a child hit a counselor or suffered a psychoneurotic breakdown. However, treatment that the children needed was not always permitted, because the children had a right to legal counsel. Lawyers, he said, had a way of swaying the courts so that many children were released before they could receive any treatment.

As Mr. Barnwell told about other programs aimed at what he called hard core delinquents, the interest of my group waned to almost zero. I was relieved when he suggested that we might begin walking through the facilities.

We went first to the reception section. "Here," he told us, "a child is first brought in by a police officer or his parents."

"His parents?"

"Oh, yes. Parents often bring their kids to us when they can't handle them at home." He returned to his description of preliminary procedures. "We ask the kid a few questions for the records, strip him, and give him a towel to put on while we search his clothes."

"The girls too?" one of the women asked.

"Sure. But over on the other side," Mr. Barnwell replied as he led us down a hallway lined with tiny windows.

"Now, these are our isolation cells. As soon as we've given him back his clothes, we put each kid alone in one of these until a doctor arrives to examine him for contagious diseases. The girls are examined by a gynecologist."

We noticed that one of the isolation cells was occupied by a very small, desolate looking boy.

"Is that boy one of the delinquents? I mean, really?" one of the Players asked Mr. Barnwell.

"Yes," he replied. Then, noticing the disbelief on the faces of his tourists, he added, "We rarely get them as young as six here."

"Six years old!" The shock moved through the group. "What did he do?"

"Well, actually, he's in solitary right now for acting up. We rarely use isolation as punishment except in extreme cases. The kids hate that most."

"But, why is he here in the first place? I thought all you had were teenagers," she persisted.

"No, we get them from six to eighteen, though the majority are from fourteen to sixteen. This kid was part of a gang that stole cars. His brother was the leader. Some forty-five percent of the boys here have been involved in auto theft or some crime involving cars."

"Is that the kind of *treatment* they get here?" I couldn't help asking. My words came out more sarcastically than I expected, but Mr. Barnwell did not seem offended.

"This is treatment, of course," he replied with more enthusiasm than he had shown up to this point. "These kids want limits. They show us that they want us to get tough with them, so we do. They never go anywhere without lining up, and we don't let them poke or fight in line. We make them answer 'yes, sir,' when they address a counselor. The older boys, especially, respond well to regimentation."

"But, do the children like the counselors?"

"No, of course they don't," Mr. Barnwell replied. "But at least they don't gang up on them. A counselor working with younger boys needs to be more personable. Actually, we find that peer communication makes the best control."

We moved on to the living sections. To get to the first one we had to walk through a large, sunny gymnasium. Its floors gleamed like a bar top as one boy, about twelve years old, scrubbed it with self-conscious diligence for his audience. Off to one side was a glassed-in ping-pong section with a single table.

"How do you keep your gym floor so shining?"

"Oh, we never use the gym."

"Never use it! Why not?"

"Too serious a discipline problem. Then, too, we can't let the boys enjoy themselves too much. For many of them the Hall is so much simpler and more pleasant than their own home life that they never want to leave here. You can see we have to discourage that sort of thing."

Noticing that he had struck an area of interest, Mr. Barnwell continued. "Let me tell you something. A few years back someone offered to donate a swimming pool to the Hall. Can you imagine what that sort of thing would do? Why, for some kids this would turn into a regular country club. Naturally we turned it down."

When we got to the ping-pong room, someone asked, "What about ping-pong? They do play that, don't they?"

"Yes," the guide answered, "but we never allow more than three in the room at one time. Things could easily get out of hand if we did."

We walked on to the long, narrow hallway that separated the boys' bedrooms. Each small room had two beds bolted to the floor. There were bars on the windows, basic toilet facilities, no decorations.

"We're badly overcrowded," Mr. Barnwell told us. "These rooms were built with enough air space for one, but sometimes we have to put a mattress between the beds and sleep three in one room. Nothing else we can do."

"How can you supervise the boys when they're in their own rooms?"

"Here. Let me show you something." Mr. Barnwell lowered his voice to a whisper. "Lawrence," he said, "can you hear me?"

We all jumped as we heard a voice come over a loudspeaker. "Sure can. Got a problem?"

"No," Mr. Barnwell replied in a voice just slightly louder.

"Just demonstrating our bugging equipment."

To us he said, "We can hear a sound as soft as a match scratching. Nothing happens in any room that the counselor on duty doesn't know about right away."

Our next stop was a classroom. Until then, we had only seen two children: the boy in solitary confinement and the one polishing the gymnasium floor. We all felt embarrassed about entering a room full of boys who were living in the situation we were beginning to see, but could barely comprehend. The boys, themselves, stared openly at us. No adult wanted to be first to enter the classroom.

It was a crafts class. The boys attended it from thirty to fifty minutes a day, twice a week. Since not much could be accomplished in so little time, the projects were kept simple. Childish clay sculptures, ash trays, and pots were displayed on a table. That day, the boys were attaching to key chains the copper enameled charms they had made earlier. The instructor explained to us that each boy had decorated his charm with a Chinese word character. This, we were told, enabled them to learn a few Chinese words in the process of their craft. We watched for only a few minutes, then gladly left. There was something about the mocking or bored looks on the boys' faces, as well as the green soap smell everywhere, that made us anxious to keep moving.

Mr. Barnwell told us as we continued that there were four full-time teachers and a physical education instructor for the one hundred thirty boys and the sixty girls who now lived at Juvenile Hall. When possible, the children had one arithmetic period, one language arts period, and two periods of crafts or homemaking a week. What few games and physical activities they had were under the direct supervision of the physical education teacher.

"There's not much point in going over to the girls' section," Mr. Barnwell told us. "It's very much like the boys'."

There was an immediate response. The Players and their friends felt unsatisfied. They made it clear to Mr. Barnwell that they had come to see as much as they possibly could.

We went through a door into a small courtyard lined with lemon trees. The fresh air and sunshine hit us with an intensity that was welcome in spite of the few moments it took our eyes to adjust to the glare. Outdoors seemed fresh and real. What was behind us seemed more like a scene from an old movie — dramatic, but somehow not quite believable.

At the other side of the courtyard was the door to the section in which Mr. Barnwell told us sixty girls lived — most of them in their teens. He unlocked the door and we found ourselves in a long hallway, much like the one we had just left. On either side of the passage were little rooms: bare, barred, devoid of human life.

Eventually we reached another entrance which led into the girls' recreation area. Unlike the boys' equivalent, this room was occupied. There were nine or ten girls present: sitting and staring at a wall, chatting with one another, or combing their hair. One girl was ironing a blouse.

The room had many chairs, but no sign of recreational equipment. There were shelves on which a number of magazines were visible.

"Aren't there any books?" asked our stage manager, who happened to be a P.T.A. Library Chairman.

"Not many," Mr. Barnwell replied. "Books represent too large a discipline problem, so we only allow their parents to bring them school books or comic books — no more than six at a time. Even then we have a problem with the children stealing each other's comic books. We have to insist that all comic books that come here become the property of the Hall."

But the Library Chairman was not to be put off. "Comic books!" she said with disgust. "It's a good thing the kids are permitted to keep up with their school work."

"Well, they actually don't keep up," Mr. Barnwell said candidly. "In reading, perhaps. There is a reading teacher here. But not in the other subjects. You see, we can't let them use pencils or pens, because any pointed objects might be used as weapons. We find that the few children whose parents do bother to bring them their school books fall behind in their school work anyway. I don't see how that can be avoided, all things considered."

Our presence seemed to make the girls uncomfortable. The hair combing continued with increasing fervor, but the girls looked at us only furtively. We decided we had stayed long enough. Thanking Mr. Barnwell for his time, we left through a door in the girls' section.

As we started toward our cars, we were silent at first, until it seemed to some that it might be unsociable to remain so. The more talkative among us began a stream of small talk — the beautiful weather, the majestic view, the hunger pangs that told us noon had arrived, and the route to our next destination. Lightness of subject matter and the warmth of the sun quickly got us back into the holiday spirit that began our day.

First we drank juice or coffee from several thermoses, then got into our cars, to eat sandwiches and cookies while we drove to the juvenile hall in the next county. It was a fair distance to the place that had once been home, if one could call it that, for both Rena and Ann. I wondered if seeing it again would help me have, even if too late, more understanding of the girls who had so changed my picture of life and of myself.

Our present destination was on the main highway of the county seat just a few miles from the center of town.

The first thing that struck us as we drove into the parking lot was the flower garden, tended casually by an adult gardener and three boys. They were laughing together, and they ignored us as we walked towards the reception entrance.

The room we entered reminded me of a motel lobby. There was a large table-desk, manned by a young receptionist, a number of comfortable lounge chairs, a cold drink and candy machine, and a display cabinet, artfully displaying woodwork, jewelry, ceramics, and paintings — presumably done by the children, but unsigned and uncredited. The windows wore bright, plaid curtains. A sign on the wall over the cigarette receptacle reminded those who waited that it was against the law for children under the age of eighteen to smoke.

As soon as he had been notified, Ted McKay came into the reception room to meet us. He welcomed us with a warmth that reminded me of that day when I first met Rena.

He said to the receptionist, "Susan — door, please," so that she might press the button that unlocked the door leading from the reception room into a hallway. Ted waited by the door until we had all passed through, then shut it tightly. He led us into the employees' lounge where he invited us to sit around the table and have a cup of coffee.

"Just a few words of explanation before I turn you over to the students," he told us. "I won't be saying much when I go with you. The main thing I want to do is to assure you that the students like to be talked to, so go ahead and ask them anything you like. They'll ask you questions, I assure you; and since they won't be embarrassed, there's no reason for you to be.

"Now, if this place seems to you to be sort of, well, disorganized, it's simply that this Hall was built to accommodate about sixty children, but sometimes we actually have close to two hundred. That's why we have beds in the halls, in the TV room, anywhere we can possibly set them up. We only have about one hundred thirty students right now.

"One more thing. If the students should mention to you the T.C., they're referring to what is probably the most significant single feature of this institution. T.C. refers to Therapeutic Community — a sort of get-it-off-your-chest session we start the day with in the separate sections every morning."

The group encouraged Ted to be more specific about T.C.

"Well, it's actually a whole way of life — a philosophy. I can only give you the sketchiest picture. The basis of it is that particular hour of the morning. It's supervised in a typically democratic manner by elected students; and every employee of the Hall is required to attend at least once a week. Any topic is open for discussion at the T.C. All gripes and grievances must be aired there — tasteless food, unacceptable behavior by other students, slights — real and imagined. Anyone can bring a problem and everybody helps with it. Outside the T.C. such discussions are not permitted, nor needed, as it works out."

"You mean the kids can insult you — or the teachers — anyone?"

"Sure. Better in that setting than in one less controlled. And, besides, we adults have the same privileges, of course."

"How does your staff like that kind of thing?"

"In some ways, not too much, I suppose. It can all get pretty emotional. But we indoctrinate all our employees thoroughly before they come to work here. If they really did object, they wouldn't take the job in the first place."

"Does the T.C. ever cost you any employees?"

"Rarely. But I think it loses us many potential employees. Some observers -- even professional observers -- seem horrified when they witness a session."

"If it's so horrible, why do you do it?"

"Because it works. The students feel better for the sessions, and group control takes on a constructive turn. I have yet to see a child who wasn't helped by this opportunity to be totally honest -- even if his only participation might be simply as an observer. Knowing other people have problems and anger sometimes helps a child work through his own more satisfactorily."

The usually talkative Jefferson Players seemed to be absorbed in their coffee drinking.

Ted asked, "Are there any more questions?"

"About books . . ." began the Library Chairman.

"Why don't you ask the students about that?" he suggested, smiling. "I think, in the long run, their point of view is the most valid in evaluating the various aspects of this place. I can answer anything they can't just before you leave. Would you like to start now?"

The party was led from the lounge through a long corridor lined on both sides with small rooms furnished for conferences such as Bill, Miss West and I used the night we talked to Ann after her first runaway. As if reading my memory, Ted said to me in a lowered voice as we walked, "Don't worry. Ann's not here. Miss West will tell you about her later."

I smiled my thanks to him.

We passed the medical center and went directly through the recreation area to the television room, which was lined with cots. There, in the middle, to one side of four ping-pong tables, was a card table covered with a white cloth, ceramic pots for coffee and tea, a pitcher of red punch, and attractive cups and saucers. A plastic plate held unevenly iced cupcakes. Standing behind the table were two teenaged girls, one Latin American, one blonde, each wearing a becoming print dress and party apron. Ted introduced us to Marie and Betty, and told us that they were to be our hostesses for the tour of the girls' section.

"Did you girls make the cupcakes?" JoAnne asked one of them.

The blonde, Betty, smiled an enormous smile and assured us that they had. "We made everything; even the table setting," she said with shy pride. "May we serve you now?"

We sat on the cots as if in someone's living room and were served punch and chocolate cupcakes while Ted related a few more points about the Hall.

"Almost everyone is in school now -- everyone except, of course, these two young ladies who are earning extra credit for their homemaking class."

"Do you have a full school program?" I asked.

"Oh, yes," he said. "We have nine full-time teachers. As we see it, all children are school children, even if they haven't ever been to school on the outside."

"What subjects do you teach?"

Ted smiled. "Why don't you tell them about the school, Marie?"

Without hesitating, Marie said, "Oh, we have all the stuff the cottage kids get at the regular school in town. They're the non-delinquents who live in the new building out back. Only we have smaller classes than they get. I made this dress in homemaking."

"And we have craft classes, if we want, after school," Betty added. "I made this." She showed us a jewelry pin made of polished stones.

"What other crafts do you have?" a woman asked between bites of cupcake.

Marie answered, "Oh, lots of things. I'll show you when we take you around."

When we had finished our refreshments, Ted turned our tour over to the girls. "Now just feel free to ask them anything you like," he repeated.

"And do you want us to say just anything?"Marie asked, teasing. "Even about the fight?"

Wincing slightly, Ted said, "Sure, if you want to."

The quiet little blonde dropped her shyness. "Do you want to hear about the fight?" she asked. Without waiting for a reply she continued, "We had an awful fight in here this morning. Two girls were all set to kill each other during T.C. Seems like one didn't like the color of the other. Whew! That was really something!"

"Sounds charming," someone said in a sarcastic tone.

"Well, it was kind of exciting," Marie admitted. "But

it nearly wrecked the T.C."

"You like the Therapeutic Community?" JoAnne asked.

"Of course!" "Sure!" the two girls said at once.

As Ted McKay fell in at the end of the group, our two young guides led us through the schoolrooms where girls of various races worked, seemingly unconcerned about us, on history reports, math problems (with sharp pencils!), laboratory experiments, reading, and other subjects. All but the guides wore a uniform: blue jeans and white blouses. The classes were small and relaxed.

The homemaking area included a full nursery with life-sized dolls, a realistic kitchen, and a dozen sewing machines.

"Do the boys have classes like these, too?"

"Sure. They use the same rooms we do, only at different hours. And they get wood shop instead of homemaking. Mostly we only get to see the boys when we're good," Betty giggled.

"Oh, come on," Ted said, rising to the bait. "You have all sorts of activities with the boys — shows that the Auxiliary puts on, folk dancing, even trips to town when your probation officer approves. And you eat together, occasionally."

"But that's the first privilege to go if we get outa line too much," Marie countered.

"That's right," he admitted.

We were shown a full athletic program, which included a spectrum of team sports. Four well-worn ping-pong tables were pointed out, "to help the students work off a little steam," the girls told us.

Lining one of the walls of the gymnasium were shelves filled with books of all levels of reading difficulty. These were numbered, but there was no evidence of a check-out system. Since this seemed to be an area of particular concern to at least one of the tourists, the girls explained how the volunteers donated all the books, kept them organized, and threw away the "beat-up" ones when better books were available to replace them.

The idea of the volunteer program fascinated some of the women among us. There was no such program at our county's juvenile hall.

"Oh, the volunteers are just great," the girls told us. "They teach us things like square dancing, knitting, how to fix our hair and walk right, and stuff like that. Some of them make birthday cakes that are kept in the freezer until somebody has a birthday. And they take the minimum security kids roller skating."

"Marie's getting singing lessons from one volunteer," Betty told us with reflected pride.

"The community cares," I said half aloud. Then, realizing that several were looking at me as if expecting more, I explained, "That's the Hall's motto."

The bright enthusiasm of our guides faded only once, when someone remarked, "How could anybody ever want to leave this place?"

Both girls frowned. "I'm leaving the minute my p.o. can find me a place," Marie said. "The chaplain's working on it too."

Our eyes turned to Betty, wordlessly questioning her.

"I'll be here a while," Betty said candidly. "My p.o. says I'm not ready yet. I might even go back to my mom's place."

We had touched on their real lives; their real feelings. People like us talk to so many others in day-to-day activities, yet actually care so rarely that when stark truth is spoken, we feel embarrassed.

The touring party seemed relieved when the smiling masks of Betty and Marie were back in place.

Like the other juvenile hall, the rooms where the girls slept were crowded and seemed further compressed by the barred windows. But here, each room was decorated with curtains, pictures, or colored paper that helped make the atmosphere less austere. Marie showed us how she had painstakingly cut out little multi-colored circles and taped them to the wall in her room for a polka-dot effect.

There were no "bugging" devices.

Just before leaving to visit the almost identical boys' section, we saw the crafts room. Here students worked on sculpture and ceramics, woodcrafts, block printing, sandcasting, lapidary, oil painting, and raffia craft. Several brought us examples of their recent or current projects for expected praise. I smiled when one brought a raffia bracelet to me.

"Oh, I have two bracelets like this," I said. "I got them from a girl who made them here, when she came to live with us."

A current like electricity ran through the crafts room.

The stranger holding the raffia bracelet said, "You had a girl from here living with you?"

"Sure," I replied. Then, flippantly, I added, "I get all my daughters from here."

There was a second of complete silence. Then the girl with the bracelet said, "Take me. Will you? Please take me."

Betty and Marie moved forward as if to indicate they had priority rights. "Take me!" both cried. "Take me!"

Soon there was a chorus that echoed down the hall as we hastily retreated leaving Betty and Marie behind, "Take *me!* Take *me!* Take *me!*"

6

JANE

We couldn't let Ann come back. In a trying session, the probation officer reassured us that we had done all we could. She confirmed my belief that in Ann's case, sixteen years was too long to have been without a family to become a successful member of a new one. Ann was placed in one of the larger foster homes that are like boarding schools. There, she would only have to cope with other girls her own age. The adults present were in a more or less impersonal supervisory role.

"Why not take some more children right away?" Miss West suggested. "We have a girl who . . . ."

"No more runaways!" I told her. Running away seems to be habit forming, and I just couldn't face that again. Not yet.

"All right," she said. "No more runaways. But you know, the teenagers at Juvenile Hall are the most difficult we have to place."

I explained that we had no reason not to want a child from the Hall, but that really, from the beginning, we had wanted a little boy just a bit younger than Steven. Couldn't they, please, find us a child with some other problems?

"How about two children? Your house could accommodate two."

"Fine. We'd like that. But, don't forget about our new little boy."

Within days we agreed to take both Jane and Vincent.

To facilitate individual adjustments, Jane, who was unrelated to Vince, would arrive about six days before he did.

A new probation officer, Mrs. Chamberlain, brought Jane to us shortly before Jane's twelfth birthday. The girl was tall for her age, skinny, pale and freckled. Her light brown hair was set in a curly style. Her face bore the All American look one might expect to find on a Girl Scout calendar. She did not smile much, but the new surroundings seemed more to interest than to frighten her.

Jane had been placed with us because she, like Ann, showed academic promise. Unknown to Jane, her father was on probation after conviction for statutory rape. His probation required that his daughter not be with him. There was no known problem between them, but the father's and daughter's closeness and mutual dependence caused some concern to the investigating probation officer.

Naturally, Jane resented what she believed to be arbitrary authority which took her away from the only human being she knew loved her.

As soon as her meager supply of clothing was unpacked, I asked, "Jane, have you ever been in a play?"

Her eyes caught fire immediately. "A play? You mean a real show?"

"Yes. I direct shows. All kinds of them. Right now we're working on a musical about a little kingdom way up in the Alps. We need girls for singing and dancing parts. Daddy is in it, too."

Jane was not ready to call Bill "Daddy" yet. The vanishing smile on her face told me I was moving too fast. I tried to put the faux pas behind me.

"You'll need a pretty new dress. Do you like peasant style?"

"Yes. I need some clothes -- mainly a coat and some dresses. We are supposed to shop for clothes, aren't we?"

"That's right. We have a hundred dollars toward some new things. Maybe you'd like to make some of them yourself. The money could go a lot further if you do."

"I don't know how to sew."

"I'll help you," I responded, perhaps too eagerly.

Jane pursued the subject of wardrobe, her face serious, her green eyes staring directly into mine. "White kid shoes are in now. They're being worn with pantihose, so I'll need some of those. And jeans — Levis, not old lady jeans with elastic in the back. Will the hundred dollars cover a cashmere sweater too?"

I told myself this girl would definitely have to learn to sew. Perhaps knit and cobble, too.

Jane settled in smoothly. It seemed natural for her to help me prepare dinner. She talked about how she used to prepare everything for her own "Daddy," including an early breakfast and a packed lunchbox with coffee in the thermos. She had been in charge of grocery shopping and dinner. Although she knew how to mix several varieties of cocktails for his guests, she said her Daddy really preferred to have a can of beer when he came home from work. The chatter continued during our dinner hour. Steven watched her with wide eyes. Bill seemed privately amused. I believe he felt compassion for Jane's loss of her place as Daddy's girl.

In bed that night, while asleep, I tried to shake off a disturbance. Bill was shaking me and quietly, insistently saying, "Grace. Grace. Wake up, can't you?"

I hate to wake up. If there were ever a fire, Bill would probably have to carry me, still sleeping, out of the house.

As I groaned and tried to turn away from him, I was suddenly aware of another person in our room. It was Jane standing tensely beside our bed, her brown hair in curlers. She looked, for a moment, like a non-terrestrial being.

"Janie! What on earth is it?" I asked, shaking my head slightly in an effort to get my brain into gear.

"The rope," she said earnestly. "I've got to find the rope."

"What rope?" I asked, trying mentally to recapture the details of a lovely dream I wanted to finish.

"The green one. I've got to have it to tie my things down. They'll all go away if I can't find it."

I dragged myself out of the warm bed and into the cold night, trying to make some sense out of what she was saying. Bill's hand detained me.

"I think she's still asleep," he whispered.

I switched on the bedside lamp and, as soon as my eyes adjusted, I looked at Jane. Her green eyes were wide open. She seemed fully awake.

"Now," I began hoarsely. "Let's start over. What is it you've lost?"

"The rope. The green one. I need it! I need it!"

"Why do you need it?" I asked with growing fascination.

"The things in my suitcase. And on the bed. They're going to fall away. They'll all go 'way. I need the rope!" She was almost wailing.

I put one arm around her and she clutched at me with both of hers.

"O.K., Janie. Let's go back to your room."

She allowed herself to be led, sobbing slightly. I put her back into her bed, covered her, and kissed her lightly on the forehead. She did not seem to notice the kiss. She said, "Daddy, where's Mommy?"

"I'm here, dear," I told her.

Her tense body relaxed and soon she breathed deeply.

Jane walked in her sleep many times after that. During the day she seemed relaxed and confident, but during her nighttime wanderings she was a frightened, lost little girl, often looking for the mother who had deserted both her and her father when Jane was only two weeks old.

Jane shopped for clothing with the knowledge of a fashion editor. She selected a red coat in a warm, lightweight, weatherproof fabric that accounted for sixty-five dollars of our county-allotted funds. My protests brought on a lecture from her about quality being a paramount factor in thrift. The white kid shoes, several pantihose, and a part-cashmere sweater brought the total to more than a hundred dollars. One pair of Levis, two dresses and three blouses later, Jane seemed satisfied.

I gave her an old shirt of Bill's to sleep in. Jane did not care what she wore in the house, but it mattered very much to her what she wore in public.

Entering school as a new girl was not difficult for Jane. The "in-crowd" took to her at once. She seemed knowledgeable about all the important things — clothes, boys, sports. After one day at school, I could see that we would soon have a telephone problem. If Jane were home, the line was sure to be busy.

My sister called long distance one morning and complained, "I can't get through to you on the phone anymore. Are you getting involved in a new show?"

"Yes, but that's not the problem. I have a new little

niece for you."

My sister reacted with silence.

"What's the matter?" I asked.

"Look," she said. "It's enough already. I carefully instructed my kids to call Rena 'cousin' and then Ann 'cousin.' They got a big kick out of new teenaged cousins, but it didn't work out to be for real, did it? My kids find this all very confusing, and frankly, so do I. I don't know how you can turn on and off this 'mother' bit, but I'm bowing out of the 'aunt' business."

We invited all the girls in Jane's class to a party for her twelfth birthday. Since Jane professed a fondness for Mexican food, we arranged to have a large table at a nearby Mexican restaurant.

La Casa del Rancho went out of its way to make the atmosphere for the party exactly right. A professional bouquet was in the center of the table with a card attached saying, "Happy birthday Jane from La Casa del Rancho." The fireplace in the center of the room had a large roaring fire that reflected in the polished floor. Jane's green eyes savored the room's decorations of cactus, basketry, and pictures of brightly dressed Mexicans.

As each guest arrived, Jane made it her responsibility to greet her, accepting any proffered gifts with sincere enthusiasm. She filled in the period of waiting for latecomers by opening each gift immediately. (How gracious her acceptance and opening of presents! What a contrast to the fearful, tense, unsuccessful study of gift opening Ann had made such a short time before.)

Jane gave full attention to each package, sweeping the contents with an eye that took in linings, linkages, and labels. Then she flashed her white, straight teeth and warmly thanked the giver, using her name. Jane had memorized all seventeen names in the two days she had been in her new classroom.

When the twenty-one of us, guests and family, had seated ourselves at the long table, a costumed waitress brought a cheese dip and corn chips. Each girl tried to call attention to herself by some playful manner of dipping and eating the chips. Steve and Bill, the only males present, watched in wonder as the girls soon gave way to uncontrolled giggling that scarcely let up during the course of the meal. Jane's gaiety merged into red-faced joy when the waitress brought a huge cake decorated with her name and twelve candles.

With much hilarity and lap piling, we managed to squeeze the entire group into our Plymouth sedan and ancient Cadillac. When, finally, we were safely returned to our living room, it seemed that there were eighteen voices going at one time with no one left to listen. The vocal chords eventually wore out, and parents picked up their exhausted children. A pleasant silence fell on the house, and Steven numbly got to bed at last.

Jane came to me and grasped both my hands. She said, "I want to thank you very much for the lovely party. Did you know that was the first birthday party I ever had?"

"No," I replied, honestly surprised. "You seemed to know exactly what to do."

"Did I?" She smiled slightly, apparently pleased with herself. "I guess I thought about it a lot. Anyhow, thanks very much." She kissed me lightly on the cheek and added, barely audibly, "Mom."

She released my hands and walked over to Bill. She smiled grandly at him and said simply, "Good night."

Several days later, Jane and Steve, now best of friends, asked me about the new little boy that was going to join our family. I told them frankly that I knew very little about him. I had been informed that he was almost nine years old and that he had been picked up after midnight by the police. He was walking with his fourteen year old sister, searching for his older, married sister's house. There had been no food in their mother's home, and she had been missing for several days.

Jane nodded knowingly. "The poor kid," she said. "I think I know how he feels. Steve and I want to do something to make him feel real welcome."

"What have you in mind?"

Steve seemed content to let the girl, not quite two years older, play boss. "That room he's going to share with Steve," she began. The colors are wrong — all pink and blue and lace curtains. Looks like a girl's room."

I saw a flashing image of Rena carefully painting that room in her choice of colors, and arranging the folds of the lacy curtains.

"Steve and I want to make it a cowboy room," Jane announced.

So the children and I, with Bill, too, when he had time, put up prepasted western wallpaper and yellow muslin curtains. Then Jane and Steven, by themselves, applied several coats of shellac to our new unfinished pine trundle bed from Sears.

"Now," Jane said, with the air of a happy housewife, after the frantic few days were over, "I can hardly wait to see his face."

The next day, while the room still smelled of fresh shellac, Vincent arrived.

7

QUINTET

Vince made our family complete, but the reality of him was a far cry from what each of us imagined.

Steven pictured the brother he had always longed for, one with whom he could discuss important thoughts, or books. He envisioned taking long, exploratory bicycle rides together, perhaps to distant cities.

Jane looked forward eagerly to having another young male in the house. She had been an only child, and at this stage in her development, boys were the one thing most worth studying, contemplating, or discussing with other girls. She believed Vince would bring home many boys, unlike Steven, who seemed to prefer his own company.

I don't know what Bill and I expected — probably another Steven. The Vincent we first met was a shock to all of us.

Nearly nine years old, Vincent looked more like five. He clung to the probation officer's arm with both hands and trembled violently. His shoulders were so stooped that we believed he was congenitally deformed. Occasionally his inhalations caught in his throat like muffled sobs.

Vince had been happy at the foster home of another couple named Morgan. They had a daughter Vincent's age whose company he enjoyed. But it was Mrs. Morgan's devotion to Vince that triggered jealousy on the part of Mr. Morgan.

Perhaps Mr. Morgan, too, expected something different from the real Vincent. He wanted a son, but Vince was more like another little girl. He was small, frail, and almost pretty with wavy hair and long, dark eyelashes. Vincent played jacks, jumped rope, and skipped rather than walk. His voice was high pitched; he often giggled.

One day Mr. Morgan called the probation officer and said, "That kid's gotta go! And I mean right now!"

Mrs. Morgan could not find the words to explain any of this to Vince, so his imminent departure was kept a secret. Mrs. Morgan packed his things at night after Vince was in bed.

The probation officer announced brightly on arrival at the Morgans' home, "Come on, Vince. We're going to your new foster home."

Vince wept hysterically all the way over to our house asking, "Why? Why?"

He received no satisfactory answer.

I think Vince always believed that this terrifying experience might be repeated at any time.

Jane and Steve watched in disbelief as Mrs. Chamberlain, the probation officer, removed first a bicycle, then more than twenty cardboard boxes from her station wagon. One by one, Bill carried each into the freshly papered bedroom. On one of his trips back to the car he whispered to me, "Do you know what's in those boxes? It's mostly broken crayons, pages from books and parts of broken toy cars. I haven't seen a complete, usable toy yet, except the bicycle, and that's practically brand new. Must be a consolation prize from the Morgans."

The ten by ten foot bedroom could not accommodate all Vincent's belongings, so temporarily, some of them were stored in the dining room. I let Bill and Steven work out the logistics while I went to where Vincent was sitting to try winning his confidence.

Jane's interest seemed torn between the sad scene in the living room and the contents of all those boxes.

Mrs. Chamberlain sounded cheerful while gently attempting to pry the weeping little boy away from her shoulder. One could hardly see his head at all. His face was buried, and a sailor hat, much too large, covered most of his long hair.

I asked, "Vince, wouldn't you like to see where we're putting your things?"

The sobbing stopped. The tear-stained face slowly turned toward me. Mrs. Chamberlain, Jane, and I were afraid to move for fear of frightening him again. As he looked up at me I noticed how deep and dark were the circles under his eyes.

Slowly, I stood up. Even more slowly, Mrs. Chamberlain stood too. I smiled, probably too brightly, and began walking toward the door of the room he was to share with Steven. Mrs. Chamberlain could not have released her hand from his if she had wanted to. She said gently, "Come on, Vince," as she followed me. Vincent moved slowly at first, but once his eyes rested on the boxes, he frowned with concern and dropped the probation officer's hand.

"Where are my other boxes?"

"They're coming, Vince," I assured him.

"That's the last one," Bill grunted while putting down a particularly large grocery carton that had been under the others in the station wagon.

Vincent's eyes made a quick survey. "They won't fit," he remarked. His words were barely audible; his voice still shaking.

"Well," I said, "some of these could go out to the garage."

"No!" Vince shouted in apparent panic. "I want all my things!"

"O.K., Vince, O.K.," I soothed. "We'll work it out." My voice sounded more sure than I felt. If there were to be any air space left in that room, something would have to go, but what? Steven was watching me, possibly wondering if I could be considering eliminating him.

Vincent's frown moved around the room. His eyes rested on the trundle bed arranged in an "L" shape. "Which bed am I going to be in?"

"The bottom one, Vince."

"No! I'll be squished! The top bed will fall down and squish me!"

"Would you rather be on top?" I asked. Immediately I was sorry I had offered that, because I knew Steven looked forward to sleeping up high.

Vincent considered for just a few seconds, then responded, "No. I'll fall out and hurt myself."

Jane, feeling ignored, stepped in at this point. "You'll like the bottom bed best, Vince. We fixed it up special just for you. See how nice it looks? Steve and I shellacked it five times. And we made it real strong. The top bed can't fall down."

Vincent looked at Jane as if noticing her for the first time. His face relaxed.

Encouraged, Jane continued. "You know what I think we should do? Let's walk all around the block so you'll get to know the neighborhood. Come on, Steve."

Vincent allowed himself to be led by the tall, self-assured girl. We were amazed at her magical effect on him.

When the children were out of earshot, Miss Chamberlain explained to us that Vincent had been reared by a sister, five years older than himself. Although Jane looked nothing like his sister, she theorized that this might explain why Vince reacted so well to Jane.

The probation officer told us little more that afternoon, preferring to make a hasty retreat while she could.

Eventually, we managed to get through dinner, find Vincent's pajamas, and get him to bed. In spite of Jane's and my assurances, he kept eyeing the top bed as if it were a guillotine poised for the slice. Once under the blankets, he rolled himself into a tight little ball.

That night in bed, Bill-of-the-watchdog-instinct shook me the way he had when Jane sleepwalked on her first night.

"Listen," he said. "I think it's Vince."

I gradually became aware of a buzzing: an alarm clock I thought at first. It was loud and irregular, varying in intensity and pitch.

"You'd better go to him," Bill said.

I arose, grumbling that Bill could turn off an alarm clock just as well as I, so why was I elected. I staggered into the hall feeling for the light, and then into the next bedroom. Steve, who ordinarily sleeps as deeply as I do, was sitting up in bed staring uncomprehending at the strange scene below him.

The buzzing was coming from Vincent. His mouth was just slightly opened and he was making the sound with his throat. It was a strained sound, somewhere between an "uh" and a growl. It moved up and down in pitch like a low siren. His body was in a kneeling position and Vincent was hitting his head again and again on his pillow. Shortly after I arrived, he threw himself with great force out of the bed and onto the floor. Vince did not wake up. The buzzing and hitting of his head continued, now on the wooden floor.

"It's O.K., Steven; he's just dreaming," I said as I knelt down on the floor beside the thrashing child. This case was clearly different from Jane's simple sleepwalking.

"Vince, Vince. It's O.K. Wake up, honey," I soothed, but he did not seem to hear me.

I took hold of his shoulders and tried to shake him the way Bill sometimes does to awaken me. Then I noticed that Vincent's right hand was inside his pajama bottom, rubbing frantically. There were spots of blood on his clothes. As I shook, I tried to pull his hand away. In his sleep, he fought me.

Gradually, Vincent calmed down. As his body relaxed, his eyes blinked in the subdued light coming into the room from the hall. As his eyes became adjusted, Vincent drew his body from a kneeling to a sitting position and slowly looked around the room to orient himself. Then he threw his arms around me, trembling violently.

I continued to say soothing things as I gradually became aware of the smell of urine. Vincent's clothing and bed were drenched.

I held him for about ten or fifteen minutes until his body relaxed into sleep. "Vince. Vince, honey. You've got to wake up, Vince. Come on now."

I managed to find another pair of pajamas; then went out to the linen closet to get some dry sheets. When I returned, Vince was totally naked. His now exposed penis was a bright, inflamed red color.

"Would you like to wash yourself before you go back to bed?" I asked.

He shook his head and finished dressing. Then he helped me tuck in the bedding. As soon as the dry bed was ready, he got in.

I thought he fell asleep immediately, and lightly kissed both boys before leaving the room. As I turned in the doorway for one more look, I noticed movement under Vincent's blankets that seemed to be a continuation of the rubbing under his pajamas.

The entire scene was repeated four more times that night and several times nightly for weeks afterward.

Eventually, Steven learned to sleep right through everything except the sound of Vincent's body hitting the floor.

I began to take afternoon naps.

We consulted Mrs. Chamberlain about our sleepwalker and our bedwetting nightmare sufferer. She assured us that this was all "perfectly natural" and that the problems should disappear as soon as the two of them had become adjusted to their new family.

She proved mistaken.

I was particularly concerned about the condition of Vincent's penis. It was red, raw and scabbed. I never saw him touch it while he was awake, but the nighttime mistreatment was so severe that Bill and I were afraid he might suffer an infection. I took Vincent to Steven's pediatrician.

Dr. Mann, an elderly lady with a German accent, had a warm, matter of fact manner with children. Vincent liked her at once and had no objection to her thorough examination. She confirmed our opinion that Vincent's penis was in serious condition. She pointed out that the more he rubbed, the more it would be irritated, in turn causing a rawness demanding more rubbing. In private, she said, "It's as if he were trying to break it off."

Dr. Mann prescribed a soothing antiseptic, but I kept thinking about her final comment. I discussed that idea with Bill, and we began to watch Vincent's feminine behavior with more interest. Bill came up with an idea that I planned to put into practice later when the opportunity occurred.

Whenever I mentioned his father to Vincent, he would quickly change the subject. He talked a great deal about his three sisters and his "mommy" with whom he slept at home. He loved the female members of his family deeply, and he missed them even more painfully than Jane missed her father. Once, when I mentioned his father in casual conversation, Vincent struck out with uncharacteristic fury. "My daddy is a bad man! He went away and left us when he knew Mommy was too sick to take care of the bar by herself. He doesn't like us and I hate him!"

Vincent, whose birth was the result of a reconciliation which did not last, had been named for his father.

We did not have to buy Vincent any clothes. There may have been no food in the home, but his mother and adoring sisters dressed the little boy in five short-pants suits, and enough shirts, socks and underwear to clothe quadruplets. Vincent wore neatly pressed slacks and a long sleeved print shirt on his first day at school, along with the inevitable sailor hat.

Jane and Steven were in their glory shepherding their new round shouldered little brother to the nearby elementary school. Jane felt important in her big sister role. Steven knew that his friends envied his ever-changing family, and he reveled in their envy.

We had enrolled Vincent earlier, so the older children knew where to find Mrs. Koch's second grade classroom. They left him at the door.

Suddenly alone, Vincent donned a protective armor we had not yet seen. He moved the sailor hat down at a slant over his right eye and walked into the room with a strut. His face bore a sneer. With overly cool detachment he moved up to the teacher's desk, put his registration card down, snorted, and found his way to the one unoccupied desk. It was too high for him. He exaggerated the oversize dimensions by squirming his body down into his seat so that only the upper half of his face was visible -- like a chipmunk cautiously peeking out of its burrow.

The armor was effective. No one in the class had any more interest in approaching him than they would have in approaching a threatening wild animal.

Vincent was a year older than any of the other second grade children, yet, he was the smallest child in his class. He had missed most of his preceding year's schooling, and tested lowest in skill subjects, including physical ones. With clowning arrogance, Vince scoffed at these deficiencies. On the playground, he sat on a bench and pretended not to be interested in the noisy games.

Mrs. Koch felt that the principal had certainly pitched her an undeserved curve with this sullen, unattractive kid.

About an hour after the closing of the school day, Mrs. Koch was busy in her classroom in consultation with the student teacher who was assisting her that year. Suddenly they were aware of a small presence, still wearing his hat. Insolence was completely gone. He looked as if he might have been weeping.

"Why, what is it, Vincent?" the teacher asked in surprise.

With a barely audible voice he replied, "I'm lost."

"What do you mean?" asked Mrs. Koch kindly.

"I mean I don't know where I live. I couldn't find my sister — or anybody — and I walked all over. I almost couldn't find the school again."

The young, dark eyed student teacher volunteered, "I'll take him home, Mrs. Koch. They must have his address in the office."

The once menacing "sailor" reached up for Miss O'Brien's hand. She smiled at him and then at Mrs. Koch who nodded her assent. After finding his address, the student teacher led the tiny boy home, counting blocks and pointing out landmarks along the way.

Vincent fell in love with Miss O'Brien.

The next day during the game period, Miss O'Brien invited Vince to join the children in a game of kickball. Vincent's mask of insolence almost devolved into panic. At her insistence, he joined the children, trying to work his way again and again to the end of the line of kickers. Mrs. Koch noticed his evasive tactic and ordered him to get up to the plate and kick the ball. Vincent tried to clown his way out of the frightening situation, but neither Mrs. Koch nor Miss O'Brien would permit it. The pitcher rolled him the ball. Vince gathered up his courage and kicked the ball as hard as he could. The ball flew high and away. While his team screamed, Vincent ran around the bases making the first home run of the day. After that, Vincent was always willing to play kickball. The children, remembering that lucky first accident, always wanted him on their team.

As Vincent felt more relaxed in school, he moved off his bench at recess time. He began to wander away from the kickball court and over to the other areas of the yard. He became fascinated with a game some of the girls were playing: jump rope.

"Can I play?" he asked shyly.

The girls laughed. "What do you mean? Jump rope is a girls' game!"

Vince donned his public armor. "I can jump harder and longer and better than any of you dumb girls. Y'wanna see?"

The laughter of the girls only made him more determined. As soon as the rope began to go around, Vince ran into it and jumped and jumped and jumped. Soon a crowd gathered. The girls enjoyed Vincent's ability, but the boys made fun of him.

"Lookit the little girl! Watcha wearin' a sailor hat for, little girl?"

The more they taunted, the harder he jumped, as if believing that he could impress them with his endurance. By the time the recess bell rang, Vince was exhausted and dripping with perspiration.

The boys could hardly wait to tell Mrs. Koch. "Y'know what Vince was doing all recess? He was jumping rope!"

Mrs. Koch glanced at the wilted, miserable boy. Thinking fast, she asked them, "Was he good at it?"

"He sure was! He was almost good enough to be a girl!" They screamed in hilarity at their joke.

"I would imagine so," Mrs. Koch replied. "After all, a boy should do it well. Men do."

"Men?" they echoed incredulously.

"Of course. Prizefighters. Didn't you ever see pictures of a prizefighter working out, for hours sometimes, with a jump rope?"

"What for?"

"I suppose it gives them strength. Helps them develop the breath and energy to stay in the ring for as long as they have to fight."

The second grade boys were impressed. Soon Vincent was being prevailed upon to give them all jump rope lessons. The fad swept through the school, making it necessary for the administration to buy enough jump ropes for boys as well as for girls.

Mrs. Koch found one thing about Vince difficult to take: his excessive lying. Unlike some liars who do not seem to know truth from untruth, Vince lied whenever he wanted to avoid trouble or save face.

He invented a glamorous family that he talked about in class — a father who was a famous actor, "always on the road," a mother who was a model, a writer, a teacher; something different every week. He did not like being introduced as Jane's or Steven's "new brother," so he avoided them while at school. He seemed to feel that his foster-child status was disgraceful — whether to himself or to his own mother, I do not know.

One day during a class discussion, a child made a remark

about everyone in the world having a dad. Mrs. Koch noticed Vincent slipping down, smaller and smaller, into his seat.

"Lots of families don't have dads," she said. "I have a daughter of my own, but there's no father in our family."

The children looked stunned. "You have a kid?"

"Why not?" Mrs. Koch laughed. "What do you think teachers do after school hours? Lie on a shelf and drink ink? I had a husband when my little girl was a baby, but he was killed during the war."

The teacher noticed with some satisfaction that Vincent was sitting up straight in his chair.

One or two other children volunteered information about divorced or separated fathers, and Vincent, though he did not add to the discussion, felt visibly better.

At home, Vincent accepted Jane's big-sistering with good humor. She, in turn, was delighted to find that Vince could play jacks and do a surprisingly accurate caricature of Al Jolson. Vince told us, "I used to do this on television all the time. I was famous. I made lots of money."

The children were skeptical. "If you're so famous, how come we never heard of you?"

"You should have heard of me. I was on *Lawrence Welk* and *Carol Burnett* and *Ed Sullivan* and . . ." The list grew a little longer every time he told the story.

But even though Vincent was skilled at jacks, Jolson, and fiction, he was most unskilled at certain things that we thought "everybody knows." Apparently he had lived on a diet of cokes and peanut butter and jelly sandwiches. He could open soft drink bottles and spread jam with aplomb, but he did not know how to use a knife and fork. Resisting an impulse to taunt him about this, Jane spent part of each dinner hour working with him on such social graces. He did not know what most meats and vegetables were called, and was uninterested in learning. Peas, particularly, struck him as far more trouble than they were worth.

He did like milk, though. If we did not watch him, he would make an entire meal of four or five glasses of milk, but nothing else.

One day I heard Steven giving Vincent lessons in the use of a telephone. It was not easy for Vincent. The boys grinned when they finally called me in to demonstrate that Vince could dial both the time recording and the weather report. Later Steven told me, "What would he have done if there were a fire? He couldn't even have told the operator!"

In turn, Vincent taught his new siblings some words and phrases he had learned from sailors in his parents' bar. When Jane and Steven came to ask me the meanings of these words, I wished I had read those family education books they say no mother should be without. There is a limit to my objectivity and scientific detachment.

Jane's father and both Vincent's parents were each permitted by their probation officers to visit their respective children for one hour a month on a specified day. Jane looked forward eagerly to seeing her father: a thin, graying man who always seemed embarrassed when Bill or I spoke to him. The warmth between Jane and her father was unmistakable. They spent most of his hour sitting on the couch, his arm around Jane's shoulder, his free hand holding both of hers. He would ask her about her school, her friends, her activities, her health. She was just as interested in hearing how his life was going without her. He encouraged Jane to "make the most of her opportunities" with Bill and me. Jane would linger at the door when he finally said goodbye. Then she would go to her room for a little while and cry.

Vincent's mother was a beautiful woman, even though she was three times a grandmother. Like her son, she was short and had extraordinarily long lashes and yellow flecked green eyes, but her long, thick hair was blonde. She did her best to keep her weight down.

Whenever she came to see Vincent, she would dress in her prettiest clothes and make up her face carefully. Her hair was brushed and shining. If her eyes might show the result of a hard night of drinking, she would wear dark glasses. Seldom was there alcohol on her breath.

They would meet at the door, and Vincent would throw his arms around her, clinging like a toddler. She addressed him in formal language, but with a soothing tone in her voice. Once they were seated on the couch together, she would do most of the talking. After telling him the news about various members of the family, Vincent's mother would spend much time telling her son what he "must" and "must not" do. Vincent hardly heard her, enjoying being close to her, feeling her warmth, smelling her strong perfume.

After her first visit, Vincent's mother asked to talk to us. She was gracious and articulate.

"I'm glad Vincent is staying with teachers," she began. "I didn't like any of the teachers he's had before. It got to the point that I refused to send him to school at all. Vincent is a very sensitive boy. He needs understanding teachers. I'm sure you can help him to catch up."

She wanted to tell us about the problems she had with Vincent's father, whom she vehemently hated, but we discouraged this, pleading a necessity to remain neutral in such matters. Vincent's mother nodded, but added, "Well, I don't know what the probation officer told you, but I think it's important for you to know that the man is living with a woman now — a terrible woman — a dope fiend."

Bill tried to move her back to the subject of Vincent. "I wish we could . . . ."

"It's true!" she interrupted insistently. "Her husband calls me up all the time and tells me about it. He won't give that woman a divorce, and neither would I even consider divorcing Vincent's father. It would be a crime to let them marry."

I was wishing Vincent were not in the room, but his eyes had a distracted look, as if he heard none of what his mother was telling us. I supposed he had heard her words on the subject of his father and "that woman" a thousand times before.

"I'm glad you're so interested in Vincent's schooling," Bill said, earnestly trying to steer the conversation back to safer channels.

"Of course!" she said, then added with significant emphasis, "I *am* his mother." She smiled and asked if there were anything she might do to help Vincent with his education.

I suggested that her encouragement for him to try hard in school would certainly help.

Bill added, "I notice that you brought him candy today. Why not bring him a book next time?"

Vincent's mother welcomed this suggestion, and for months to come she always brought a book with her. The first was a dictionary picture-book. Subsequent books were simple, phonetic stories. Part of each visiting hour was spent reading each gift book together. They seemed happy for something specific to do.

Vincent's father rarely came. When he did, it was a strain for everyone concerned. Vince and his father hardly knew each other, so they had little to talk about. The father attempted to make up for this lack by bringing expensive toys with him. Vincent would be polite, but he also tried not to get interested in the electric trains, games, or skates. The short, balding man would sit down on the floor and bend his head over the new toy as if fascinated. Eventually, Vincent's curiosity would bring him down to the floor, too, as a more-or-less interested spectator rather than as a participant. The father scrupulously obeyed the one-hour time limit, glad, I thought, to be through the difficult situation. Before he went out the door, he regularly left several dollars as a parting offering with his protesting son.

After his father was gone, Vince would come into the kitchen or wherever he could find either Bill or me.

"I'm not going to eat anything for dinner tonight."

"Yes you are."

"No, I'm not. And I've decided not to make my bed any more in the mornings."

"What on earth is the matter with you, Vincent?"

He would then try any obvious lie or a string of profanity until he could manage to get punished in some way, such as being sent to his room. Once punished by Bill or by me, he seemed satisfied. It took us quite a while to realize that the more he enjoyed his father's visit, the more he felt the need to be punished.

The buzzing nightmares after a visit from Vincent's father were many and extreme.

Jane and Steven, determined to help Vincent in his schoolwork, made up flashcards of simple number combinations. It was Steven's idea, remembered from the time we had to help Rena learn the same things. The three children made a game of the nightly practice. Vincent enjoyed the attention. The flashcard practice became a favorite delaying tactic at bedtime for all three.

One night, after a most enjoyable session, the euphoria that followed their comradeship made the inevitability of bed seem particularly remote. I set my face hard and spoke sharply to Steven and Jane, sending them scurrying. But Vincent required a more gentle approach. I stayed in his room, helping him to get ready.

"Jane's nice," he said happily, slowly removing one tiny shoe. "And Steve's nice, too."

"Mm hmm."

"You know, Steve's the first boy that's ever been as nice to me as my sisters. I like him."

He got into bed, sleepily. "I wish I weren't a boy," he confided.

Thanks to Bill's earlier suggestion, I was ready for that. I said, "Not a boy! Are you *crazy*? Why, if I could be a boy, I'd jump at the chance!"

Vincent's sleepiness vanished. He sat bolt upright with his eyes wide. "Why?" he asked.

"Because it's a man's world," I told him, sounding as sexist as I could manage. "Men rule countries. They get to do what they want much more than women do. And they're stronger; they get the most interesting jobs; they travel more. I always wanted to travel, but a woman can't do that as well by herself."

"Why not?"

"Because she needs a man along to protect her."

Vincent could hardly believe what he was hearing. "Would you really rather be a boy? Honestly?"

"Of course!" I said, apologizing inwardly to Betty Friedan. "You want to trade places? I'll take you up on the offer right now."

Vincent slid down under the blankets, but his eyes stared widely at the ceiling.

I kissed him lightly and, to press the point, said, "Good night you lucky boy." Then I kissed Steve and assured him that he was wonderful, too.

There were no nightmares at all that night.

Vincent began to make friends with boys at school. One day while playing kickball, he met David.

"You know something? Indians played ball, too," David told him with authority.

"How do you know?" Vince asked.

"I read about it. I have lots of books on Indians. They had a game something like baseball. And they taught the Canadians to play la crosse, too."

"What's la crosse?"

"I'll show you in one of my books. Y'wanna come over after school?"

"Mom says I have to come home first, because she worries," Vince related with some pride. "But if you'll come over to my house first, then I can go to yours."

David was delighted to discover where Vincent lived. He knew Steven well. He told Vince, "We used to go with Steven to plays when he had a sister named Rena. Are you his brother now?"

Vince was surprised and unhappy that David knew of his "disgraceful" foster-child status. "I guess so," he replied in a barely audible voice, his shoulders hunching more than before.

"That's *fantastic,*" said David. "I wish I could get new brothers and sisters all the time. I've had my same old sister for ages."

David spent many afternoons reading to Vincent from his collection of books about Indians. He was also pleased to find someone to enjoy his favorite at-home game -- the masculine equivalent of dolls. David had hundreds of miniature men, animals, and houses. Vincent and he would set up cities, bringing in sand, rocks, twigs, and weeds. Each toy man was assigned a role in their town, and placed appropriately. Together the boys made up histories of the towns, the buildings, each individual inhabitant.

Once they discovered a way to climb up to our garage roof. Here they found a complete planet, set apart from mere earth, where they could build an entire country without having some mother come along and demand that "all toys be put away, *now.*" The game went on for many afternoons, until a heavy rain ruined everything. The little garage-top world was flooded, and the boys wept together as the Lord, Himself, might have wept surveying the flood of Noah's time.

David introduced Vincent to the wealth of the public library, and Vincent brought home as many books on Indians as the rules would allow. Those he could read, he read. The others I read aloud to him at bedtime. The romantic, colorful, seemingly free world that the books painted filled Vincent with dreams of another, lovelier existence.

He found a bird feather, and occasionally, while home, he would remove his sailor hat and replace it with the feather, tied with a piece of his own long hair to the back of his head. He used water to try to straighten his wavy, black hair, but he could never get it to stay straight. Vincent's curved back, held as straight as he could hold it, also belied the image he longed to represent. As if to drown the sight with sound, he would scream, whoop, and run through the house and yard in a strange, twirling dance.

Vincent's leaping around made me pay attention to an announcement for a boys' Modern Dance class and another for girls being offered at the community center. The teacher was a fine, local male dancer. It occurred to me that the exercise might help Vincent's pitiful posture.

We offered dance lessons to all three children. Steve was not interested in the least. Both Jane and Vincent were delighted with the idea, so we enrolled them in their respective groups.

Jane went to class only once. "Mom, that class is terrible! We have to stretch and stretch and jump around. Why, it's work! I can't imagine why anyone would want to bother!" she declared. Then her eyes brightened, "Say, you don't suppose they'd let me join the boys' class, do you?"

Not only could Jane not join, but the boys' class teacher maintained a rule of "no females of any kind, including mothers, anywhere around the premises while we're practicing."

After the first session, Vincent, face aglow, ran out to the car where I was waiting for him. "Mom! That class is great! I didn't know I could do so many things. I can jump in the air and turn around almost three times. And I can fold my legs like an Indian and bounce my head way over my knees lots of times. And when I jump, I can jump a long ways. You oughta see me! I'm as good as all the other guys!" He looked three inches taller.

That day when we got home I had a surprise for Vincent. In straightening up things in the garage, I had come across a costume that had fit Steven three or four years before — a tunic, hand painted with Indian symbols and fringed with plastic leather on the hem and sleeves. There were beads around the neck. The costume included a matching feather headband. My elderly aunt had painstakingly created these things for Steven to wear over jeans several Christmases previous. Steven wore them a few times, but he had a serious soul, never given much to make-believe. He outgrew them before they had seen much use.

Vincent could scarcely believe his good luck. The sailor hat hit the floor as Vincent changed with the speed of cinematic transformation. Stimulated, rather than worn out by his dancing class, he ran out to the back yard, up and over the ancient, unpainted fence, and into a neighbor's yard -- a shortcut to David's house.

Spring grew warmer, and Jane was hard pressed to keep up with her social life and still finish her pink and white peasant dress in time to wear in the Jefferson Players' *Paxania*. I was pleased to see her follow through on the sewing, but appalled to find that Jane had absolutely no singing voice.

That did not stop her, however. In every chorus number, a loud, awful monotone could be heard clashing against the other voices. It was Jane. I couldn't tell her to keep quiet. She croaked her "Paxania! Here's to YOU!" with pink faced enthusiasm.

The Players pretended not to notice.

In mid-May I received a phone call from the instructor of Vincent's Modern Dance class. "I'm sorry," he told me. "We're going to have to give up the class."

"Oh, no!" I wailed. "Vincent seemed to be getting so much out of it."

"Yes, I know what you mean," the young man told me. "I wondered about his back during the first few sessions, but I now believe that with proper exercise, it could straighten out completely. He loves dancing, and so did all the other boys."

"Then, what happened?"

"Social convention," he replied bitterly. "Sexism. The boys were given a bad time at school when they mentioned taking dancing. In every case, they were teased so unmercifully that they quit. All except Vincent. Hasn't he run into anything like that?"

"If so, he hasn't told me."

"In most cultures, dancing is considered a male occupation. It takes hard work, a strong body, and lots of self-discipline. I think it's ridiculous that it should be called 'sissy.' "

When I told Vincent that the class was cancelled, he nodded. "I wasn't going to go anymore anyway."

"Why not?"

"The guys at school say dancing is for girls and that if I like dancing, I must be a girl. So I don't want to go anymore."

I felt simultaneously delighted and sorry. Vincent was telling me he wanted to be a boy! Conventions might not help his shoulders straighten up, but perhaps his new masculine pride would.

I asked him, "Does David say that?"

"No, not David. He just felt sorry when I had to go away in the afternoons. Now I can spend more time at his house."

Jane came in, verbally brushing Vincent aside. When she wanted to be heard, she wouldn't let anything interfere.

"That man!" she began. "Who does he think he is, anyway?"

"My dancing teacher?" Vincent asked innocently.

"No, stupid; the principal!"

"Has there been any trouble?" I asked.

"He says we can't have a graduation party. He says that sixth grade graduation really doesn't mean any more than graduating from kindergarten these days."

"Well, maybe he has a point," I told her. "After all, you've been going to that school yourself for less than three months."

Vincent, sighing as if bored, left. Jane watched him go, and then gave me her how-can-you-be-so-ignorant look that I was beginning to see more and more often.

"*Everybody* has a party when they graduate," she informed me with authority. "We're entitled to a party. Why shouldn't we get one?"

"Well, I don't know, Jane. What do the other kids in your class think?"

"I'll tell you what they think. They're mad, that's what. But, we've decided to go about this thing democratically."

"What do you mean, democratically?"

"Suzie and me, we're starting a petition. We're going to write it in the most legal words we can find, and then we're going to get all the sixth grade kids to sign it. I know I can get the boys to. We're going to demand a party!" Jane declared with the conviction of a natural revolutionary.

Then she diluted the effect by adding in a small voice, "You don't suppose we could get into trouble, do you?"

"I don't think so, if you go about it in a grown-up manner," I said. "Maybe 'request' would be a more diplomatic word than 'demand.' "

Tall, pale Jane worked together on the petition with short, black Suzanne, the daughter of one of the Jefferson Players. With executive-like efficiency they located one person to act as chairperson in each classroom, with or without the teacher's knowledge. By checking, double checking, and consistent perseverance, Jane and Suzanne eventually had the signatures of more than one hundred sixth grade students on their petition. The girls decided it was time to make their big presentation.

Jane said, "I'm going to wear my *Paxania* dress this morning, Mom; is it clean?"

"The dress you made for the show? But Janie! How can you wear such a light cotton? It's cold and raining outside."

"I don't care. I think it's important for that principal to remember I'm an actress."

Actress or not, the man was not impressed. He read the petition politely, smiled at the girls, reminded them that he was, after all, the principal, and the answer was no. No party. That was final.

"It isn't *fair!*" Jane shrieked as she came slamming into the house after school. "I thought this was a democracy!"

"America may be," I told her, "but school is not."

"Isn't school a part of America? Shouldn't we be learning how to be citizens? I don't believe there is such a thing as a democracy," she said bitterly. Then she added, "Will you go down and talk to him for us, Mom?"

"I don't think that would do any good now, Jane. He said his 'no' was final, didn't he?"

"We've got to have a party," she wailed. "I promised all the kids!"

"Then keep after it," I advised. "The principal may not be the only one who can say yes or no."

"Yes, he is," she said. "He's like the way things really are in this country. I don't think I want to be an American anymore."

Jane sulked for the rest of the afternoon. The weather had cleared by the time she walked over to Suzanne's after dinner. Following serious deliberation, the girls decided against a trip to the Board of Education, and planned, instead, to give a graduation party of their own -- at our house, naturally. They would invite every signer of the petition.

Limited by funds and Bill's firm veto of the original plan,

the party included only Suzanne's and Jane's class. With the same executive skill they had demonstrated getting their petitions signed, the girls arranged for food and music, paid for it from their own savings and allowance advances, and rearranged furniture for the proper balance of sitting and dancing space. Relaxed and gracious hostesses, they enjoyed their celebration enormously. At eleven o'clock, the boys were sent home. The girls spread blankets and sleeping bags over the living room floor. Music continued all night, amid giggles and talk. Vincent and Steven peeked in at the glamorous affair until they were spotted and banished indignantly.

The annual summer visit to Bill's mother took on a special glow that year. Jane announced that the trip was her "graduation present," and acted as though she believed it. She supervised the packing of the boys' suitcases, and later, the car. Steve and Vince indulged her bossiness pretending they, too, believed the trip to be Jane's own.

Before we got into the car, I made my final tour of the house to check windows and lights. I found Vincent in his room, frowning as he looked at his sailor hat and Indian headdress.

"I don't know which one to wear," he said seriously.

"Maybe it's time you stopped wearing a hat at all, Vincent."

"I'm not a sailor anymore."

"No."

"I'm an Indian. But it might look funny."

"Yes, it might."

"I don't know what to do," he wailed. "Tell me what to do."

"I can't always do that, Vincent," I said, inwardly praying he wouldn't take the feathers. "Some decisions you must make for yourself."

Bill began blowing the horn. Vincent looked at me desperately, but I wouldn't let him out of it.

Vince picked up his sailor hat. Then he put it down again. "Yes," he said. Then, "No. Yes." He was perspiring. "Please tell me what to do!"

Bill blew the horn again. I started out to the car. "Come on, Vince," I said.

When I got out to the car, Vincent came running up behind me. In his hand was clutched the old sailor hat. His large, green eyes were full of tears that he kept trying to blink back. Steven noticed Vincent's distressed state, but he said nothing about it.

The children talked and laughed for the first few miles; then they began to sing. They started with the old songs everyone seems to know, and then launched into a medley from *Paxania:*

In the middle of the morning when you're drowsy;
Feelin' frowzy -- just lousy. . .

in Steven's sweet soprano, Vincent's clear, baby-like voice, and Jane's exuberant monotone. When they were tired, Steven and Jane slept, but Vincent's wide eyes took in everything. He was definitely "the appreciator," remarking, "Ooh! Look how those rocks go into the dirt. Like they were growing there!" or, "Look what the sun is doing to that water — it's sparkling! Do you see it?"

The town where Bill's mother lived was a sad little place, still dreaming of a day, thirty years past, when Hollywood's elite visited regularly to soak up the sun on the desert sands by her fresh water lake. The sun overcame the lake, and when it vanished, so did the tourists. Most of the citizens moved away; businesses boarded up one by one; houses fell into unloved disrepair. All the hotels closed except one. Its Spanish brick facade was faded and crumbled in sections, but unlike the town, decay added to its beauty. The effect was like that of an historic old mission, long forgotten but once alive with priests, soldiers and Indian converts.

We parked on the hotel's brown front lawn. Jane, Steven and Vincent, hot and stiff as they tumbled from the car, took in the picture with awe.

The large, empty lobby was dark. It took a while for our eyes to adjust after the bright sunlight outside. In answer to the ringing of the bell on the desk, a slim, tan man of about fifty years registered us and showed us to three large rooms. Consistently, the rooms boasted memories of wealthy, exacting guests, but the wallpaper was yellowed, the plumbing old fashioned and noisy, and the windows raised or lowered only with much encouragement.

We told the children to unpack their things, then we unpacked our own. Bill and I went back to the kids' rooms where we found open, still full suitcases, but no children.

We went out to look for them.

Down the hall we heard running footsteps, then Jane's voice, "Oh, Mommy! This is beautiful! There's almost nobody here but us, and it's just like a creepy old castle."

"We found a secret passage," Steven volunteered.

"And a railing that almost fell down when we leaned on it," Vince added. The other two children glared at him.

"Well, it did," Vince said in a small voice.

"You broke something? Already?" Bill asked in horror.

"No, of course not, Dad," Steven explained. "We just almost did. Boy, we could explore this place for days."

We conventional parents sent the three youngsters straight back to their unpacking with admonitions about "other people's hotels."

Later, we went down to Mom's dry lake site home to pick her up for dinner. She was not ready when we arrived. While Steven showed Vince and Jane around, Mom indicated she wanted to see Bill and me alone in the kitchen.

"Why are you staying in the hotel? Don't you like to stay with me?" she asked.

"Of course we do, Mom," Bill assured her. "You're the only reason we come down to this town, and we want to spend time with you. It just seemed to us that to descend on you with five people was too much."

"I could have made room. I could borrow a cot."

"It's much better this way," I added. "The kids love the hotel. They have rooms to themselves and even a swimming pool."

I did not add the main reason we chose the hotel. A nine year old bedwetter who regularly had noisy nightmares plus a twelve year old sleepwalker would be a lot for Mom to cope with. An experienced hotel could take such phenomena more in stride.

Mom liked our new children at once. The lovely, immature face of Vincent, set off by hunched shoulders, gave him a vulnerable air that appealed to most maternal people. Jane's bright smile and social know-how could be counted on to win over anyone she wished to win, and she had never known a grandmother before. Mom made the children chocolate chip cookies and apple turnovers, and sat with them for hours telling them stories containing obvious morality messages. Steven was proud of her.

The weather was hot. After a week, we suggested that

Mom join us for a drive to her favorite vacation hotel near Santa Monica beach.

"No," she told us. "I would interfere with your vacation."

"What do you mean? We came here to see you."

"No," she said again. "There are lots of things the children should be seeing. You might take them to San Diego — maybe even to Mexico."

"Won't you come too?"

"No, I don't enjoy much car travel. But you go."

We did extract a promise from Mom, however, to let us pick her up on our way home so we could drop her in Santa Monica on our way back home.

In San Diego we found a two bedroom plus couch motel suite that worked well for us, in spite of Jane's protests about having to sleep on the couch "right out in public." The first morning there, I awakened to squeals of laughter. Bill had awakened before me and had gone in to check on the boys. By the time I got there they were engaged in a three-way free-for-all. They were twisting arms and throwing each other violently, but everyone was laughing.

"Vince! Hold down his legs! I've got his shoulders!"

"Oh, no you don't — I've gotcha! Hey, no fair crawling under the bed. Hey!"

As the two hundred pound Bill flattened himself to reach for Vince, Steve succeeded in rolling his adversary over on his back. Bill used both arms to imprison the squirming Steven as he rolled up on his knees. Then, in a surprise attack, Vince was up on Bill's back. Bill dropped Steve, who also got up on Bill's back in a second. As both boys hung on miraculously, Bill stood up and ran around the room giving them a kind of wild piggy-back ride.

I was laughing in spite of my concern that someone was sure to break a bone. I suddenly became aware of Jane, standing beside me at the door in the old shirt she used for a nightgown. Her face was pale and she frowned slightly.

"What is it, Jane?" I asked quietly.

As if she had not heard me, Jane watched the melee for a few more seconds, angry that she had been left out. She then turned and went back to her couch.

Our motel could not have been more idyllic if it had been on a Pacific island. The children planned cookouts on the beach, proudly making all arrangements themselves. Vincent seemed fascinated with the sand. First he dug wildly in puppydog fashion, buttocks high, paddling sand furiously through his spread legs with both hands. Then Steven got him interested in an elaborate sand castle construction.

Jane alternately splashed in the warm waves and lay in the sun "working on her tan." In a lazy voice, she began to reminisce.

"Daddy and I used to go to Clear Lake. It wasn't warm like this, but it was real nice."

"What would you do there?" I replied as I smoothed sun tan oil on my legs.

"Oh, Daddy is a good fisherman. Sometimes we'd rent a motorboat and go out on the lake all day. Sometimes he'd tow people he knew who liked to water ski."

"Can you water ski?"

"No. Daddy wouldn't let me go in the water at all because I can't swim. But some day he'll teach me how."

San Diego Zoo -- an impressive collection of animals when seen through the eyes of adults: a paradise to children. In such a settng it can be a joy to wonder at children's wonder.

Vincent's eyes watched, wide open like his mouth, while the brightly colored birds made stacatto movements in the bird house. His body unconsciously copied them, jerking or moving gracefully as he watched them walk or fly. Like a cat, he crept slowly to be as close as possible to the most shy of them. Uncannily, they recognized his intent gaze as admiration and allowed the small, sailor-hatted human to come much closer than his medium-tall companions.

From another direction, Jane squealed, "Mommy! They're not cats at all -- they're real baby lions! And we can go right over and play with them, see?"

In an adjacent compound, Steven looked serious and tall as he mounted a bored tortoise's back, Steve imagining himself at first as an heroic epic hero. Then he took off his little golf cap, made circles with it in the air, and let out a whoop like a movie cowboy.

Jane told him scornfully, "Hey, dummy. You better get on a mule for that. The turtle's not going any place."

Jane chattered constantly. Steven was glowing with the fun of her companionship. Vincent studied everything he saw as if some day he would have to describe it in detail to a celestial court. He tried to communicate with the animals by making soft copies of their sounds.

Bill and I saw little of the zoo, itself. The happiness of the children pushed itself inside our own skins, and Bill and I held hands like newlyweds, squeezing them occasionally with unspoken mutual messages. We were magically in their world; the happy world that children were once supposed to inhabit continuously, but rarely do. We had to keep very quiet in order not to let our presences be felt, spoiling it all. We took pains not to let our young guides know how our feet hurt, or how our breath felt shorter and shorter.

Together we left that enchanted land to visit another, the amusement park on the San Diego pier.

The joyful mood of the children enveloped us; we decided to accept Mom's earlier suggestion and drive to Mexico.

Steven and Jane talked or slept during the drive while Vincent took in the arid landscape, the unbelievable blue of the ocean, the wild array of colors in the rustic roadside shops for tourists.

The poverty, evident everywhere in Mexico, troubled the children. "Do you mean people really live in those places? But they're only signboards nailed together. How do they keep the rain out?"

We got as far as Ensenada. There, local police concurred with the manager of the motel that the roads south of Ensenada were impassable. We turned back, disappointed, heading for California to fulfill our promise to Bill's mother that we would take her to Santa Monica.

Mom enjoyed the trip to the beach as much as we did. She, too, fell under the spell of the children's gypsy joy. Before we left her she told me privately, "These are good children. I like them very much. Only one thing I have to tell you: be careful. Don't let the new children rob Steven. They'll take a lot of your time, and I know you want to help them. But Steven must never feel cheated."

Years later I asked Steve if he ever did feel cheated by our attentions to Vincent, Jane, or even to Rena or Ann. Steven seemed surprised by the question. Apparently he had come to believe that the children were with us because of him, and Steve loved his expanded family.

Reluctantly, we left Mom and began our homeward drive. As we rode, we sang, joked, and played games. We were barely half way home when Bill suggested, "How would you kids like to drive really north? We've never been to Canada."

The joy resounding from the back seat was the answer he wanted. I began to sound like an authoritarian, reminding them, foolishly, that they would have to stay well-behaved, be understanding about late dinners and non-existent rest rooms, have their clothes packed the minute Bill was ready to leave the motel, and all the other admonitions that seemed important at the moment.

We stopped at our house only as long as it took us to pick up a suitcase full of warmer clothes. We did not even eat there, but hurried away before there could be any risk that our spirit of adventure might wane.

Along the Oregon coast, pervading fog hung about us in ghostly veils. The children's banter subsided; they grew quiet. It was time to stop.

We found a place with cabins made of wood so weathered that they looked like driftwood. Inside were great, squeaking, vintage brass beds. Since the only heat was supplied from quaint wood stoves that none of us knew how to use, we slept in our clothes. We were all in one room, and the twang of the bedsprings let none of us sleep well.

In the morning I was aware, in a kind of half sleep, that Jane was whispering to the boys, "Get up. You gotta be all ready when Mom and Dad wake up."

"Why?" croaked Steven, as he tried to turn over and sleep some more.

"We've got to be extra good. We got to be all packed and ready so we can show them."

"Show them what?" Vince asked in a louder voice.

"Shh!" Jane warned. "If we act just perfect -- if we do better than we're expected to -- maybe we'll get a *real* trip next year."

"This is a real trip," Vince said, puzzled.

"You mean camping?" Steven asked, now fully awake.

"Sure. Why not?" Jane replied. "Or maybe even around the world. But we have to show them that we are good travelers."

I opened one eye and looked at Bill. He had heard the discussion too, and thank goodness, he was smiling at Jane's attempted manipulations. He shook his head slightly as a signal for me not to say anything, and we both pretended to sleep while the childen, like the shoemaker's elves, crept about the cabin, shivering while they prepared a makeshift breakfast and packed their suitcases.

Our trip along the Oregon coast continued into mist and clouds as we climbed upwards, up and up, until we were through and above them. The more rarified and cleaner air intoxicated us, as did the vistas of clouds below us. There were no advertisements to clash with views of wet grass and bright flowers. Together we shared an eerie feeling of moving along an extended peak in an unfamiliar sky. Only a need for meals that could not be indefinitely ignored forced us to drive down through the clouds and on to a town that offered tourist cuisine.

We did not stop again until we reached Seattle where my high school friend, Elinore Lindberg, lived with her husband and six children.

The Lindbergs were anxious to show us the tourist attractions of Seattle, but our kids were quite content to abandon the car and stay in that home and neighborhood rich with children.

The Lindberg kids had the best "cart" in the world It was simply a box attached to a long piece of lumber, two axles and four wheels. The front axle could be pivoted by pulling right or left on a rope attached to either end. Steering was simply a matter of pulling the rope while pushing with one's feet as they rested on the front axle.

Out the back gate of the Lindbergs' house was an alley. Vince, Steve, Jane, and the Lindberg boys pulled the cart through the alley to the top of a hill that overlooked the schoolyard. The lucky one whose turn it was to steer would sit in position and call, "Ready!"

Several hands would start him down the hill, faster and faster, directly toward the school basketball poles, the air whistling in his eyes and ears and hair. Then with his eyes wide open, it would be up to the driver to maneuver fast between the basketball poles, like a slalom. There were only inches of clearance on either side as one drove through. The driver would zig zag in and out as long as the momentum would keep up, in and out, in and out, pushing with the weight of his feet and shoulders to keep the cart from slowing down too soon. After the inevitable halt, he would reluctantly jump off and let someone else try it.

And they were off again, their excited voices carrying into the house.

"Hey, Dave, get off the back! How can I steer with you back there?"

"Aw."

"Hey, you guys. What would happen if somebody crashed into one of those poles?"

"Get smashed up, I guess."

"Who? Him or the cart?"

"So, why don't you smash it and see?"

We hardly saw the children until they came in, breathless, sweaty and hungry.

"Gee," Vince said. "When we get home, let's build us a cart. O.K., Steve?"

"Sure."

After promising the Lindbergs we would return the following year, we moved on to British Columbia where the warm welcome we received from everyone we met made us wish we could stay for the rest of the summer. It was there that Vince first demonstrated what was to become a peculiar reoccurrence.

We were walking over a rustic, wooden bridge in one of the many wild parks near Grouse Mountain. Vincent was enjoying the way the water moved around the rocks. He climbed over the railing so that he could hang on, but still be closer to the stream. Then his hold slipped, and he fell into the water, not hurting himself, but getting his clothes completely soaked. While he shivered audibly, we hurried back to the car, covered him with a blanket, and Bill drove as fast as he could back to the motel to get the boy a change of clothing.

About two days later Vincent fell off a diving pier and into the icy ocean off Vancouver. He could not swim, but the water was shallow on the side he "chose" to slip into.

A week later, at a mountain family camp sponsored by our city, Vince cast a borrowed fishing line for trout, and followed the bait right into the stream.

Vincent loved natural water. Perhaps he was trying to get as close to it as possible. Boats of all kinds fascinated him, so primarily for Vincent's sake we rented a rowboat at the family camp. I expressed concern about Vincent's safety on the middle of the lake, so Bill kept him busy at the oars. Vince was too small to handle them alone, so Steven or Bill would take one oar while Vince struggled with the other. The little figure's skinny arms strained to push the oar out, then up; out, then up. The handle of the oar hid his face for the seconds it was up high, then again on its way down. He did not complain or want to stop for a minute, although the effort was obviously taxing his diminutive energies to the utmost. The strategy worked. Vince did not fall into that lake until we had already returned the rental at the dock.

When we arrived home from our magical journey, only the adults were tired. The kids wanted to get started on their various projects right away.

While Jane moaned over her old wardrobe and began cutting out a new blouse, Vincent and Steve could hardly start soon enough on their own cart like the Lindbergs'.

They went into the garage to look for materials. Steve said, "We'll have to work with what we have around here. Let's just make it a piece of wood with wheels."

"No," Vincent disagreed. "We should make our cart just like the Lindbergs'. We'll have to have a box on top."

"Vince, where are we going to get a box that'll fit me or Jane? We'll be all cramped in."

"But, it's gotta be just like the Lindbergs' or it won't go as good."

"Mr. Lindberg helped his kids," Steven reminded Vince. "Our dad doesn't know how to do things like that."

The argument grew to a heated pitch, each boy insisting on having the design his own way.

"O.K., you go do it your way and I'll do it mine," Steve told Vince; and as if to illustrate his determination, Steven left the garage and went straight into the house to look for Jane.

Vincent, who had anticipated help from the stronger boy, was taken aback as he watched Steven resolutely walk away. He blinked back tears, resisting an impulse to run after Steve. Then he remembered David. Of course! David was not as tall or as old as Steven, but Vince knew that he could work with his best friend. He ran off to locate him.

Steven found Jane in her room staring at bright fabric

on the floor of her small back bedroom. The material was slippery and kept moving around under her paper pattern. She was about to give both the fabric and the pattern some of her most angry words when Steven came in.

"Jane, why don't you let that go for awhile and help me build a cart like the Lindbergs'?"

"I'm busy," she said sulkily, glaring at her frustrating project. "Besides, three people would be too many at one time."

"Vince is gonna make his own."

Jane looked up, suddenly interested. "Why?" she asked.

"I don't know. Just wanted to do it his way, I guess." Then he repeated for emphasis, "Vince is gonna make his own alone."

"You and me could make a better one than Vince can," Jane said as she stood up with enthusiasm that surprised Steve. Jane's potential blouse was already forgotten.

"Sure," Steven said. "Then we can ride it on Short Street."

"We'll show him," Jane said as she hurried from her room and out the back door toward the garage.

Watching carefully for the black widow spiders that everyone warned them lived in woodpiles, they picked through scraps of lumber that were being saved for our fireplace. Steven groaned when he found that Vincent had already claimed the only two wheels in the garage — rusted red ones that once were part of a wagon. The third and fourth wheels had vanished long ago.

Jane and Steven made the rounds of the markets and liquor stores trying to find a wooden box large enough to hold one fair-sized child, but the local merchants either needed all the wooden cartons they had or simply preferred cardboard. When they were about ready to give up, Steven remembered his old toy box. It was sturdy, made of wood, and certainly large enough. Jane and Steven triumphantly brought home a large cardboard box into which they placed Steve's rarely used games, balls and miscellaneous wheel toys. In the process of the transfer they found a pair of old strap-on roller skates that was transformed, by a simple loosening of each center bolt, into four separate pairs of wheels.

Jane and Steve felt really excited now. With more enthusiasm than skill, they removed the lid and mounted the toy box onto a crude T-form. They nailed the skate wheels to the back of the box and to either side of the front axle. Neglecting to ask permission, they removed the clothesline from the garage walls and used it to make a steering device.

While Jane and Steve were in the process of knotting the line to the outside edges of the axle, Vincent returned to the garage with David. The two friends were weary after spending the entire day searching for two more wheels to match the ones they had. The city dump and the hardware stores yielded nothing for them. Finally, a bicycle repair store was discovered where the wheels they needed waited tantalizingly, but at a price so high they despaired.

"Hey! You did it! You made a cart!" David said.

"Not yet, silly," Jane squelched. "It has to be tested and sanded and painted."

"Does it have to be painted?" Steve asked, suddenly deflated. "I thought we could use it today."

"Well, if you don't mind splinters," Jane replied in her most authoritarian tone.

"We'll be careful," Steve said, growing excited again. "Come on. Let's go test it out on Short Street!"

"Can we come?" Vince asked.

"Sure!" Steve answered quickly.

"If you'll do what we say," Jane added, recognizing her advantageous position.

The test on Short Street indicated two major problems. First, there were no brakes. Also, they had forgotten to allow for some sort of pivotal action in the steering axle.

"I guess we're going to have to tear it apart," Steve said unhappily.

"No! I know how you can steer without changing a thing," Vince told the others.

"How?" Jane asked.

"Let me show you. I'll have to take it up to the top of the hill."

"Hey, don't do that. It's dangerous," warned the cautious David.

"I know what I'm doing. Let me go," Vince said, taking hold of the rope and beginning to pull.

Fearing he would see his brainchild damaged before he had a chance to ride in it himself, Steve asked, "Are you sure? Real sure?"

Vincent was already at the top of the slightly inclined Short Street. With obvious satisfaction, he pushed the cart to start it, jumped in, and began maneuvering it down the sidewalk. As soon as some momentum was established, Vince yanked up hard on the right side of the rope, bucking the contraption like an awkward horse. It obligingly began to move to the right. Then Vince yanked on the left side, and bucked the cart to the left. He zig zagged that way down the hill, picking up velocity. His friend David ran toward the speeding contrivance with Jane and Steve. They were all shouting, "Yay!"

"Let me try it, Vincent!"

"Neat goin'! Go faster!"

"Don't forget who it belongs to, Vince. Vince!"

The boy was flushed with success and the thrill of speed. Having demonstrated his jerky, but effective, steering system satisfactorily, he simply let the vehicle coast to the bottom of the hill. When he got to the corner, he jerked left once more to round the corner. He jerked up hard. The edge of the axle crashed down on the sidewalk in a countermovement, breaking off the right front skate wheels. The added force tilted the cart suddenly to the right, throwing Vincent out of the toy box. He let go of the rope and tried to catch himself with his hands, slapping them flat on the sidewalk as he flipped over on his back.

The cart was not damaged at all, except for the detached skate wheels, but Vincent fractured both his wrists.

With two casts on his forearms, Vincent made quite an impression on his new class that September. Every time he told his story, he embellished it a little more, making himself sound increasingly heroic. Like combat medals, the casts bore silent witness to his tales.

I had a conference with his new teacher early in the semester. Clearly she liked the small, round shouldered Vincent with his two wrist casts. He did not fool her for a minute with his cocky way of facing any trying situation, nor by his rakishly tilted sailor cap.

"I've met lots of little guys like Vince," she said laughing. "I grew up in a Puerto Rican neighborhood in New York. I'm Puerto Rican myself. Remember *West Side Story*? I could have been Maria!"

I recalled her remark the night we took the children to see a revival of *West Side Story* performed "in the round."

The central staging technique employed by the company managed to involve the audience in the tragedy more fully than might otherwise have been possible. The chorus worked behind and beside the audience as well as in front of it. No one could help but get caught up in the joy of the dance "America." The mounting tension of "the rumble" engulfed us all. When "Maria's brother" was killed and fell at the feet of Vincent and Steve, both boys screamed and lifted their feet into the air with simultaneous terrified movements. Jane, who was sitting next to me, grabbed my arm with both hands and buried her head into my shoulder until the lights went off and "the corpse" quietly stood up and moved out of the room.

The experience of *West Side Story* deeply affected the children. "Mama," Jane said to me on the way home, "I don't understand what the point of it all was. Why did anybody have to get killed?"

"Nobody *had* to get killed," Steven answered quickly with some bitterness. "That was the point. Fighting is dumb."

"Some fighting might be right," Vincent argued. "All that in the show was wrong, but some fighting must be O.K."

"Not when it gets to killing people. People are the most important thing in this whole world — even people you don't like," Steven insisted.

"But sometimes you have to fight," Vincent said. "Like when you're in the Navy and there's a war. Then it's right."

Steven looked hard at the small boy sitting next to him in the back seat of the car. He asked, "Vince, do you think you could kill anybody? Ever?"

Vince reflected for a minute. Then he said, "No. I never could."

Jane said, "Lots of people kill, sometimes. My daddy fought in the war. I never asked him, but he must of killed someone."

Vincent replied with an earnestness I rarely heard in his voice, "Maybe it's all right for some people, but Steven is right. I couldn't do it."

"What if somebody was going to hurt you?" Jane asked.

"Even then. I think I'd rather die than really hurt somebody else."

"Me too," Steven said, and he put his arm around Vincent's shoulder.

The children grew a great deal in the next school year. Steven was placed in a class of "high achievers," and his teacher planned to make a full year's project of writing complete books -- one book from each student. Steven took the assignment seriously, and consequently had little time for Vincent or Jane as he researched, wrote and rewrote his own *Lost on Pirate Island*.

Deprived of Steven's company, Jane spent as much time as possible with her friend from sixth grade, Suzanne. Jane hated her new junior high school with its grim "We're here to *work*" approach. She suffered through it, though, with stoic determination and Suzanne's sympathy. The two of them did as little schoolwork as was compatible with passing their courses, while they gave maximum attention to the discussion and pursuit of adolescent boys.

Vincent was still far behind academically. To motivate him, his teacher found every opportunity to praise his every effort and achievement.

One day for their art period she assigned an abstract design project. The children were to scribble over the paper with pencil, then fill in with crayon the areas within the scribble lines. Vincent's resultant work showed his usual feeling for color values. The teacher seemed pleased. She sent Vincent to the principal's office with his work to show "the great man" his talent. The principal, perhaps impressed, but more likely in order to please the diminutive non-achiever, asked if he might frame the work and put it up in his office. Vincent could not have been happier if it had been hung in a major gallery.

His keen and appreciative eye led him to put more and more of what he saw and felt onto paper. He was fascinated with trees and water, and perspired with effort as he tried to catch their fluidity on the static paper. He experimented with chalk and water colors separately; then combined media. He strained his limited ability as he groped through any how-to-draw books he could find in the school or public libraries. His artistic skill grew, and with it, his abilities in all other school subjects.

As spring grew warmer, we discovered that Jane was saving bubble gum wrappers to send away for a camping lantern and compass. From his allowance, Steven was purchasing books with titles like *Your First Camping Trip.* Vincent was asking questions about where he might locate lakes and streams as subjects for his new paintings.

There was a plot afoot.

8

THE AMERICANS

An American is a person who works all year for a vacation during which he piles all those he thought he loved best into a station wagon and drives himself and them to exhaustion.

--Terribly Old Joke

Neither Bill nor I had ever tried camping before, but the costliness of motel rooms and their occasional unavailability encountered on our trip last summer gave us the incentive we needed to consider it. The excited children assured us they "would do all the work."

We purchased a four year old station wagon, an umbrella tent, three sleeping bags, and a cotton filled mattress tailored for the rear section of a station wagon. To these we added collapsible or folding eating utensils, a folding table, Coleman camp stove, and a tarp and rope to tie everything to the top of the car.

Before we left, the children practiced assembling and collapsing the tent in our back yard until they could achieve the former in about ten mintues and the latter in less time. They slept out in the tent one night and declared the experience "great," adding, somewhat sheepishly, that perhaps we could also invest in a few air mattresses.

A joyful feeling filled us as we drove away from our home that first day. As if by prior agreement, we all fell silent, savoring our feelings. We expected adventure. We would get acquainted with our country, and perhaps even slightly with the land to our north. We felt like we were on our way to shake hands with God.

We had not known what to do with the bountiful crop of plums from the tree in our back yard, so the children gathered and washed more than a hundred of the sweet, black fruit and put them into a shopping bag to bring along. Young appetites emptied the bag in a few hours, causing us to need rest rooms more than restaurants that first day out.

The weather was sunny but not hot as we traveled the road we remembered from the previous summer, taking in new details of traffic, small towns, amorphous clouds and smog-free skies.

For our first night of outdoor sleep we located a public campground in the southwestern tip of Oregon that was both a wood grove and a beach front. It was quite late in the afternoon when we located a tent space convenient to the bathrooms and showers.

Bill untied the huge, odd-shaped lump on the car roof, and Jane became building superintendent for the instant house.

We felt free, walking together along the beach and enjoying the sunset that night. The spell of the morning was still with Bill and me as we watched our three, escapees from the car, like former prisoners, running, climbing, throwing small stones into the sea, pretending to threaten one another with salty soakings, and falling, exhausted, onto the sand for thirty-second rests that magically gave them the energy to start their nonsense all over again.

It struck me that Vincent's shoulders did not seem to be quite so rounded as I remembered them. Perhaps he was only growing taller.

Surprised by sudden darkness, we groped our way back to the campground. The darkness was more total than it ever was in the city, and we had not thought to carry a flashlight. Gas lanterns on the picnic tables of other campers who read or played cards gave us a clue to the whereabouts of our green, fabric house.

"Mommy," Jane began in the tone I now recognized as an earnest prelude, "do we have to brush our teeth to-night?"

"Yeah," Steven added. "And a shower tomorrow when we can see would be better, too."

"Where's the bath room?" Vincent asked for the twelfth time.

In the tent, the children got into their sleeping bags without their usual bedtime ritual while Bill and I tried to work out the logistics of undressing in the car and crawling onto the mattress in the back.

"Hey!" Bill shouted as he hit his head hard on the ceiling of the station wagon. "That *is* a hard top."

Throughout the night he kept hitting his head whenever he tried to turn over. By morning, Bill was pretty irritable.

Rubbing his aching head, he announced, "O.K., you guys. From now on the back of the station wagon belongs to you."

"No!" howled Vincent and Steve in chorus.

"Yes!" Bill replied. "Either that or we're turning around right now and going back home."

Jane's eyes grew wide. Quickly she said to the boys, "It's O.K. You'll like it in the car." She noticed Vincent's upset face. "You can see the stars with the back door down, Vince," she added with unusual gentleness. "And smell all the lovely trees and plants."

"But Indians sleep in tents," Vincent said, crushed.

"No, they don't," Jane told him. She was groping for some way to keep her dream of a summerlong camping trip from ending abruptly. "I mean, they don't sleep in tents in the summertime. They sleep outside under the stars. It's kind of like part of their religion!"

"In station wagons?" Vincent asked rhetorically.

Jane was stopped for only a moment. "Well, if you stick your head out, you'll feel like you're outside." Suddenly she turned to Bill. "*I* don't have to sleep in the car too, do I?"

Our author of *Lost on Pirate Island* looked unhappy, but said nothing.

That night, the boys tussled into the station wagon, placed their pillows at the very edge of the lowered rear door, and gazing at the stars, talked themselves to sleep. Jane retained her place in the tent. She slept in a corner opposite from ours.

We stopped in Seattle briefly — just long enough to

take advantage of real beds at the Lindbergs'. While Bill and I rested and chatted with our friends, the children took a new, more critical look at the Lindberg children's cart.

It was raining the next day when we left Seattle, and raining still when we got to Vancouver. The thought of setting up a tent in a downpour pleased none of us. We looked for a motel room, but found that only the most expensive ones were still available. Discouraged, we located a small restaurant that was still serving dinner, although it was past ten o'clock at night.

The waitress was tired. She mumbled only the most important words for her task until Bill mentioned something about our coming from California.

The waitress' eyes stopped darting about the room and looked at our little quintet with new interest.

"California!" she echoed, savoring the syllables. "You came up *here* from California?" She stopped herself just before she asked what was really on her mind — why?

Bill answered her unspoken question. "We were able to visit here for only a few hours last year, and we fell in love with what we saw. We made it a special point to come back just as soon as we could."

The young woman seemed as pleased as if we had said that she, personally, was the reason for our visit. Her interest in all of us seemed to stimulate the sleepy children.

As she hurried to turn in our order, Vincent, who was sitting beside me, said, "Mom, please don't tell her my real name."

"Oh, for heaven's sake, Vince. What's wrong with your name?"

"I mean my last name," he told me frowning earnestly. "I don't want her to know I'm — well, you know."

"Why not, Vince?" Bill asked gently.

"'Cause I don't like for people to think I'm weird," he answered bitterly. Vince pulled his body back into his chair and hunched his shoulders as if trying to curl up into a clam shell.

Jane frowned and pulled her lips into a tight little line, but she said nothing.

Between courses, the waitress questioned us about our trip. When Bill mentioned our housing problem, she thought for just a moment and then remembered a friend who knew someone in Parliament who was away for the summer. She seemed certain that we could use the apartment.

We ventured from the book-lined, centrally located apartment without waiting for the rain to stop. We enjoyed museums, endless totem poles, our first la crosse game, dinners in boats converted to restaurants, an opera, and a Giraudoux play which the children liked far more than they expected to. Warm, friendly people who could never do enough to make us feel welcome, constantly apologized for the incessant rain. Finally, it stopped.

Now we could visit Vancouver's outdoor attractions. We went up the ski lift at Grouse Mountain and strolled the many beautiful parks. We were struck with the way people used and appreciated parks there. They read, picnicked, or just sat and drank in the beauty, even in the still overcast or drizzling weather. In California, people seem to feel that they must do something active when they are in a park.

Vincent sketched whatever he saw. Most of his sketches failed to please him, however, and ended up scribbled over and dropped into garbage cans. The few he saved were exciting in their subjective appraisal of details that most of us had completely overlooked.

"Honey, why don't you send one of your drawings to your mother or dad?" I suggested. "They would probably appreciate hearing from you."

"No," he said as if shocked. "These things are no good."

"They're terrific, Vince. Honestly! But, if you really want to save them, let's pick out postcards to send to your parents."

"No," he answered again. "It would only make them feel bad that they couldn't be here too."

When I suggested to Jane that she might write to her father, she replied similarly. "I never went any place before without my daddy."

"Don't you suppose he's glad that you're taking such a nice trip?"

"Yes, but getting a letter or a postcard would only make him feel that I was real far away. A letter's not the same thing as talking together."

"Are you worried about him, Janie?" I asked her.

"No. He seems to be doing fine with me not there. Only sometimes I miss him real bad."

We did not bring up the subject of parents again on our travels, but unknown to the children, I, myself, sent a few postcards to their parents. Vince and Jane sent cards to their friends David and Suzanne.

As soon as the weather cleared, we left our comfortable city apartment and took a ferryboat to Vancouver Island. The zest of the boat trip and the charm of Victoria, a city with hanging flowerboxes along the streets, captivated us. Even the gas stations had little gardens. Wherever we went, the windows of fantastic bakery shops lured us inside. We dawdled with little appetite for dinner that night at a costly restaurant near the strikingly lighted Parliament House.

Bill was the first to notice that time had escaped us. "It's one hour to midnight and we haven't found a place to camp yet!"

The campground near Victoria is called "Goldstream," because, we were told, there is a stream running through it where one might still pan for gold. The total darkness in campgrounds that never failed to surprise us completely enveloped the wooded area. We inched the car along like a supply truck on its way to a battlefield. The headlights did little good because of the lack of a clear-cut road. Trees seemed to keep looming up in front of us.

I got out of the car to look for a tent space, while Bill followed, maneuvering the car among the trees as best he could. The children were dozing in the back seat.

I was trying to shout quietly things like, "Bill! This way — no, over here!" in a kind of stage whisper. At that hour, most campers were asleep.

I was startled to hear a loud voice calling from the darkness, "Are you folks looking for a place to camp?"

"Yes," I responded, trying to adjust my volume.

"You can share ours, if you like," said the voice which I could now recognize as that of a young man.

Having been brought up in a metropolis, I am inclined to be suspicious. I told him, "There are five of us — my *husband* and three kids."

"Grace, what's going on out there?" Bill called to the back of my head.

"Nothing, Bill. Just a minute, O.K.?"

Another voice came out of the darkness, and I could soon make out a shape coming toward me. "There're two of us, and we only have our bicycles and a pup tent. We don't need the whole camp space. Why don't you set your things up here?" I could barely see that the two shapes that owned the voices were around sixteen years old.

The back door of the car opened and Jane bounded out with the instinct of a politician recognizing an opportunity to make a speech. "Thanks a lot," she told them as if she were in charge. "We'll be happy to join you."

"Jane. Jane. . .," I tried, but she was already on a new subject, ignoring me.

"You guys from around here?"

I slipped into the front seat to discuss the situation with the driver. At that hour, Bill could see no alternative to accepting the offer to share a camp site; and so he began to inch the car into position.

He left his parking lights on and got out of the car. "All right, Janie. Get your brothers up while I take down the equipment."

"Oh, Da-a-ddy. Not tonight. It's too late," Jane told him. Then, as if it were settled, she turned back to her more interesting business.

"Come on, Jane."

Really annoyed now, Jane said, "We can't set it up tonight. I'll sleep on the front seat of the car. Why can't you and Mom sleep outside for once?"

"This whole area's still wet from the rain, Jane. Now, come on," Bill said firmly.

Jane made a disgusted grimace for the benefit of her new audience, then came over to Bill. Quietly, but insistently, she told him, "No. Not tonight. It wouldn't be polite not to talk to those boys after they were so nice and everything. I'm not going to set up the tent and that's it."

Jane could turn on a real tantrum when she felt she needed to, and her tense face was giving storm warnings.

"Jane," I said, "how do you think it would look if you were to get a spanking right here and now?"

It is forbidden for foster parents to strike their wards, and we never did it, but at a moment like this the threat alone served the same purpose.

Jane turned her head back to the Canadian boys, smiled, and said, "Be with you in a few minutes!" Then with a furious look at me, she turned to awaken Steve and Vincent.

Half blindly, our two boys helped Jane set up the tent. I don't believe Steve ever did wake up completely, but he went about the motions of his routine like a robot.

Jane glanced over frequently as our hosts went to rekindle their campfire. The lights and shadows that the blaze produced fascinated Vincent. The minute the last stake was pounded in, Steven went back to sleep with his clothes on in the rear of the station wagon. Jane hurridly returned to the serious business of enticement, while Vincent played the role of little-brother-underfoot.

Like the waitress before, the young Canadians were impressed by the fact that we were from California.

"How long have you studied French?" they asked Jane.

"French? What do you mean, study French?"

"I mean, in what grade do you start it?"

"We don't study French. What for?" Jane asked, bewildered.

"What for? Well, why do you study anything? Because it's important; I guess."

"I don't want to take French," Jane told them.

"You mean you can take anything you want?" they asked, apparently surprised.

Vincent, uninterested in this discussion of pedagogy, tried to turn to subjects more in line with his interests. "How come you guys are out here with only bikes?"

"Our parents let us come as a kind of a test. If we make out all right here near our own town, we can take a really long back packing trip later on."

"By yourselves? Where will you go?" Vincent asked, wide eyed.

"Oh, I don't know. Into the wilds, I guess. We'd just kind of explore."

Vincent continued to press them for details of their proposed journey as Jane, feeling upstaged, quietly grew more and more upset. When Bill and I were ready to settle down for the night, I approached the campfire to thank the boys for their consideration and to tell Vincent and Jane to get to bed. Prepared for outraged cries, I was surprised to see Jane stand up and go directly to the tent with only a, "See you tomorrow."

Once she was inside the tent, Jane began to rage. "It isn't *fair!*" she began. "They're *my* friends. Why do you and Vince have to interfere?"

"Oh, Jane, for heaven's sake. Life goes on, boys or no boys."

"But it isn't fair! Why did Vince have to butt in?"

"Because he likes people too," I told her.

"Baloney. He was only trying to ruin it for me."

"How did he ruin it?"

"Those boys liked me until Vince came. Then they ignored me. I think Vince did that on purpose."

"Oh, come on, Jane. Get to bed. You'll feel more human in the morning."

She didn't feel more human. In the morning, by the time Jane was dressed and beautiful enough to pass the critical test of her purse mirror, the young Canadians were almost finished with their campfire cooked bacon and eggs. They talked a few minutes with Jane, then left the campground on their bicycles. Once they were gone, Jane set her lips in a tight, small line, and hardly said a word to anyone.

After breakfast, Vincent and Steven ran down to the stream to try to figure out how to pan gold. Bill and I took an exploratory walk to enjoy the clean greenness, and Jane stayed behind to sulk.

By lunchtime, Vincent and Steven had decided that they were not going to get any gold without some lessons to improve their panning technique. We ate cheese sandwiches, and drank milk made with skim milk powder and stream water. Then Bill was ready to drive east.

"O.K. Come on, kids. Let's pack up," I said in my schoolteacher voice.

"Oh, no," Jane whined. "We just set it all up."

"Come on, Jane. It's time to get moving."

Jane's sulk exploded. "No! I won't! I'm tired of you always makin' me work. You never let me have any fun! I'm not going to do anything more." She began to weep loudly.

Tantrums were not new with Jane, but this one did seem to top her former efforts. I went over to her, put my arm around her and asked, "Honey, is your period due?"

At that, Jane really blew up. Her crying, sounding almost like a scream, reverberated through the camp. I half expected to see a mounted policeman come riding up to see who was torturing whom.

Jane ran over to the picnic table, put her head onto her folded arms and continued weeping. Her face now covered, the dreadful sounds were quieter. I was ready to ignore it and let her have her fun, but not Bill. He walked over to Jane and said, "Now look here. Either you get up and do your share right now or once we're off the ferry boat I'm turning the car around and driving straight home."

"No!" said Vincent and Steven in chorus.

"I mean it," Bill said. "We all have our part to do. Mine is driving. If we can't all work together we might as well know it right now and give up."

"Go ahead," said Jane, calling his bluff. "I'm not having any fun, anyway."

"Last chance," Bill tried again.

But Jane ignored him and went back to her tantrum.

I helped the boys collapse the tent and get everything up on top of the station wagon. Bill, whose arms ached from the job, tied up the bundle with yards and yards of clothesline.

When we were ready, Bill turned to Jane. "Well, we're ready. Are you willing to join us, or would you rather stay here all alone?"

Walking proudly while wiping her nose on the back of her hand, Jane took her place in the back seat. The boys stared at her mutely. Bill started the car and drove straight to the ferry boat.

The passengers and driver were all silent, trying to devise some way to get out of the situation without losing face. Jane, feeling far better for her outburst, was willing to do anything except admit she was wrong or apologize. I knew Bill had been looking forward to the journey as much as any of us, but he believed in keeping his word as well as his authority.

During the ferry boat ride the boys explored the deck and watched the swelling sea. Jane sat quietly alone.

As soon as we disembarked, Bill drove following the signs that pointed to the American border.

"Dad," Steven began in a small voice. "Please let's

not go home."

In a voice only slightly louder, Vincent said, "Yeah."

Bill did not reply, waiting to hear from Jane. She said nothing. The drive continued in silence.

When he got to within a few miles of the border, Bill swung the car east. Everyone noticed, but pretended not to.

After a few miles I ventured a question, "Where are we?"

Bill did not answer at once. Then he said, "We can turn back at any point. There's no need to go exactly the way we came."

The rest of the day's drive was largely in silence.

By nightfall we came to one of Canada's many campgrounds. Bill pulled in and got out to untie the line. Without a word, the three children set up the tent in record time. When the cooking utensils and other equipment were in their places, Jane took the clothesline that was used to tie the bundle to the top of the car and knotted it tightly around a clump of trees. Then she hung our three largest towels on the rope. Smiling sweetly she said, "See? Now with a little bit of water warmed on the fire, a person can take a real shower in here."

Our journey continued.

We had heard of a Quaker settlement in British Columbia called Argenta. That was our next major goal. We knew no one who had visited there, so we were not prepared for the rugged logging trails that led to the town of Argenta. In Canada at that time, any road with asphalt was indicated on the map as a "highway." The next best roads were "improved roads" which simply meant that they had leveled them and poured oil and gravel. About half way up to Argenta, the roads were not even "improved." We drove around bumpy curves in clouds of dust, feeling as if one wheel must be hanging over precipice after precipice. Bill, who had never driven in such country before, confided to me that what really worried him was the possibility of meeting a logging truck coming down. As the truck would probablly be too heavy to back up the mountain, we would have to back down. "Now, if that happens," Bill said, "I would want all of you to get out of the car and follow me on foot."

We did not encounter that situation, but we did have

one almost as serious. On a particularly steep incline, the motor of our car died. It was not overheated, but the loaded station wagon just decided it could not or would not take such a steep road, so it quit. With the motor, the power brakes also went out. When Bill tried to restart it, the car responded only by rolling slightly downhill.

"Everyone out," Bill said, while beads of perspiration began to form on his forehead.

"Where can we go?" I asked him. "We can't scale this mountain or hang over the side."

"You figure it out," Bill said. "I have enough problems right here."

The children and I got out. There seemed to be a shoulder several hundred yards back, so we walked downhill and stood there while Bill wrestled to get the motor going again. The car choked, rolled, blew black smoke out of its twin exhausts, and eventually moved forward. Bill gunned the motor and continued forward until he was around a bend and out of our sight. After waiting a few minutes, the children and I started the steep hike up the hill to join Bill on a somewhat more level stretch.

"Are you sure you want to go to Argenta?" I asked him when I was back beside him.

"What do you suggest I do now?" he asked. "Turn the car around on this narrow road? I'm afraid we're committed." Then he added, "But, I'm beginning to get an idea."

About a half an hour later, we arrived at a small town on the edge of Lake Kootenay. Bill left the miserable road and drove into the town as if he knew exactly what he was looking for. He drove directly to the edge of the lake where there was a small harbor with boats tied up.

"We're going to rent a motorboat," he announced.

"But, Bill! You don't know the first thing about driving a motorboat. That's a good sized lake, and the water looks pretty choppy to me."

"There couldn't be too much to learn about driving a boat. And it couldn't be any more risky than that poor excuse for a road," he answered. "Come on."

The children were glad for an excuse to run, and became involved in a sort of improvised tag game while Bill went inside the building labeled Kaslo Boat Rentals. I walked out on the pier to take a closer look.

The lake was full of fish. It seemed to me I could have reached in and grabbed one, Indian fashion. Nevertheless, there were no other boats or fishermen in sight. The lake was not at all calm. Wind was coming up hard. I turned back to the children. "Hey, kids — how much do you remember from those swimming lessons you took last summer?"

"Are we going to swim up to Argenta?" logical Steven asked incredulously.

"I hope not," I said with more sincerity than I wanted to show. "But just in case, how about putting on your swimming things underneath your clothes?"

Jane went to the car at once to comply, but Steven and Vincent looked unconvinced.

"Mom, do you think I'm going to fall in like I did all the time last year?" Vince asked.

"It's not that, dear. It just seems to me to be, well, a precaution. You might want to swim in the lake once we get to Argenta."

Steven was sold. "Sure, Vince. It's a real nice day for around here. They must have a beach there, and it'd be easier to wear stuff than to bring it. Come on!"

I went inside to see how Bill was doing.

He greeted me, "Hey, hon', good news. We're even going to have a chauffeur for the rest of the way."

The pleasant, slow moving man behind the counter smiled. "Well, he's really more of a pilot, I guess. The fact is, my son's never been up to Argenta. It's time he went."

I felt immensely relieved until I saw the man's son. Our "pilot" was about eleven or twelve years old.

The children grinned as Tommy took over the driving. Jane wished he were just a bit older, but used her charm on him just the same, for practice.

Tommy didn't know what to make of all her attention. He was a quiet boy, serious about his responsibility for the safety of his father's boat. His blue eyes took in everything, but he showed no apparent interest in talking about what he saw or did.

The lake seemed endless. We sped across miles of choppy little waves. Once the novelty of the motorboat and the spatter of spray upon us wore off, we began appreciating the wild, wooded shore rushing past. After more than an hour, Tommy cut down the motor and drifted into the first small dock we had seen.

"We're here," he said simply. He held the small craft while our family disembarked shakily. Then Tommy carefully tied up the boat and leaped out himself.

Once we found footing on the dock, we looked around. We could see a small, flat farm to one side, and a little house near a lumber mill across from it. But the town appeared to be deserted.

Simultaneously Bill and I realized how ridiculous our present situation was. What were we supposed to do now? Walk up to the door of some total stranger and knock? What could we say if we did meet anyone: "Hello. Here we are. Please entertain us." Even sight-seeing would be limited since we were on foot.

We looked at one another and laughed. Then Steve said, "Well, we might as well go swimming." That idea caught on, and all four children tore off their clothes. Tommy wore his undershorts. I was glad to find that our three did remember at least the rudimentary rules of swimming. Tommy, of course, swam very well.

Lake Kootenay, which had before been only a cold, blue-gray highway, natural yet sterile, like the dirt roads we had abandoned, was now alive with youthful exuberance. In water, children can teach us something about creativity. They don't soak themselves, or simply swim back and forth. They experiment with movement, with wetness, with human contact. The primitive and the godlike merge in their unselfconscious fun.

Bill and I sat crosslegged on the wooden dock. Bill sighed. "Wish we could join them?" he asked me.

"No, Bill. I'd rather watch this time."

My husband nodded, relaxed, and enjoyed the children's enjoyment, our unaccustomed isolation from other human beings, the quiet pine backdrop, and the clean, crisp air. Bill and I felt very close to one another.

As if he were a spirit conjured up from the dock itself, we suddenly became aware of another presence. Standing behind us, his mouth open, breathing hard but not puffing, was an enormous Irish setter. His tail wagged very slightly.

"Well, at last the welcoming committee has arrived," Bill said.

The animal took his words to be some sort of signal,

and tried to communicate a response. He moved close to us, as if in recognition, then walked a little away. Then he moved back to us, walked away, back and forth.

"Does he want us to go with him?" I asked.

"Seems so. Maybe something is wrong."

"No," I replied. "He seems relaxed — not the least bit upset."

The children had noticed the setter, and were out of the water, dripping on the dock.

"Who is that?" Jane asked rhetorically.

"He's sure beautiful," said Steven, who had wanted a dog ever since the death of Tippy. "Do you suppose he belongs to someone?"

"Of course he does," Vince said. "Look at how clean he is. But this isn't just a dog. He's somebody's friend, and he understands everything we say."

The animal did, indeed, seem to respond to our words. He began his back and forth sign language again.

Vincent, our sailor-hatted Indian, understood the pantomime. "He says he's our guide," Vince told us with shivering conviction.

On cue like Lassie, the Irish setter wagged his tail harder.

"Let's hurry up and get dressed," Steven said, beginning to dry himself with the towel I offered from my oversized handbag.

As soon as we could, we left the dock, following the reddish brown creature who seemed to know exactly where he was going.

"He's probably taking us to his master," Bill said.

"No," Vincent told us. "His master isn't at home. That's why he's so glad to see us."

Her tone heavy with sarcasm, Jane asked, "How do you know?"

Vincent didn't answer. He just smiled at the dog and I shook off an impression that the dog smiled back. There is a kind of telepathy that often develops between a boy and his own dog, but Vincent and this new acquaintance were already communicating like old friends.

I noticed that we all spoke of the setter as "he" rather than "it."

The dog led us up a trail to the right, past the lumber mill and little house. He sniffed at every fence, tree, and rock along the way, keeping an eye on us, never going too far ahead; never lagging behind. The road led us up the hill, past a number of small, rudely built cottages and two permanently installed trailer homes.

"Do you suppose someone dragged those trailers up those terrible roads?" Bill asked me.

"They must have. They certainly couldn't have fit them into motorboats."

After some twenty minutes of walking about and looking at the quiet, rustic town, we followed the dog, running ahead of us, to a building that did not look like the others. He began chasing his tail as if to signify that this was a place to linger.

It was a two room schoolhouse built by hand of lumber from the surrounding trees. Ground level, it had a covered porch with a welcome drinking fountain, chairs turned upside down, and a telephone with a hand crank.

The children used their hands to shade their eyes in order to peer into the rooms, each of which was dominated by a large portrait of Queen Elizabeth II.

I was fascinated by the telephone. "Do you suppose it works?" I asked.

"I guess so," Bill replied. "But, whom could we call?"

I picked up the receiver. There was no dial tone such as I was accustomed to.

"I think it doesn't work." I turned the handle. It made a ringing sound that surprised me and caused me to stop turning before I had completed two rounds. I listened. There was a voice on the line, very distant and unclear. I could not understand the words.

"Did somebody answer?" Jane asked.

Quickly I hung up the receiver. "I think so. It sounded like somebody, but I couldn't understand what he said."

"Maybe it was a ghost," Steven said with a trace of humor.

His words made me aware of a growing discomfort. We had not yet seen one human being in this town — only a dog who acted as if he owned everything himself. The voice on the line could, indeed, have been that of a ghost.

Tommy grinned at our naivete, but did not offer any comment or help.

The children followed the dog out to the rear of the

building where they found a rudimentary playground. The slide was a smoothly sanded and varnished piece of long wood, almost straight except for a hump in the middle. It was tilted on two high wooden horses placed just under the hump.

There was also a wooden swing tied with stout rope to a tree branch, and no other equipment except a single, wooden frame outhouse.

The dog sat down in the middle of the playfield while all four children tried out the slide, the swing, and the outhouse. Vincent was most interested in climbing a large, witch shaped tree that had grown in such a way as to be tailored for climbing.

Glad for a chance to sit down, Bill and I found a bench. I rubbed Bill's feet and he rubbed mine.

By the time we felt refreshed, the dog indicated to us his conviction that it was time to move on. Most dogs could not have exercised such authority over Bill, but this setter made him curious. We went back to the road and continued to follow our glowing mahogany red guide.

The area was so beautiful that it added to our growing sense of unreality. Water caught lights and made patterns among rocks, changing its pace from gentle to torrential within only a few feet. Ferns and flowers abounded like a garden from another era. The few houses we saw blended into the mountain as if they, too, had grown there. Vincent kept muttering, "Why didn't I bring my paper? Or even one piece of charcoal? Why was I so stupid as to leave them in that darn car?"

"Vince, I have my camera. You tell me what to shoot and I'll take a picture of it that you can copy later," I suggested.

Vincent sighed with overstated exasperation. "Mom, photographs are dead things. To get a real picture, you have to catch it while it's still alive."

"Oh, come on!" I said, in no mood to speak tactfully. "What makes a charcoal sketch any more 'alive' than a photograph? You're always complaining you can't catch lights and movement, anyway."

Vince walked beside me quietly for a minute. I was afraid I might have said something to deflate this newly budding ego, but Vince was only trying to think how best to explain to one as ignorant as I.

"Mom, a drawing — even a bad drawing — is how somebody *feels* about something. A camera is only a machine. It can't feel anything, and its pictures show it."

"It seems to me," I said, "that a picture can remind you of something and that memory can include feelings."

Vince considered my words, then answered, "Yes, but only if you have looked at whatever it was very closely the first time you saw it. Peole don't usually really see something until they try to draw it. I think pictures from a camera are mainly phony."

We walked for what seemed like hours. Strangely, none of us felt like eating the cheese, bread, and apples which I carried, although the thermos of water needed regular replenishment. We felt thoughtful, perhaps like pilgrims, but happily so. The good humor of our red-haired guide kept our weariness from turning to moroseness.

The dog's mood changed suddenly to anticipation. He began to turn his attention from the scents of the road back to our little party. He jumped wildly, and ran to and fro as he had done when first he tried to get us to follow him.

"What's he trying to tell us now, Vince?" I asked.

"I don't know," he answered, as if the question were perfectly normal. "But I think it's good, whatever it is."

When we rounded a bend, we saw a low, ranch-style house that looked like it might have come from a California subdivision, except that it was surrounded by chickens and two unfenced and unfettered goats. The livestock ignored us, but watched the dog nervously as he tried to lead us upward to the door of the house.

We stood back, strangers, unwilling to impose on the people who lived in the attractive, shingle-roofed house.

Steven said, in a matter of fact tone, "The dog wants us to go in."

"What's the matter? Don't you trust him?" Vincent asked.

"I wish I'd stayed in the water," Jane remarked.

Frustrated at our hesitation, the dog began to bark. The goats started and ran, but the Irish setter ignored them, concentrating his barking toward us.

The tree shaded front door opened, and a small, dark

haired woman said, "Why, Jonathan! Hello there. What's the matter, boy?"

The dog ran back to us while the woman's eyes followed him. When she saw us, she smiled. "Hello! Did Jonathan bring you with him?"

There was no mistaking her friendliness, so we went toward the door. "I guess that's what he did," Bill replied, "if you mean the dog."

"Yes, that's Jonathan, the Stephenson's dog. They're the people who live in the little house by the lumber mill, and ordinarily, they look after visitors. But when they're away, Jonathan takes over the job for them. Won't you come in?"

The setter, seeing that his responsibility was discharged, turned his attention to the goats, which he teased joyfully.

"Will he hurt the goats?" Vincent asked.

"Oh, no. It's only a game he plays whenever he sees them. Actually, he and the goats are good friends. Jonathan often comes up here to play with them."

We entered the simple, unpainted, and booklined living room. The sun made designs on the floor as it came in through one of the windows past a half-protecting tree. "Please sit down," the woman told us as if we had been expected. "You must be very tired. Where did you leave your car?"

"In Kaslo," Bill told her.

"Kaslo! How long have you been walking?"

"Not too long," Bill, who rarely walks if he can avoid it, told her, smiling. "We came up here by motorboat. Tommy, here, is our chauffeur — pardon me, our pilot."

Bill then introuced the rest of us and himself. Before he was through, two boys, two girls, and a tall, thin blonde man entered the room.

"We're the Herberts," the lady told us. Then, to her husband she said, "Jonathan brought them. I guess everyone else is at Friends Yearly Meeting in Vancouver."

"Great!" Mr. Herbert said. "Ever since those magazine articles, many visitors come to Argenta, but we rarely meet any of them."

Jonathan had chosen well. After Mrs. Herbert gave us cold fruit drinks, she sent her children out to show ours the little cave down the hill where they slept in the summer.

We learned that Mr. Herbert was in charge of the school we had seen along the road. That was a government school, not the Quaker boarding school for which Argenta was known — thanks to glowing, if not entirely accurate, magazine articles about the "idyllic" alternative education and life style. Actually, the Quaker school was beset with problems — ideological, pedagogical, and financial. Although it might have seemed like a conflict of interests, Hugh Herbert, a former Anglican pastor, was trying to help the small, experimental school get itself on a firmer footing. Bill and Mr. Herbert talked shop happily for about an hour.

Jean Herbert, looking relaxed and interested in the discussion, did not say much. I watched her with admiration. When people just pop in at my house, I feel somewhat frantic and probably show it.

The children came in looking refreshed.

"Mommy, you ought to see it down there," Jane bubbled as she burst through the door. "It's all hidden and there are berries and animals around and — it's real great!"

"Yeah," Steven added dryly. "And they have mountain lions, too."

"Mountain lions! This far north?" Bill asked in alarm.

Hugh Herbert smiled. "Well, we see an occasional mountain lion around here, but when we do, we just notify the forest rangers and they send someone to hunt it down. Since all the children have a long walk to school, we do have to be a bit careful, you see."

"How about that?" Jane breathed. "Wouldn't it be great to worry about mountain lions instead of cars?"

"One of the reasons we moved up here was so that the children could have some experience with being close to nature before it was too late," Hugh Herbert told us. "They'll probably spend most of their lives in cities; and sidewalk is no substitute for earth and grass. At least, not for a whole lifetime."

Jean Herbert grew serious. "Well, that was one consideration, but not the primary one that brought us here."

"What, then?"

"Oh, you don't want me to get off on that," Hugh Herbert said quickly, smiling again.

"Why not?" his wife said. "You always say that it's important for everyone to understand about the Doukhobors."

"Weren't they the people that were having nude parades? I read about that in Vancouver," Steven said, squatting unceremoniously on the bare floor.

We all got comfortable as Hugh Herbert, puffing now on a pipe, began to tell us the story of a long persecution of Russian immigrant followers of Tolstoy's philosophy. Although his voice was soft and his manner deliberate, he held the interest of all but his own children throughout the recitation. The Doukhobors took shape in our minds as a stubborn people who held rigidly to their old ways in spite of every effort to Canadianize and to secularize them. The "nude parades" we had read about were an extreme measure to call attention to their convictions.

"A few sent their children to regular public schools, but not many," Hugh Herbert said. "A conservative mood has crept into the Canadian government, so some misguided power elite decided to force these 'peculiar' people to send all their children to Canadian schools. Those who refuse have their children taken away from them — provided the children can be located and locked up.

"Nobody is happy with what has happened," he continued. "The admirable Royal Canadian Mounted Police are now put into the outrageous position of having to chase down children in the woods and bring them, kicking and screaming, to the boarding schools the government has set up for the purpose. Actually, these are a kind of juvenile jail."

Steven began to look embarrassed, but Jane and Vincent were spellbound.

Jane said, "I know how those kids feel."

"How could you?" Hugh Herbert asked, his own passion against the injustice blinding him to the changes in our three children.

"I know," Jane replied simply. "There is no worse thing in the world than to be taken away from your parents. It feels . . . scary. You hope you're not awake . . . like you're walking in your sleep. All the grownups you see are like they're from some other world and don't really care about you any more than a mouse. It makes you mad, but you can't do nothing."

Mrs. Herbert was looking at Jane seriously, as though recognizing her for the first time. She said gently, "But many adults do care, Jane. We care. We moved up here so we could be as close to our Doukhobor friends' settlement as possible, in case they needed us. We've tried to let them know we're still their friends in every way possible. We even go to Vancouver to the courts and represent them when they let us."

Vincent kept his eyes down to the floor while he said to Jane, "Some kids are better off some other place. Not everybody should be with his own mom and dad -- even if it hurts a lot at first."

I blinked back tears.

Hugh Herbert, now aware that the conversation had taken a turn he did not understand, changed the subject.

We spent another joyful hour with the Herberts, who then insisted on walking back with us to the dock. Jonathan awoke from his nap in the sun and joined all of us, following this time rather than leading.

We snapped pictures, promised to write, and were about to get into the boat when I noticed a handmade sign tacked up prominently on a tree. It said, "You are entering Argenta. Are you lost or crazy?"

The last we saw of Argenta from the rocking boat was a large Irish setter, still watching from the end of the dock, wagging his tail slowly, steadily.

We camped in many places in southwest Canada, marvelling at her clean air, learning to enjoy swimming in her icy lakes. Finally we swung the car down into the United States.

In the otherworldliness of Yellowstone, Steven and Jane explored the trails together. Jane, fascinated by the wildlife, ignored the warnings of the forest rangers and chased any bear she could see, shouting enough to frighten them thoroughly, "Here, bear bear bear bear bear!"

Vincent was too busy staring at the bubbling pools, geysers, and odd combinations of colors to be able to sketch them. "Nobody would believe it, anyhow," he reasoned.

We left Yellowstone, exchanging its earthy trails for asphalt highways. With each evening's stop, we found our new campground different from the preceding one; refreshed, we arose with the first pink of morning and moved on.

We didn't camp in St. Cloud, Minnesota; motel rooms were a necessity. Mosquitoes swarmed as thick as Los

Angeles smog. We dropped our things into the room quickly and went out to purchase further protection, insect repellent, which we applied generously to ourselves before going to a night baseball game to watch Curtell Motton play.

Curt, a former student of Bill's, was an outfielder and star pinch-hitter for the Baltimore Orioles. Some years before, Curt had clinched a pennant for the Orioles. In the deciding game of the championship play-offs against the Minnesota Twins, it was he who, in the final inning, drove in the winning run off Ron Perranoski.

Temporarily, Curt had been sent to Baltimore's farm team in St. Cloud as a player-coach; he was both batting instructor and center-fielder.

Few people were at the ball park that night, probably apprehensive of those clouds of insects. The small crowd was as relaxed as if the game were being played in a neighborhood park. Bill had no qualms about swinging his large body over the railing and down to the field where the team was warming up.

When Curt saw Bill he let out a loud, wild whoop that sounded like, "He-e-e-e-e-ey!" Curt raced over to where Bill stood as if he were trying to take an extra base. He grabbed Bill's hand in both of his.

The children watched their animated conversation with awe.

When the game was about to start, Bill swung back over the rail to join us. Curt's team won the game easily, with Curt hitting safely every time he was at bat. After the game, Curt insisted on taking us to his favorite restaurant for fruit salad. The children couldn't have been more pleased if they had been invited by a movie star.

Curt was never one to talk much about himself. He appeared to be more interested in talking to each of the children in turn. He asked questions of Steven about the book he wrote in school. He questioned Jane about details of our camping trip, pretending interest when she went on and on about the "cutest boys" she had met along the way. Curt had a skill in drawing out Vincent that I had not observed in any other man except Bill.

"I've decided to be an artist," Vince told the seemingly engrossed Curt. "Maybe I'll be a ballplayer in the summer."

"Great," Curt replied. "It's a good life for a man.

You'll have to work hard now to get ready, you know."

"Yeah," Vince agreed. "But, I'm not too hot at games. And I wish I was taller."

"Taller? Not necessarily!" Curt reassured him. "They need us little guys on the team to field those grounders. *I'm* not very big, didn't you notice?"

"You're a lot bigger than I am," Vince mumbled miserably.

"But I wasn't always," Curt told him. "I was littler than you are when I was your age. How old are you, anyway?"

"Ten," Vince replied.

I caught momentary surprise on Curt's expressive face, but Vince, thank goodness, did not notice. Ten year old Vincent looked about six or seven.

"You keep playing ball every chance you get," Curt advised. "And eat lots of fruit salad, like me. You'll grow; I guarantee it."

"Don't the other ball players like fruit salad?" Jane asked.

"Sure. Why do you ask?"

"I don't see any of the other guys from your team eating here."

"They eat at another place," Curt told her. "There was a little, well, unpleasantness when I was first here in town. I got the impression the restaurant owner would rather I ate some place else."

"Why?" Jane asked, suddenly wide-eyed. "You're a big star!"

"Not so big," replied Curt, smiling. "Not so you could notice. Anyhow, I don't like to cause trouble."

"Curt," Bill said frowning. "Are you saying that there's some problem about your being black?"

"Well, *I* don't consider it a problem, but you know. Once in a while, sure. It happens, and it's worse some other places. Even in my own home town where I was brought up and went to school, I couldn't rent an apartment a couple of years ago."

Jane was thunderstruck. "I thought that only happened a long time ago! I don't know anybody who acts like there's something wrong about being black."

"Well, believe it," Curt told her smiling, "I do."

"That isn't *fair!* she said, using her favorite phrase in reference, for once, to a problem that did not directly involve herself.

"I know," Curt replied simply, as he got up to pay the check.

Jane was introduced to prejudice twice more that summer, and we could see the seeds of militant activism sprouting in her outraged spirit.

First there was "Aunt Joyce," an old friend of Bill's and mine who was working on the editorial staff of *Time* magazine. She was tall, black, sophisticated, and strikingly beautiful. She wore elegant clothes that looked as comfortable on her as blue jeans did on our lanky daughter. Jane fell naturally and completely in love with Joyce, whom she called "the most beautiful lady I ever saw in my life." In spite of genetic improbability, she introduced Joyce proudly to everyone as "my aunt." Joyce responded with characteristic pleasure.

We stayed with Joyce's mother for a few days on Martha's Vineyard where the incident occurred. Our party was refused service at a "Clam Shack." Bill was furious and looked ready to tear the place apart.

Jane was on the verge of tears.

Joyce, sensing the depth of their shocked naivete, did exactly the right thing: she laughed. "Oh, come on," she said. "Is that really the first time that ever happened to you? Where you been? Why, that polite little war's been going on for a long time, but don't you worry. Our side wins a few battles too."

"Like how?" Jane asked.

"Well, for instance, there were those who didn't want us to use the beach where you kids built a sand man yesterday. So, they put up a sign that said, 'Members only.' Members of what wasn't exactly clear — members of the white race, I suppose. So, a bunch of us went down there at about three o'clock in the morning and stole the sign."

"Didn't they just put up another one?" asked realistic Steven.

"Sure," Joyce answered. "They kept putting up signs and we just kept taking them down. Finally, they quit bothering."

With humor she told of other incidents that could have generated anger if narrated by someone else. But, when

Joyce told it, the absurdity of separateness made us all laugh.

For Jane, Aunt Joyce could do no wrong. Once Vincent told her, "Aunt Joyce, you've got an accent."

"No, she doesn't," Jane told him defensively. "All of *us* have accents. Aunt Joyce talks just right."

"Thank you," Joyce said, smiling. And she meant it.

We took Joyce and her nephew, Norman, camping with us in Boston, because they had never camped before. There is a beautiful campground on the outskirts of Boston which most Bostonians, then, didn't know about. Consequently, we had a large, beautiful plot of wooded land practically to ourselves.

After sleeping outdoors one night, the four children decided to build a rude wooden lean-to for themselves to sleep in the second night, "to protect us from wild animals." They labored at their task, gathering wood and clumps of vines, piling them systematically higher and higher. Soon, a small group of other young campers perched on nearby stones to watch the effort. One of them addressed twelve year old Norman, "Hey, boy, are you a nigger?"

He ignored them. Our three had never heard a question like that before and weren't sure how they should respond, so they took their cue from Norman.

"Hey, nigger," the spectators taunted, "how come you're playin' with white kids?"

They kept it up until Bill, finally growing concerned, had to interfere. Later, after we had gone into the city for a seafood dinner, we came back to find the little wooden retreat completely demolished. Norman assured everyone that he loved sleeping outdoors at night, but the incident permanently scarred the memory of Boston for Steve, Vincent and Jane. They felt that Norman, their guest, had been insulted and that they, somehow, were at least partly to blame.

When we returned to New York we stayed at International House. This student residence, where races and languages mingle freely, had a healing effect on the children's disenchantment with white Americans. Over the door was engraved, "That brotherhood may prevail," and the people who stayed at International House lived those words.

That summer, Bill, an old alumnus, and the two boys

shared a room in the men's wing while Jane and I shared one on the women's side.

As Jane and I were in the elevator coming up to our room, an East Indian girl wearing a sari turned to Jane and said in an excited voice, "Isn't this wonderful? Isn't this a beautiful country? All my life I've wanted to come here and now I'm here I can hardly believe it. Don't you feel that way?"

"Sure," Jane said. "I like this country just fine."

"Where are you from?" the young woman asked Jane.

"California," Jane replied. "But I feel just like you do about New York."

As we left the elevator, thirteen year old Jane looked at me with eyes aglow. "Oh, Mommy," she said. "That girl. That lovely girl in the elevator. She talked to me just like I was a person."

"Aren't you a person?"

"No, not really," Jane replied. "Not like someone grown up."

The Arab young men also treated Jane like an adult. They hurt twelve year old Steven's feelings by making fun of him so that they might have Jane to themselves to talk to, to dance with at nightly parties, to sit with in the coffee shop, and to ask for dates. The attention both pleased and frightened Jane. She knew she was not pretty in a conventional sense, and the older men made her feel uncomfortably challenged. To help her feel more secure, we kept the family together as much as possible.

Nevertheless, strain developed between Steven and Jane. She began to see herself as a young woman encumbered by two little brothers. Steven, who had been inseparable with Jane throughout the trip -- to the growing exclusion of Vincent -- felt hurt and bewildered.

Increasingly, Vincent was showing more interest in art. Naturally we wanted him to experience as many museums as possible, and New York is a museum addict's paradise. Their grandeur rather frightened him, and Vince would not venture through their cold halls unless I was at his side, preferably holding his hand. Many times Bill and the two older children would go elsewhere while my feet blistered on endless concrete gallery floors.

Our fifth museum was The Museum of Modern Art. There,

while going through at a pace too fast for any real or serious study, Vincent suddenly stopped, tensing his body. He sucked in his breath holding it.

I followed his gaze to a painting so rich in color and movement that it virtually sang. Bright yellows glowed with life through circles of lighter yellows, dark blues, browns, and greens. Under the blazing yellows lay a quiet town, mostly blue, with tiny houselights barely reflecting the excitement of the sky above. In the left foreground, a dark cypress reaching almost to the top, resembled smoke. Each stroke was small, measured, like the beats of a musical composition.

"That's by Vincent Van Gogh," I whispered almost reverently to the rigid boy.

"He's Vincent?"

"Yes. His name is like yours," I answered.

"I could have painted that," Vince said, barely audibly.

I smiled. "Honey, you paint beautifully, but you have a long way to go before you'll be an artist like Vincent Van Gogh."

"But, I will," Vince said. "I will be."

That night we were in Greenwich Village and saw a young man, long haired, shabbily dressed, with a guitar under one arm and an easel under his other. That cinched it. "When I grow up I'm gonna live right here and paint like Vincent Van Gogh. And in the summer I'll play baseball," Vince proclaimed.

Bill whispered, "He just might, too."

We did the usual tourist things — sometimes with Joyce, sometimes on our own. The children enjoyed the United Nations Building, although the art work presented there was too modern for Vincent's tastes. The awesome practices and theories of that august body did not impress the children. They enjoyed the Empire State Building far more. We were surprised at the fascination of the three for the Statue of Liberty, which we did not visit, but saw from the Staten Island Ferry.

It seemed natural to follow New York with a visit to our nation's capital.

The woman at the Tourist Information Office in Washington seemed annoyed that we preferred to camp. She pointed out that the weather was far too hot and sultry for sleeping in a tent. Nevertheless, we found a government operated campground right on the Potomac River within walking distance of the Jefferson Memorial.

Washington, D.C., offers most of its sights, sounds and entertainment freely to anyone under twenty-three. Young tourists are given the impression, rightly, that all of those buildings, documents, and ceremonial bands are theirs in a sense more real than the clothes they wear. They are welcomed like absentee landlords.

The place that made the greatest impression was The National Archives. There, displayed like The Ark of the Covenant, in an alcove all their own, are America's three gospels: The Declaration of Independence, The American Constitution, and The Bill of Rights. A serious faced, young Marine stands guard.

Steven, Vincent and Jane each stood alone, wrapped in his private emotions, unaware of the rest of the family quintet. Their faces mirrored the slight frown of the Marine guard. Jane's eyes glazed, as if she were trying to remember something told to her long ago when she was only half listening. Vincent's eyes moved fast over the documents, while the rest of his body stood very still. He seemed to be memorizing the atmosphere and textures in order to borrow them at some future time for his own purposes. Only Steven attempted to read the strange penmanship on each sheet of manuscript. After a few minutes, he sighed and gave up.

Awakened suddenly from her trance, Jane moved on tiptoe to the ladies' room where she had apparently been compellingly summoned. By the time she came out, the rest of us were walking down the hallways, looking at the other significant documents and photographs from America's courageous, sometimes foolish, often imaginative past. Jane took my arm and whispered loudly, "Mom, you should have seen that bathroom. It was a mess! There were towels and toilet paper all over the floor, and some people had even written things on the walls. How can people do things like that in a place like this? It's like messing up a church!"

Most of the buildings and monuments caused some expression of awe, but Arlington Cemetery depressed us all. Beautiful as the landscaping and sculpture were, particularly the stone reproduction of the Marines setting up the flag on that windy Pacific island, there was no escaping the row upon row of white crosses: some with flags, several with withering bouquets.

"That's a terrible thing to see in such a pretty park," Jane remarked.

"That's a terrible thing to see any place," Steve mumbled.

Vincent said nothing, but drew his lips into a tight little line.

The drive back west was a blending montage of mountains, lakes, small towns, livestocked farms, county fairs, museums in old buildings which once served some other function, delicious meals and occasionally unpalatable ones, rural Quaker meeting houses, and tires bursting at inopportune times. When we got home, all we wanted to do was sleep. We notified no one that we had arrived until we brought our feet back down to the realities of our own familiar community.

When my sister finally came to see us, she smiled knowingly at my glowing reports and said, "I know how you feel. Seeing this country through the eyes of children is to really see it. Older people like us forget how to see."

It had been exhausting. But I wouldn't trade that summer for any "adult" vacation imaginable.

9

CHOICES

School could have proved an anti-climax after our love affair with the campgrounds and cities we visited. But it turned out to be the beginning of significant changes and growth in Jane and Vincent.

Jane's best friend, Suzanne, was given a more academic program of classes than Jane, so the only time they could see one another was at lunch. Jane found it hard to make friends at her junior high school, and the regimentation bored her. Even the boys now seemed immature after her royal treatment at International House. The energetic girl looked forward only to her physical education class.

The thirtyish, trim, blonde gym teacher wore shorts that served to advertise the benefits of regular exercise. She lined up the girls and told them, "Now, since this is your second year here, I assume everybody already has her gym suit, right? Good. Then let's get our locker assignments right away. We're a little short of lockers, so everyone find a friend and come register in the office with her so you can share your locker with someone you know. I'd like to finish that portion of the paper work today so we can get down to some real work tomorrow. Let's get started!"

Jane looked around at the sixty strange faces in her gym class. Oh, if only Suzanne could have gotten her gym period at this hour! With a sinking feeling, Jane realized that she didn't know any one of the girls in her class. Freed to do so, every girl quickly found a locker partner to bring into the teacher's office -- everyone, it seemed, except Jane.

How could she tell the gym teacher her problem? I'm sorry, Ma'am. I have a friend, but she's not here. No. What happened to all of her friends from sixth grade? Had they changed so much that she couldn't recognize them?

Angry and embarrassed, Jane walked to a bench to sit down and think of a way out of her dilemma. Gradually, her gaze moved away from her feet as she became aware of another girl sitting beside her. The stranger was short, rather heavy, and black. As Jane turned to her, the girl smiled shyly. She asked Jane, "Don't you know anybody either?"

No. I mean, sure I do, only they're not in this class. Don't you know anybody?"

"No," the girl replied. "I'm new. This is my first day here."

"Y'wanna share lockers with me?" Jane asked, beaming.

The two hurried toward the end of a line of chattering girls who were being issued combination locks by the teacher. Jane and the new girl were the last to receive one. The teacher watched them, frowning slightly, as the girls left her office to find a basket for gym clothes to go with their padlock.

After a minute of deliberation, the teacher picked up an unassigned lock, left her chair, and followed the pair to the locker room. Having made her decision, she moved swiftly; not quite running. "Oh, Jane! May I see you just a moment? No, dear, just you alone."

Surprised, Jane left her new acquaintance who was practicing the lock combination. "Yes, ma'am?"

"Jane," the teacher began in a voice slightly lowered, "here's another lock for you. You may have a basket to yourself."

"That's O.K.," Jane replied. "I don't mind sharing."

"Well, honey, your mother might mind. I mean, well, you know. We get lots of complaints from mothers about their daughters having to share facilities with colored girls. We wouldn't want any trouble, right?"

Jane was stunned. Without realizing it, she took the proffered lock. "What should I tell her?" she asked.

"You don't owe anyone any explanation, I'm sure," the teacher said, and left Jane standing alone, more lonely than she had felt before.

Jane put the lock into her purse and went through her remaining classes like the sleepwalker she still was at night. The more she thought about the situation, the more upset she became. By the time she got home she was almost screaming.

She told me of the incident, adding angrily, "Mommy, she should have known better! After all, she's an adult!"

"What do you want to do about it, Jane?"

"I want to complain. I want to go to the principal and to the Board of Education. I think that teacher is just terrible!"

"How do you think your new friend will feel if she finds out about this?"

The question hit Jane like a slap. "I hadn't thought of that. I wouldn't want her to know. She has to have that teacher all year. But, Mommy, it would be wrong to just let it go, don't you think so?"

"Yes, Janie. I think so. Sometimes *no* action is an acceptance of things that are wrong. . . . I suppose you want my advice."

"Yes, of course!"

"I think you should do something, definitely. But I also think you, yourself, ought to decide what it should be."

"Should I maybe ask Suzanne?"

"You decide."

Jane thought about the matter for the rest of the afternoon, muttering as she wandered aimlessly around the house until it was time to set the table. After dinner, she went to her room, and painstakingly composed two identical letters describing the incident and her reaction to it. She took the position that no matter how many mothers might complain about their daughters "sharing facilities," the school had no right to condone any prejudicial behavior or slightest form of segregation.

Jane showed me the letter. I corrected her terrible spelling, but made no verbal comment about the contents. I was proud of her, and I think she knew it.

Jane mailed the two letters that night — one addressed to the principal and one to the Board of Education.

Thursday, at work, Bill received a call from Mr. Bagsley, the principal of Jane's school. Could Bill come to the school office after work that afternoon?

When Bill arrived, the principal handed him Jane's letter. "You haven't seen this, have you?"

Bill read the letter quickly, smiling slightly. "No," he replied, "but I did know about it. I was teaching an adult class the night she wrote it."

"I'd like to know why your wife didn't stop her, then."

"My wife? Why should she stop her?"

The principal turned on a tone of voice he used to lecture unbright juvenile offenders. "Mr. Morrison. As an educator, you must realize the implications and dangers of this sort of challenge to authority."

"I believe there are many authorities," Bill replied. "Jane never challenged authority. She appealed to it."

Mr. Bagsley was aghast. "I can't believe you fully comprehend the situation," he told Bill. "You do know she sent this same letter to the Board of Education, don't you?"

"Yes, my wife told me."

"What do you expect the Board to do? How does this make my position look?"

"Mr. Bagsley, why did you ask to see me? Have you talked to Jane?"

"No, and I don't intend to. I have as little as possible to do with those Juvie kids."

"Juvie kids? You mean, those from Juvenile Hall?"

"I looked up her record. I know all about her," the principal said with unmistakable implications.

"Then you know she's no delinquent," Bill said, beginning to feel angrier than he liked to feel.

"There now, take it easy," the principal said, adopting a more conciliatory tone of voice. "One can't be exposed to disease without becoming at least slightly infected, can one?"

"Then all you can make out of her letter is a challenge to authority by a Juvie kid, is that correct?" Bill asked without taking it easy at all.

Mr. Bagsley shook his head. "I certainly had not expected this attitude from an educator. I guess there's no point in our discussing her behavior at all."

"*Her* behavior!" Bill fairly exploded. "What about the

behavior of the gym teacher?"

"That is not a point at issue," the principal said.

"It certainly is as far as I'm concerned." Bill began to feel all the frustration he had kept inside himself at the Clam Shack in Martha's Vineyard.

He lectured Mr. Bagsley on the responsibilities of the schools, on the immorality of prejudice, on the importance of seeing children as individuals rather than as labels. When he was through, he assured Mr. Bagsley that if he should be asked, he would say the same things to the Board of Education.

We did not hear from the Board of Education. Jane was changed to another gym class where she had a locker by herself. The teacher never spoke to Jane about the incident nor about anything else.

The change of gym periods necessitated a change in art class, and Jane met the handsome, enthusiastic Mr. French. It had been he who had insisted that Rena put gum on her nose and sit in front of the class, getting her off to a poor start. Perhaps he was wiser now; or perhaps he recognized the name of Jane's guardians; but for whatever reason, Mr. French did his best to treat Jane kindly. She had no artistic interests at all, but the young teacher awakened something inside her. He became the unwitting object of Jane's first crush.

She tried to think of things to talk to him about, privately, if possible. He subtly saw to it that they were never alone together, but he listened to her adolescent chatter as if whatever she had to say were of great importance to him.

One day Jane told the art teacher about Vincent. Mr. French invited Jane to bring "her little brother" after class to meet him.

The very next day, Jane practically dragged Vince to Mr. French's classroom. The teacher dropped what he was doing and concentrated on the small boy who was holding some rolled up sheets of art paper.

Critically, Mr. French looked at each drawing. "Now, Vince, you show in this one an excellent feeling for color."

"That's how the mountain really looked," Vince told him. "There were all kinds of purples and browns and blacks in it until you got up close."

"Yes, and you caught the mood very well, too. But there's

one thing wrong here. Can you see what it is?"

Vince smiled and nodded. "I knew it as soon as I was finished. It's where I put the sun, isn't it?"

Jane squirmed as the two went painstakingly over each drawing, analyzing purpose, details, and overall impressions. Vincent began to open up and talk energetically about his seedling dream of artistic achievement.

Mr. French encouraged him, pointing out both rewards and sacrifices. He did not laugh at Vince's new signature, "Vincent," at the bottom of each composition. Vince felt taller with this sympathetic listener.

"Vince, I have some oil paints here, and some brushes and stretched canvas. I want you to see what you can do with them."

"No, I don't want them," Vince said.

"Why not?" burst Jane. "They're expensive!"

Mr. French urged, "It's time you tried to see what you might do with oils, Vince. You're ready for them."

"No," Vince said, louder than before. He was hunching over again, retreating.

Mr. French could not understand the vehemence of the child's protest, and pressed the proffered materials into Jane's willing hands. The magic of full understanding between the little boy and the young teacher vanished.

Jane and Vince walked home together without saying a word.

When Vince came into the house, he ran into the kitchen to find me. "Mom, you should have met that Mr. French. He's great! He has long hair like me and he knows just about everything about art. He thinks my things are real good!"

Jane came into the kitchen with the gifts Mr. French had placed in her hands. "Mr. French gave Vince this stuff, but Vince didn't want to take it."

I asked, "Why not, Vince?"

He looked down at the floor. "I don't like it when people give me stuff," he said. "It kind of makes everything different. I don't need anything, anyway. I got all those boxes in the garage."

To Jane, Vincent's attitude was stupidity, but I think I understood. The boy's parents were always ready to give him toys, clothes, money, books, any *thing* the child might use. In that way they attempted to buy his forgiveness for holding back the one gift he wanted most desperately -- themselves.

Jane's father's visit was scheduled for the last Sunday in each month. When he was due for his September visit, Jane spent the afternoon prettying herself and preparing a display of Vincent's artistic impressions as well as her own snapshots of our summer trip.

The father and child had not seen each other since June, and both glowed with the happiness of being together again. Jane clung to the gray-haired man standing in the doorway for several minutes until he gently removed the thin arms that were crushing his chest. He smiled as he put his arm around her waist and led her to the faded brown couch where they usually sat during his monthly hour. I said a few polite words of greeting and left the room to face the endless mess in the kitchen.

Several minutes later I heard Jane's voice raising higher and higher until she was crying. Assuming that whatever problem had come up would soon talk itself out, I did not interrupt them.

Bill, who had been reading in the bedroom, came into the kitchen. "Do you hear that?" he asked me.

"Yes, but I don't think we ought to interfere, do you?"

"Yes," Bill said. "I'm going to have a look."

As Bill walked into the living room, Jane's father, tall and thin like Jane herself, was just going out the door. He turned only long enough to nod a polite goodbye to Bill, and was gone before he could be questioned.

Jane was still sitting on the couch, sobbing, her nose and eyes running and unwiped.

I came as soon as Bill called me. I took the sobbing girl in my arms and let her have it out. Finally she said, "Mommy, you wouldn't believe what he said!"

"Well, for goodness sake, tell us, honey."

It took a while for Jane to calm down long enough. Finally she said, "I was telling him all about our trip, and he seemed real interested. And I was showing him the pictures I took, and I got to the ones of Aunt Joyce and Normie, and he nearly had a fit. He told me, 'No daughter of mine associates with niggers.' That's what he called

Aunt Joyce and Norman, Mommy, '*niggers*!' I couldn't believe it. My own daddy!"

Quickly, before Jane could get hysterical again, I said, "What did you say to him, dear?"

"I told him my very best friend, Suzanne, is black and then he really got mad and told me I was never to speak to her again. I said that wasn't fair, and he just got up and left."

"Jane," Bill began. "A father is a person. Like any person, he may be wrong sometimes."

"*That* wrong?" she wailed. "He was so wrong I can't believe it. Mommy, what am I going to do? I can't break up my friendship with Suzie just because he says so."

"Jane," Bill spoke gently, "try to understand it from your father's point of view. He was raised in another part of the country and in a different time when people thought differently than they do today."

"So were you," Jane countered.

"Yes, but I've been luckier. I've met many people like Aunt Joyce and Norman and Suzanne. I've worked with black people in public housing and in teaching. Maybe if your father's life had been different, he would think differently, too."

"He said I'm no daughter of his," Jane almost whispered.

"Just saying that doesn't make it so."

"Janie, you're not the first daughter to see things differently from her father," I reassured her. "My own father and I disagreed many times on many things we both considered important."

"But this is the first time for me," she said. "I feel like I don't belong to anyone anymore."

Jane changed after that Sunday. She began to call Bill "Dad," but grew quieter, more withdrawn. She no longer got along well with Steven, and open hostility grew up between Jane and Vincent. Much of the problem was probably Vincent's fault. He found it easy to tease Jane and began to take great delight in it. We could not leave the children alone in the house any longer. They were too old for babysitters, and yet, could not get along without either Bill or me to referee. Sibling rivalry was something with which I had no experience and felt little talent in handling.

One night, when Bill and I were trying to get the checkbook to balance, Jane and Steven came into the dining room, where we had our desks. Jane said, "Mom and Dad, we have something to talk to you about. It's important."

Reluctantly, Bill put aside his check stubs and scratch paper and tried to look as attentive as such a pronouncement warranted.

Jane said, "We have decided that it's time Vincent should leave. We don't want him around anymore."

Bill and I were flabbergasted.

After a few seconds to collect his thoughts, Bill asked Steven, "Is this your idea, Steve?"

"Well, no, but I agree with Jane," Steve said. "Vince is getting to be a pain in the neck."

"In what way?" Bill asked.

Jane began, "He's always nagging and teasing and acting silly . . ."

"I asked Steven," Bill interrupted quietly.

"Well, you know. Like Jane said," Steven stammered. Then he continued with more assurance. "My room is real crowded with him and all his stuff in there. And he always wants to talk, even when I'm reading. His nightmares wake me up sometimes, too."

"He doesn't have nightmares very often, anymore," I reminded him.

Bill said, "Steven, these things have always been true, ever since Vincent arrived. Why has it suddenly become so unbearable?"

Steven looked helplessly at Jane for support. She said, "Whenever I want to do anything or Steven wants to do anything, there's Vince, always getting in the way. He mocks me, too, and I don't like it."

"So the only solution is to 'get rid of him,' is that the way you see it?" Bill asked.

"Yes," Jane replied quickly. Steven nodded, casting his eyes first down at his feet, then looking at his parents — perhaps challenging them.

I was glad Bill took charge of the discussion. "What if this were an ordinary family where all the children had always been brothers and sisters? What would happen then?"

"Lots of parents get rid of their children if they don't want them," Jane said bitterly. "I met a lot of kids at

Juvie whose folks brought them there themselves."

"Jane," I broke in. "Do you think that your father did that to you?"

"No," she replied in a tone I found unconvincing. "But he might could."

"Might *have,*" I corrected, inwardly cursing my pedantic reflex.

Ignoring the personal reference, Jane launched a new tirade on the problems of having Vincent in the house.

"Where do you propose that Vince might go?" Bill asked her.

"They'll find him a new foster home. They found him two already; they can do it again."

"You know it isn't that easy, Jane," I told her, disgusted at her apparent lack of feeling. "How many girls did you meet at Juvenile Hall that had been waiting months for placement? How many times have we gotten phone calls asking us to take in just one more boy or girl?"

"They did it before; they can find him a place again," she repeated, this time more sullenly.

"We'll have to think this over," Bill said, ending the matter abruptly. Steven looked at us with an expression that might have been surprise; might have been pleading.

"What do you think?" I asked Bill after the two children had left the room.

"I don't know," he said. "We must think about Steven first, but that doesn't mean he's the only consideration."

"I guess we'll have to talk to him further," I sighed.

"Yes, but right now, let's get back to these figures."

Bill's point about where Vince might go if he left our home made quite an impression on Steven. He remembered the hysterical little creature who first appeared in our living room clutching an arm of the anxious probation officer, and it troubled Steve to think of Vince going through that experience again.

"But, Mom," he said later when just the three of us were alone in the living room, "I am so sick of having Vincent in my room. He's always so much there that I don't feel like there's any room left for me. Even when he's not there, his stuff is all over the place. I can't study. I can't think. I can't even get into the bathroom half the time. He takes forever in there."

"Do you like Vincent?" Bill asked.

"Usually I do. He's fun to play with. I like football out on Short Street much more now that he's in the game; and I've gotten to like his paintings and sketches. But, sometimes he just makes me so mad! And he acts so silly. I don't know. Maybe it would have been better if he'd never come here in the first place."

"But he did," Bill said. "There's no changing that."

Steven just shook his head.

"Whose idea was it to talk to us?" I asked.

"Jane's," Steve admitted. "But I still think it was a good idea."

That night I wrote to the probation officer. Bill and I could not decide what to do. We knew we needed help.

By the time Miss Chamberlain came to see us, we had decided one thing. Contrary to what our foster home license said, our house was not really big enough for a family of five. Not any more. What worried us was what the future held for a child who would naturally feel he had been rejected by the people he had so trustingly been calling "Mom" and "Dad." Vince was only just beginning to eat well, to look forward to the future, to stand straighter, and to do well in school. Might not the shock of a new placement blunt that new growth?

Miss Chamberlain suggested another possibility. "Have you considered keeping Vincent and sending Jane to live elsewhere?"

We had not.

"As I see it," she told us, "Vince is the one who really needs you most right now. Jane still sleepwalks occasionally, I know, but other than that, she shows no signs of maladjustment. She makes friends easily and adapts rather well. Perhaps I could even find a relative who would be willing to take her, now that she's almost fourteen."

"What about Steven's feelings?" I asked.

"Might not a lot of the problems be ironed out once Vince and Steven each have rooms of their own?" Miss Chamberlain pointed out. "After all, Steven had a private retreat for ten years — until Vincent came. Maybe Steven's real problem is sharing his privacy."

The new idea made sense to us, but we were still unhappy.

We loved both our foster children. Our happiest years as a family had been these last two. Our most vivid family memory was the American-Canadian trip we shared. Shared memories, shared experiences, even shared problems and arguments make people belong to one another far more than accidents of heredity. Then, too, the fear of pain -- the kind I suffered when Rena and Ann ran away -- played a role in my hesitation, if not in Bill's.

"Did it hurt you when we lost our first two girls?" I asked him then for the first time.

"Of course it hurt," Bill said.

"Then, why did you want to take Jane and Vincent?" I asked.

"Just because it might hurt to lose them is no reason not to have foster children," Bill stated in his matter-of-fact way. "We're the adults. Ignoring those kids doesn't make their problems go away. They need us — and perhaps we need them too."

We kept putting off any action. About a week after the probation officer had talked to us, Jane could bear it no longer. She brought Steven in to see us and ask us where we stood.

"We've decided Vincent has to stay," Bill told Jane. "He has no place else to go."

Steven looked stunned. "Steve," I said quickly, "we're going to look for a bigger house. Maybe if you two have separate bedrooms, you'll find him easier to live with."

"No!" Jane nearly screamed. Then, more quietly, "You're going to have to make a choice. Either Vincent goes, or I go."

"We don't want to lose you either, Jane," Bill said, unruffled.

"I mean it," Jane said, encouraged. "I'll write a letter to Miss Chamberlain tonight and tell her I want to go away."

Steven looked at Jane in amazement. "Jane, don't do that," he pleaded.

"I will so. Now, will you get rid of Vincent?"

"No," Bill replied, more firmly than before.

Jane gave Steven a little shove as she swept past him and out of the room.

A long, strained week followed during which Jane refused to talk to anyone in the family no matter what approach was tried. Bill-the-Reasonable felt particularly frustrated by her stubborn refusal to discuss the situation any further.

One overcast Wednesday, Jane had her bags all packed when Miss Chamberlain finally came for her. Both foster mother and foster daughter were on the verge of tears, so neither trusted words that morning. It just happened. One minute Jane was in the house; the next she was beside the probation officer in the county-crested car. Then they were gone.

I wept a little before anyone came home from school, yet I felt different this time. It wasn't like the loss of a prized possession I mourned as with Rena and Ann. I was troubled more by a sense of failure. Somehow I never really had become the mother this girl could trust enough to share with another child. I loved her, and yet I had not met her deeply felt needs. She was hurt, of course. I hurt too, but not, I discovered, anywhere nearly as much as when I lost my other daughters.

By afternoon I was ready to face my three men as if nothing had happened.

10

VINCENT

If either Steven or Vincent reacted strongly to Jane's leaving, neither showed it. Both accepted Vincent's move to a room of his own as a matter of course. The small back bedroom was soon filled with art supplies, and the rug grew decorated with sundry careless splashes of paint.

Once Steven asked me, "Did Jane decide to leave because of me?"

"No, dear, I really don't think so. Why?"

"Well, I kind of bragged about my grades. They were real good this year, and hers weren't so hot. Maybe I shouldn't have bragged."

"Don't worry about that," I told him. "Anybody might think of ways in which he could have been kinder; that always happens when somebody goes away or dies. I can't believe Jane would have stayed with us no matter who got what kind of grades."

Jane was placed first in a girls' home, later with a childless aunt. We were told she was getting along well. She never wrote to us, and we soon lost all track of her.

Neither did we see any more of Miss Chamberlain.

When Vincent's father moved to a new county, Vincent's case was transferred to that jurisdiction. Since that county was distant, our local juvenile probation office was asked to provide an advisory officer to report monthly on Vince's progress. Any decisions she might consider were to be approved by the distant and faceless authority of the new county.

Ms. Brown, a young probation officer who took her job most seriously, seemed frustrated by this lack of actual control, as well as annoyed at the addition to her already heavy case load. She set about trying to "rehabilitate" Vincent's mother, who lived nearby.

At first we saw much of Ms. Brown. She was a direct person who had a great faith in the power of truth. She talked to Vince about the reasons for his placement, his feelings about his parents, and his foster home. Vincent hated her visits and grew particularly angry when she hinted that his mother might have a problem with alcohol. Vincent preferred to ignore unpleasant truths. After Ms. Brown left, Vince would ride his bike rapidly around and around the block, or rush over to David's to get a baseball game started.

June 11, 1976

Dear Mr. Mills,

Your letter of June 6th came as something of a surprise. I was under the impression that most of the information you requested for your county had already been sent to you through Ms. Brown of our county's probation department. However, I have no objection to giving you my impressions as well.

About Vincent's health: It is now just about perfect. He eats well, plays hard, and has the best resistance to the diseases that go around of anyone I know. He got through last winter with no more than one sniffle. He takes excellent care of his teeth and has had no cavities during the last year or so. (His teeth were in horrible shape when he first came to our home just over two years ago.)

His social adjustment is also good. He has many friends at school and is well liked by his teachers and by our adult friends. He tends to blame everyone and everything other than himself whenever he encounters difficulties, but much of that is undoubtedly typical for his age.

His progress in school has been phenomenal, thanks largely to excellent teachers, but also thanks to Vince, himself. From pre-primer reading level, he has advanced to fifth grade level and is now wild about books, especially biographies. Occasionally his perfectionist inclinations keep him from finishing his assignments at school, but he does understand his subjects and is reliable about eventually doing his assignments.

You asked about his parents. Vince used to resent his dad bitterly. During his visits, Vince was polite, but shortly after his father left, Vincent usually had a tantrum. This was particularly true when his father brought along the woman with whom he is now living, Carolyn, or her daughter. However, the last two visits were quite friendly. Vince seemed to be establishing much more rapport with his dad, although we have not heard a word from him in several months.

Vince adores his mother. He does not show that he misses her at all, but is always delighted to see her, which he does about once a month. Ms. Brown is considering extending the time his mother can spend with Vincent.

He has a real talent for all forms of art that he has tried, although lately he seems to have lost his interest. He picked up folk guitar quickly from our other son, Steven, and the two often perform together. He is also taking clarinet lessons at school, but shows little enthusiasm for that. Most of all, Vincent loves baseball (which he plays well), other sports, and tramping through any wild country. Lately, he has taken up gardening.

Our summer plans are somewhat hazy at the moment. Last year we drove and camped across more than 11,000 miles of southern Canada and northeastern United States. This year we don't feel quite so ambitious.

I hope I have adequately answered your inquiry. Please do contact me at any time that you wish additional information. Or drop in if you happen to be nearby. You really should meet Vincent.

Cordially

Vincent loved animals. He had a mysterious way of making friends with them immediately, seemingly talking their language. One time, when visiting Monterey, we walked out onto the pier.

"I bet there are seals around here," he said idly.

"No, young man, not at this time of the year," volunteered an old man who happened to be standing next to us. "They come around here when it's warm, but when it's cold they swim out many miles."

Vincent smiled one of his sweet, almost apologetic smiles, then turned to face the bay. He began to bark raucously. In a few seconds the sound was returned. Minutes later we could see shining black bodies cavorting around below us. With no hint of self-consciousness, Vince was talking to the swimming mammals as if they were old friends he hadn't seen for years.

But he didn't like cats. "Cats are traitors," he advised us, and would have nothing to do with them. So, of course, we had to get a cat.

I've always had a theory that kittens are nature's trick to make people take cats. Kittens are irresistible, and our new little calico, Ginger, readily won Vincent over.

In no time at all, Vince was inventing games to play with the willing kitten, and teaching her modest tricks. She was the first one he looked for when he came home from school, and many hours that peaceful summer at home were spent playing with her.

One Friday, while Vince was reading in the living room, Ginger, who had been sleeping on the floor in the sun, stood up, walked slowly over to Vincent, and vomited beside his feet.

The boy had her in his arms within a moment and screamed for me. I was elected to clean up the mess while Vincent, a look of panic on his face, stroked the limp figure in his arms.

"What's wrong with her, Mom?" he asked, his face pulled into a deep frown.

"Probably something she ate, dear," I assured him. "She'll be all right soon."

But she wasn't. Ginger got worse and worse until, alarmed, Vincent and I wrapped her in an old blanket and took her to the veterinarian. "Feline distemper," the doctor told us. "She should have been vaccinated."

He told us to take her home. She probably would not last out the weekend. If, however, by some miracle she did survive, we were to bring her back to him on Monday.

The reference to a future date decided Vince. He took charge of Ginger and scarcely left her side for a moment.

It looked hopeless to me. Her hair was matted and wet with perspiration. Her eyes were open and glazed.

She lay very still except for occasional vomiting which Vince, now, cleaned up.

Vincent kept the limp animal on his lap unless he absolutely had to leave her. He stroked her occasionally, talking to her constantly. He rambled on about the things they could do just as soon as she got well. He told her how wonderful she was, how her three toned fur was the most beautiful he had ever seen, and how he was going to paint a picture of her. I drew the line at letting her sleep on Vincent's bed, so he slept in a sleeping bag on the floor of the living room to be nearer to her.

She pulled through. Vincent was her only medicine. After that, she was very much Vincent's cat. A few months later, he midwifed her five black and white kittens.

Bill mused one day, "Do you suppose Vincent should become a vet? The school tells us he's college prep material now."

"Should?" I asked, sounding almost angry. "How do we know what he should become? Haven't we learned anything yet about how parents' sense of responsibility can become imposition?"

"All right!" Bill replied in a soothing tone. "But it wouldn't hurt to suggest it to him, would it?"

December 13, 1976

Dear Mr. Mills,

Thank you for your letter of December 11th. I am glad to know that there is "someone up there" who actually cares about Vincent, and I also appreciate opportunities to "brag" about him.

We rarely see Ms. Brown, although she occasionally phones. From what she told me, I believe she tried hard to "rehabilitate" Vincent's mother, but her efforts proved unsuccessful. This may have prompted her suggestion to both of us that Bill and I should become Vincent's legal guardians. She explained to us that "permanency planning" was a concept her department has adopted enthusiastically. If your county is in harmony with this philosophy of permanency as it might apply to our situation, we would be pleased to discuss it with someone from your department. We would need to clarify matters such as financial help (we would still need that), and natural parents' visiting rights. I hope that we would be empowered to sign papers on Vincent's behalf if we were his legal guardians. Years ago, when we had another foster child, we went through a terrible time tryng to get someone to operate when she had appendicitis. The legal and financial complications were alarming. They finally operated, but only when they were sure her life was at stake. A legal guardianship might have solved this particular situation.

Now, about Vincent himself. I am enclosing his report card and a recent insight that seemed so meaningful to him that he felt he had to write it down. (See next sheet.) The "Two Sayings," he tells me, came to him while he was "in a grumpy mood." As these indicate, he has done a lot of thinking about himself and the world he lives in lately, and he seems to be at peace with both.

Vincent shows signs of becoming a bookworm. He reads every male biography he can get hold of. He has recently read about such diverse personalities as Benjamin Franklin, Woolworth of the variety stores, the Wright brothers, Babe Ruth, and Mahatma Ghandi.

Vincent was selected as part of a study that the University is doing through their psychology department. This is supposed to be "a study of the two-party relationship," but I'm unclear about exactly what they hope to find out. We are only told that the University pays a male student three dollars an hour to make friends with a fifth or sixth grade boy (carefully selected, of course). They get together for about three hours, twice a week to chat, to go somewhere, or to do something. The University student is called a counselor, but he isn't meant to do any counseling; just be a pal. Vince's counselor is an eighteen year old Chinese-American student of physics. His family has always had one or more foster children. (Vince told us this with the comment, "That's good. He won't think I'm a weirdo.") Vincent loves all this attention. After his sessions with his counselor, he is in a magnanimous frame of mind, even feeling sorry for our older boy because he does not have such a wonderful advantage. Vince loves to talk. He can go on for hours. Here is someone who listens.

When Vince isn't talking, he is concentrating. His power of concentration is something to behold, and a thing of some concern to his teacher. When he is working on math, or a painting, or reading, you have to shake him to get him back to this world. Amazing!

It used to be that Vince saw his mother for one hour a month. Now Ms. Brown has made that one full day a month. This has changed Vincent's attitude toward her visits. Apparently they have little to offer one another. Vince is annoyed when he has to "give up" a Sunday in this way. Often, they merely go to her apartment and watch television all day. He is quite fond of her, but no longer speaks of "Mom's place" as synonymous with heaven.

It has been many months since Vincent last saw his father. Possibly a year. Every time he comes, there is a big to-do about his bringing along his "other family." Ms. Brown says he absolutely must not do this. The father feels that he wants Vincent to accept them, so he sneaks them in one way or another. Recently he called to say he was coming. I reminded him, politely I hope, that he was welcome any time but that his family was not. He reacted quite angrily and even threatened legal action. Then he said that if he couldn't have his family along, there was simply no point in his driving all that way, and he would not come. He didn't. Vincent was visibly relieved. He said to me, "Well, I don't want to see all those people, anyway. After all, they're not related to me."

Vincent really does not know his father, and shows no desire to. Once when his father "sneaked in" his baby, pointing out joyfully that here was Vincent's little brother, Vince ignored the child completely. Later he asked me if "a lady can keep from having a baby if she wants to."

If you ever get to our area, why don't you drop in? You're welcome any time, of course, although a preliminary phone call is probably a good idea. Vince is a delightful boy in a number of ways. You should meet him.

Merry Christmas!

Cordially

"TWO SAYINGS

Did you ever stop and
think how imperfeck
the world is, and how
perfeck you seem to
yourself.

"And did you ever stop
and think how imperfeck
the world is, and how
imperfeck you
seem to it."

Mr. Mills rarely answered my letters. We were disappointed that he apparently had no inclination to pursue the idea of our becoming Vincent's permanent guardians. I don't know if Vincent needed that added security, but we, having lost three children already, probably did.

That Sunday before Christmas, the four of us went to my sister's home for our annual family celebration. During the party it struck me how much a part of the family Vincent had become. He was beginning to look more like Bill than Steven did. He was standing straighter now and copying Bill's walk and pet phrases.

At the same time he seemed to be accepting himself. "I'm a direct descendant of Plato, Socrates, and Aristotle," he told my sister's children, proud of his Greek ancestry.

In the afternoon, the cousins took Vincent and Steven to an amusement park at a nearby beach. They swam, shivered, argued, giggled, and improvised games. At an amusement booth, Vincent won gifts for everyone by pitching baseballs to knock down plastic milk bottles. Standing far back, he concentrated on his job so intently that he soon attracted a crowd of curious onlookers. He didn't even notice them.

To complete the afternoon, the children clowned for a souvenir photo in a set labeled "City Jail."

That Sunday was the real holiday for us.

December 25th, itself, was bleak. Ms. Brown had arranged for Vincent to stay at the home of a married older sister over Christmas eve. His mother would also be visiting there. For Bill, Steven, and me, the day without Vincent felt incomplete. We missed him. "Won't Vince *ever* get home?" Steven asked, before going to bed.

Vincent arrived very late. A car squeaked to a stop in front of the house, stopped briefly to discharge its passenger, then drove away before the boy could turn to walk up the front steps.

Bill and I could hardly open the door quickly enough.

Vincent's arms were full of boxes. His shoulders were hunched again, worse than they had been in many months. His long dark lashes swept up momentarily, then he looked down again. We could see he had been crying.

Vince walked into the living room, dropped his packages without looking at them, and sank wearily onto the couch. We waited for him to volunteer something, but he just stared, atypically quiet.

"Do you want to talk about it, honey?" I finally asked.

"I'm not going there any more. I hate my mother," Vince told us.

"Hate's a pretty strong word, Vince," Bill stated quietly.

Vince lapsed back into silence for several minutes. Although we watched him, neither of us felt we should intrude upon his thoughts. Finally Vince said without looking at us, "Did you know my mother drinks whiskey?"

"Yes, we know," Bill replied in a matter of fact voice. "Didn't you?"

Vince did not answer directly. He began to talk in a monotone. "There were lots of people there last night. My grandmother, my uncles, some of my sister's friends. It was a big party. I noticed my mother was drinking out of a bottle instead of a glass. She kept the bottle in a bag, but you could tell. She started to look sick like she used to look all the time. I thought she was going to throw up. Then I knew she was just real drunk. Nobody else noticed.

"I walked over to her and I said, 'Please, Mommy, stop drinking that stuff.' She looked like she didn't understand me at first, then she said, 'O.K., if you don't want me to.' But she lied. She just went out into the hall where nobody could see her and went right on drinking. She didn't stop for a minute. And she promised me!" Vincent's voice was getting higher now.

"Vince," I began, "don't you kow that there are some people who can't stop drinking even if they want to very much?"

"But she promised me," Vince said stubbornly.

"It was a promise she probably wanted to keep, Vince," Bill told him, "but she couldn't. Some people say it's an illness. It even has a name, 'alcoholism,' and it's one of the hardest illnesses in the whole world to cure."

Vince looked up, frowning. "Why are you on her side?" he asked darkly.

The question took us by surprise. Annoyed, I asked, "Since when did it become a matter of sides?"

"She lied to me, don't you see? I asked her to stop drinking, and she promised me she would, and then she just sneaked out and did it anyway!"

He was not to be swayed from his feeling of betrayal. The hypnotic note came back into his voice. He continued, "Later, she fell asleep on the sofa. She was snoring real loud, but I don't think anybody noticed. Anyway, they were all drinking, too. All except my sister. She doesn't drink anything but cokes. Then my uncle started making fun of me. He tried to get me to smoke one of his cigars. He said he would burn me with the cigar if I didn't smoke it."

"And, did you?" Bill asked gently.

"No, of course not. I hate those things. I just took off and started to run. My uncle took off after me, and we ran all the way up the street and around the block, him yelling he was going to burn me with his cigar. I was scared."

"Where was your sister all of this time?" I asked.

"She tried to stop him, but she couldn't. My mother could have, but she was on the sofa and never woke up for a minute. If she had kept her promise and stopped drinking whiskey, she might have stopped him."

"Did you get hurt, Vince?"

A ghost of a smile flashed momentarily on his face. "No. I'm a real good runner," he said. He was so hunched over and half buried in the upholstery of our brown couch that his appearance made his words seem unlikely. "I ran back into the house and locked myself in the bathroom. He kept banging on the door and yelling that I should come out and take it like a man, but I just stayed in the bathroom all night."

"And how about Christmas morning?" I asked, wanting now to get him past the painful period.

"Everybody was asleep," he replied, "except for my sister and her husband and the kids. We all opened our presents, and I played with my niece and nephew. But they're really too little to have any real fun with." He arose wearily, ignoring the boxes still strewn around the couch and floor. "Well, I guess I'll go to bed now," he said. He started out, then turned and announced, "This is my only home now." Ordinarily reluctant to kiss anyone, he walked back to kiss me. Then he asked, "Can I change my name to yours?"

It took much talking by Bill, Ms. Brown, and me to get Vince to agree ever to see his mother again. Ms. Brown had her most successful session with Vince, forcing him at last to face the fact that his mother had been a heavy drinker even before he was born, and could not seem to help herself. Ms. Brown prevailed upon Vincent's naturally kind nature and convinced him that his mother needed affection now as much as ever.

But things were never again the same between Vincent and his mother. The nightmares returned punctually on the nights before each of his scheduled visits with her. She did not appear with as much regularity, usually calling to say that her car had broken down. When this happened, Vincent would sigh audibly, then rush out to start some game with Steven or David.

That year he stopped painting altogether, and seemed to withdraw somewhat. He read more, tried writing fantasies, and proposed long bicycle trips with Steven; sometimes they pedaled to beaches ten or more miles away. After dinner he would go into his room and play his guitar for hours without stop -- usually the same melody over and over again, and occasionally, original compositions.

He got along well with his fifth grade teacher, whose only complaint was Vincent's atrocious spelling. Vince also maintained a friendship with his remedial reading teacher, Mrs. Snodgrass, although her special help was not needed by him that year. In June, he impulsively wrote her a little note on lined notebook paper. She showed it to me years later.

"Dear Mrs. Snodgrass," he wrote. "thank you for helping me to read and I also thank you for makeing reading something witch I can enjoy with out stumpling threw every sentenence. I will allwas be greatful to you Mrs. Snodgrass.

"Sincerely Yours, Vincent, ROOM 207."

My thoughts and Bill's, during that year, were taken up with a problem more our own. Powers That Be decided a new freeway was more essential for the public good than our home. We were ordered to move.

Bill and I loved our sixty year old house as much as if it had been ancestral. So much of our lives seemed to reside there. We had painted or papered every room ourselves; the cowboy wallpaper in Steven's room put up in anticipation of Vincent's arrival; sea print paper behind a tropical fish tank in the bathroom; white textured walls offsetting a worn blue rug where most of the traffic moved. After our kitchen ceiling had fallen down and been repaired, we put up glowing red brick scrubbable wall covering to hide the scars. The kitchen looked like a hamburger joint.

On the south side of our house fourteen rose shrubs survived in spite of periodic neglect. The plum tree in our backyard, which overwhelmed us with abundance every June, grew in a shape ideal for climbing. Short Street, nearby, was where we always found the kids when their fun made them oblivious to time.

We hated to see it all torn down. Not all change is progress. Residents on our block grew more neighborly, sharing the sense of tragedy. Somehow, everyone looked to our house as a rallying center to halt the destruction.

Bill planned his defense of the condemned neighborhood and took it to the City Council. His eloquence impressed a newspaper reporter who interviewed Bill in the hallway after his presentation.

The reporter's story was printed the next day headlined, "Ideal Home Clashes with March of Progress." It began:

The new roof on the Morrisons' home glistened as usual in the sun today -- but it didn't quite ring true.

For the roof and the recently remodeled kitchen and even the green front lawn all stood as little more than an exercise in frustration.

This home may be in the way of progress. As plans now stand, it is one of many in the path of a newly proposed freeway.

For twelve years the Morrison family has lived in that home. Both sons, aged 13 and 11, were raised there. . . .

That last line was an assumption by the reporter. He knew nothing of our somewhat unusual family — one of only three foster homes in the entire city then. Perhaps he might have had one more story there.

Bill's pleas at City Hall did not keep our neighborhood intact. One by one the neighbors accepted the slightly less-than-market prices offered for their homes and moved away. We felt a growing sense of despair and isolation as we half-heartedly began touring other people's houses.

January 10, 1978

Dear Mr. Mills,

I apologize for not having written to you much earlier regarding Vincent's development, etc. I was not ignoring your request, but felt that I might have more to tell you after last month's Christmas visits to both his father and his mother.

Basically, there is nothing different or significant to report. Vincent is, to all appearances, a healthy, active, popular, well-adjusted twelve-year-old. This might seem an oversimplification, but it is the overall picture. What follows is not meant to indicate problems of any magnitude, but rather to paint a somewhat deeper picture.

This year, Vincent does not care much for his teacher. She complains that he does not pay attention in class; he complains that she is "prejudiced" in favor of girls -- particularly oriental girls. For the first few weeks of school, Vincent was inventing maladies so that he could stay home and paint all day, or read, rather than go to school. I quickly diagnosed these "sudden illnesses" and visited his teacher to discuss the matter. This seemed to help. Although Vince does not have his usual enthusiasm for school, he now accepts it. In all his subjects he is doing average or better work, in spite of a tendency not to complete his assignments if they do not interest him.

Vincent's happiest moments are spent either painting or playing ball -- preferably baseball, but he will accept any organized team game. For some time his interest in painting seemed to be diminishing, but it has flowered again. He spends hours in his room painting, and he sings while he paints. His skill grows notably. Due to the large number of family members that he has, Vince was overwhelmed with the challenge of getting everyone a Christmas present. I suggested that each adult would appreciate one of his signed paintings. Vince's reaction was a shocked, "I couldn't do that! Why, I'd never get to see my paintings again!" They're like "his children" to him. Nevertheless, he did give an oil landscape to his father.

Vincent regularly picks up the guitar and plays. We are now providing him with private lessons, and he is doing well; but he prefers to improvise his own "flamenco," as he calls it. His strumming often reflects his moods -- contemplative, as well as happy or sad. Sometimes he sings along; more often he does not.

Vince writes imaginative stories. He did an especially fine one about a crew of sailors on a life raft that got swallowed by a giant whale, only to find that within the creature there was a whole city with a thriving culture ruled by none other than Captain Kidd.

He is developing a deeper closeness with our thirteen year old son, Steven. They always "stand up" for one another when one is having difficulty or is being "chastised."

Remembering last Christmas, Vince dreaded this one. He was getting very nervous about the possibility of having to see his mother in an intoxicated state again -- a spectacle that literally makes him sick. So when his father suggested a visit to his place, Vincent was delighted until Ms. Brown, our local probation officer, pointed out to him that his mother would have to know. Vince knows his mother's extreme resentment toward his father, and he could not face her probable reaction to this visit. Ms. Brown helped Vince to decide what he really wanted to do. He spent four days with his father (the first such visit that has ever been permitted), Christmas back with us, and then about six days at his sister's home with his mother as another guest in the house. All of us, especially Steven, missed Vince, and we worried about how these visits would go -- especially the time spent with his mother.

It was pouring rain at his father's place, but nevertheless, Vincent had a glorious time. He played cards and developed a rapport with the other children living there. The family went on a shopping spree and bought Vince a complete new wardrobe. Vince met the man who heads your county's Juvenile Probation Department and told us "he was a real nice guy." The ride home must have been joyful, judging by the high spirited people that arrived here, although

Vince appeared to be somewhat shaken on his way home by the awesome sights of floods caused by torrential rains. Vincent sees things with an artist's eye -- that is, in more detail than most people do.

Christmas here was a happy day for everyone.

Vince had a satisfactory visit at his sister's, also, except for some boredom. Vince's niece and nephew are only three and five years old, so they are not much company for a boy of twelve. Again, it rained, and he was stuck in the house.

His mother did not stay the entire six days, and apparently she was sober while she was there. Vince tells us he was able, for the first time, to talk to her honestly about such things as her drinking, his visit with his father, and a recent "run in" his mother had with the law.

Did you know about his mother's incarceration? Ms. Brown told us, and apparently, Vince's father could not wait one day to tell Vincent about it. According to the newspapers, Vincent's mother stabbed her boy friend while both were intoxicated. She was jailed on an attempted murder charge while the stabbed man was hospitalized. It was touch and go for more than a week, but he did recover and refused to press charges, so she was released. I suppose you can get more details from the police records if you should need them.

There is one new thing about Vincent, but again, I do not mean to imply that it represents problems of any great magnitude. Personally, I attribute the following to the simple fact of being twelve years old. I've observed similar behavior before, and so far, it has seemed to pass.

Vince is somewhat harder to live with. He loses his temper. He screams, "That isn't fair!" when things don't go as he would like them to. He has been caught several times in lies, lately, but maintains steadfastly that he never lies. It's simply that "we didn't understand what he meant." Sometimes he is reasonable; sometimes, very unreasonable. Occasionally he goes out of his way to start an argument over nothing at all. I might add, because it supports my "phase" theory, that he currently requires far more sleep and food than is usual for him. At times, he goes to bed willingly as early as 7:30. He can and often does put away a complete meal when he gets home from school in the afternoon, puts away a substantial dinner, and asks for a large bedtime snack.

Another thing, though, that I doubt I've ever told you about Vincent. He is absolutely honest about money and property. If he doesn't buy milk at school, he returns the dime. If money is left lying around the house, he never notices it nor touches it. He has never even borrowed anything out of Steven's or our room without asking first. Generally speaking, "things," that is, material things, hold no interest for Vincent unless they are absolutely vital to his art work or to his ball games.

Our house has been condemned for a new freeway. This means we must move before September. We are house hunting, so far without enthusiasm. We will, of course, notify you of our new address when we have one.

I hope I have covered the matters of interest to your office.

Cordially

March 12, 1978

Dear Ms. Brown,

I would very much appreciate your help, probably in the form of a letter. We have a problem which is not yet severe, but which, I believe, could get that way.

When Vincent's mother phones, she usually talks only to Vincent. She always phones to tell him that she will arrive, on schedule, on the first Sunday of the month. Usually, she does arrive.

Last Sunday morning, however, she phoned at about 9:45 to say that she had to work and couldn't come. She told Vince she would come next Sunday. Fortunately, I was in the room and, guessing what had been said, I took the phone. I explained to her that all of us already had plans for next Sunday.

At that she really blew up. She had a tantrum on the phone telling me, at the top of her voice, that "Who did I think I was? After all, Vincent was <u>*her*</u> *son and she had every right to see him whenever she wanted to." When I could get a word in, I suggested she might call you to discuss the matter. This, as you might guess, only brought on a new tirade against you -- particularly on the subject of your letting Vince visit his dad. Now, I admit that I am as susceptible as the next person to a full blown tantrum-- especially when it comes from an adult, so when she quieted down a bit I suggested that she might come Saturday. This idea she liked and said she would. Then she began a long recital of her personal problems which I cut off as politely as I could, because I had a class to teach. She accepted this and assured me that she would call me on Monday to tell me all her problems. (She did not, thank heaven!)*

Yesterday, Saturday, she called Vincent and explained that "her car broke down" (again!) and that she would come to see him next week. I was home. She did not ask to speak to me.

Now, I realize that things happen and one cannot always keep appointments. And I do think she enjoys these visits with Vincent. I want her to be able to see him; really I do! But, I would like being able to count on the first Sunday of the month. I would rather keep it that way. Also, if there ever had to be a change, I feel that I, and perhaps you -- not just Vince -- should be consulted.

I would sure appreciate anything you might do to prevent this kind of thing from occurring in the future.

Sincerely

Ms. Brown sent me a carbon copy of a letter she wrote on March seventeenth. That letter said:

"Dear Mrs. V,

"There appears to be some confusion regarding equitable and reasonable visiting arrangements.

"In order to be certain there is no cause for confusion, I must insist that you adhere to the original arrangement of your plan to visit with Vincent on the first Sunday of each month. I realize circumstances will arise indicating a change of the day would be reasonable, but I think it would be more equitable for all parties if you were to cancel completely if you cannot make it on a given first Sunday. If you wish to see Vincent twice a month, then we need to establish another specific day of the month, so that the foster parents and the boy would know what to expect.

"It is not our aim to make things particularly difficult for you but rather to have a program which is reasonably tolerable for all -- that requires compromise.

"Thank you for your assistance.

"Very truly yours,
"G. Brown
"Deputy Probation Officer"

At the bottom of that carbon copy she penned by hand in red ink:

"Dear Grace,

"I trust the above will suffice. I didn't want to get too specific nor to make her any angrier than she already is. Don't panic at the idea of a second visit. This is more in the nature of being -- shall we say -- conciliatory. If she takes me up on the offer, I'll be very much surprised.

"G. Brown"

I wasn't surprised. Vincent's mother immediately took up Ms. Brown's offer of two visits a month, to the dismay of Vincent and the rest of the family.

With persistent searching, we found a home on the bay that everyone approved. We had to wait for its completion, however, so I set about building furniture at night school for the new, larger house, while Vincent and Steven tried their hands at home boatbuilding. In spite of their surface enthusiasm, it was clear to Bill and to me that both boys hated the idea of moving. Vincent's nightmares returned. He stopped painting entirely.

One Sunday, Vincent's mother called to tell us she would be unable to get to our place before noon. I suggested she might pick Vincent up at the Friends' Meeting House and gave her instructions how to find it. She agreed to that arrangement.

Our meeting went as usual that Sunday; more quietly, perhaps, than some meetings. Towards the end, I noticed the door opened and Vincent's mother came in. She did not sit down, but stood in the rear for the final several minutes. After the usual shaking of hands that ends the meeting, I pointed his mother out to Vincent. The two of us went back to join her. She did not return my smile.

"What kind of a place *is* this?" she demanded, a bit too loudly.

I indicated we should move out of the meeting room. Once outside, I asked her, lowering my voice, "What do you mean?"

"I can't believe you could bring my son to a place like this!" she stormed. "That room is full of hippies! I don't know how many beards and sandals I saw. In fact, *nobody* even bothered to dress properly for church. It's the most disgusting thing I've ever seen!"

Without another word the attractive blonde woman took Vincent's hand and dragged him down the front steps of the gray, wooden building.

She never again showed more than cold politeness toward Bill, Steven, or me.

Bill contracted to teach at a special federally funded teachers' institute at a college in Oregon, and we were all glad to get away from the neighborhood of boarded up houses and empty streets where we still lived. We gave the house to two girls who were university students, rent free, with the undertanding that they were to keep the roses and lawn watered and take loving care of Ginger, our cat.

In Oregon, Steven discovered competitive swimming, and Vincent joined a local baseball team. The quiet, small town life appealed to all of us more than we had expected it to. We rediscovered wildflowers, neighborly visiting, walking, and fishing. Vincent studied every boat he saw for construction details and diligently worked on his rowing. No one we knew had a sailboat, but Vincent assured us, "Anybody can sail."

The boys and I returned home before Bill, because I had promised to help with an educational conference in early August. We took the train home; an extraordinary experience. Vincent and I, with shared reverence, watched as mountain gorges, rivers, waterfalls, and tiny towns rushed by. We forgot all about food until it was too dark to see outside the train. Steven, only occasionally impressed, read an entire science fiction novel.

I had written of our planned return to the house-sitting young women, encouraging them to stay on as long as they liked. We took a cab to our house and were surprised to find all the lights out. With more of the neighborhood houses boarded up than when we had left, our place looked doubly desolate.

As we unlocked the front door, Vincent began to call, "Ginger! Ginger!" It did seem strange not to at least be greeted by our affectionate cat.

We started to hang up the wrinkled clothing from the suitcases. About forty minutes after we had arrived home, a young woman I had never met before came into the house with a man. She seemed startled to see us.

"Oh, are you the people who live here?" she asked.

"Yes. Who are you?"

"I'm one of the tenants," she told us.

"Tenants? How many of you are there?"

"Five," she said.

"And do you pay rent?" I asked.

"Of course," she told us. "Two hundred dollars a month."

The two girls to whom we had given the house had not informed us about their "subletting" business.

"Where's Ginger?" Vincent asked the minute he could interrupt.

"Ginger? Oh, you must mean the cat. Could you excuse me just a moment? I have to say goodbye to my friend here."

When she finally returned, Vincent could stand it no longer. "Where's Ginger?" he repeated impatiently.

"Well, you see," she began slowly, "we actually have no idea. She kind of disappeared."

"Disappeared? What are you talking about?"

"Well, there was nobody here most of the time, so she just wandered away."

"Why weren't we notified?" I asked. Anger was bubbling up inside me.

"Well, we didn't see any point in worrying you," she answered.

Vincent was already in tears, and Steven's lips were tightened into a narrow line.

"Didn't it occur to you that I might have had some idea as to where to look or how to advertise or something?" I asked, my voice rising.

"Well, it wasn't my problem," she replied coolly. "I never even saw your cat. Sorry." And with that she went to bed.

I spent the next hour calming both boys, unpacking, and trying to convince myself not to let anger cloud my judgment. The first two things I did reasonably well, but my temper was high when the girls to whom we had entrusted our house arrived home at 3:00 a.m.

They told me they had received word of our arrival, but decided we could manage for ourselves. Yes, the cat was gone. Too bad, wasn't it. And yes, they had sublet part of the house. Why not? It was left in their care, wasn't it?

I told them to vacate by the next morning.

They said they could, but that the five tenants could not, since they had signed contracts until the end of the month.

I assured them I would call the police if necessary.

All the girls were out of the house by the next afternoon.

The loss of the calico cat he had once nursed back to health was a tragedy that Vincent could not accept for weeks. He walked all over the ghostly neighborhood calling, "Ginger! Here, girl!" uselessly.

August 4, 1978

Dear Ms. Brown,

I would appreciate a call from you as soon as possible re Vince's visits with his parents.

His dad called tonight. Seems he's a neighbor of Mr. Mills, the probation officer I have been asked to send occasional reports to. Vince's dad claims that Mr. Mills said it was quite all right if he had Vince for "two, three, four, or even five weeks." He was all set to come right over. I reminded him of my need for official verification, and he assured me that I would be hearing from Mr. Mills very soon. He said that he didn't know if Mr. Mills would be writing to you, too, or not. "Probably not."

We notified Vincent's mother as soon as we returned from Oregon. I expect to be hearing from her soon, too.

I asked Vince if it were all up to him what he'd like to do. After some consideration, he said that he'd like to see his mother for one day, his dad for no more than ten days. The main thing that worries him is how such an arrangement would worry his mother. He very much enjoyed the visit with his dad last December, but does not feel ready for an extremely long visit at this time. Please call. Thanks.

Vincent's visiting began the way he had suggested. Steven was miserably lonely. Most of the children in the neighborhood had moved away or were on vacation. Steven's face began to show the sad expression that he had when he was little and used to ask, "Mommy, why don't you get me a sister or a brother like Kathy's mother did for her?"

When the education conference began, I sent Steve to stay with my sister and her three children.

I commuted daily to the conference from my quiet house on the deserted street. I wondered if I had overreacted sending away the university girls who had lived there in early summer. When I felt too alone, I would telephone Bill in Oregon and run up a large bill.

The sponsoring Institute announced a special jazz concert on Thursday night for participants in the conference. I was glad to go.

Around the corner from our house, on Short Street, there lived an eighty year old widow in a one room, rebuilt garage. She was lonely, very fat, and talkative. We usually avoided Mrs. Hill because she complained a lot, particularly about children and cats. It is difficult to explain to some people why children find it necessary to take running leaps over their shrubs rather than use a sidewalk, and why cats like to stalk birds. But now that we were the only human beings left on the block, our relationship was growing more friendly.

On the night of the jazz concert, Mrs. Hill was sitting alone, as usual, watching television. Suddenly the set and the lights overhead began to flutter. They flickered just a little at first, then went out and came on for longer periods of time. A few minutes later, her doorbell rang.

"Who is it?" Mrs. Hill called in her more than ample voice.

There was no answer.

"Who is it?" she called again.

"Electric Company," a male voice replied. "Let me in. We're having some trouble with the electric lines now that so many of the houses have been torn down."

Mrs. Hill opened the door, but her screen remained

securely locked. "You're from the Electric Company?"

"Yes," the young, casually dressed man replied. His hands were empty.

"Show me your identification," the naturally suspicious woman demanded.

"It's out in the truck. Look, this will only take a minute. Have you noticed any trouble with your lights?"

Mrs. Hill refused to be sidetracked. "Where's your truck?" she asked.

"It's way around the corner," he told her. Then, impatiently, "I'm not going back there now. If you don't believe me, why don't you call the company?"

"I will," she replied. "What's the number?"

"Ask Information."

Mrs. Hill went to the telephone and dialed the Information Operator. Suddenly a weight smashed through the screen door. The elderly woman's screams were temporarily stifled by a strong arm around her throat.

I got home at about 11:30 that night. There was a police car parked in front of my house. When I pulled up, a policeman got out of his car and, before I had closed my car door, he began asking me what I thought were a lot of silly and personal questions. When he was satisfied that I had a perfect right to be there, he told me, "Now, I don't want to scare you or anything, but there was an attempted rape around the corner tonight."

"Who? Mrs. Hill?" I asked incredulously.

"That's right. She's O.K., though. I guess she's a lot stronger than that guy thought. She screamed her head off and managed to run two blocks for help. By the time we got there, he was long gone. I don't think he'll come back, but I suggest you phone us if you hear anything strange."

"Everything sounds strange, now," I told him. "Our house makes all kinds of noises, and the half torn down house next door keeps dropping things."

I went inside and phoned Bill at once. I did not tell him about the attempted rape because I knew he would have gotten into his car and been with me in record time, teaching contract be damned. With my coat still on, I told him I missed him, and chattered on and on about the conference and the jazz concert. After I hung up, I looked around the house. The back door had been removed from its hinges. It lay, foolishly, on the dead lawn in the back yard.

The next night, fourteen year old Steven was home sleeping in a sleeping bag on the floor of my bedroom. He was exhausted. The two of us had spent the day re-attaching the back door and packing our thousands of accumulated belongings.

It was time for us to begin a new life in our infant house on the bay.

11

LETTING GO

The small, silver forms darting around so close to the surface of the water outside our new back door fascinated us all. Unpacking was nearly forgotten in the joy of soaking up the new beauty and novelty. It was enough merely to be alive.

The fish seemed so eager to be caught that the boys tried to oblige with a fishing tackle. Vince stayed dry, unlike his experiences during earlier fishing attempts, but the fish weren't too interested in the bits of meat the boys used for bait. Bread interested them more, but the prey easily nibbled the crumbs from the hooks and swam away triumphantly.

Vince and Steve came up with another idea. They sprinkled bread crumbs over a small area in a shallow part of the water. Then they waited. The smaller fishes' enthusiasm brought their larger brothers, and Vince and Steve easily scooped up their choices into strainers or old cans.

But Vince could not eat them. He had known them alive, and it seemed to him immoral to eat his victims. While Vince watched in horror, the rest of us enjoyed the fresh fish as thoroughly as a farmer might enjoy the first crop from a new, rich acreage.

None of the boats the boys had attempted to make in the back yard of the old house did anything but fall apart when faced with the reality of currents. This dampened Steven's interest, but Vince seemed to enjoy such challenges.

He poked around amid the debris from building and unpacking and lashed together a raft made of plywood and two inner tubes. To this he added a metal pole and a sail cut from black plastic we used as a ground cover when camping. To our amazement, the craft sailed nobly. Vince used the sail, alone, to guide his strange looking creation. About a month later the idea of a rudder occurred to him and he soon made it a reality.

Other boys, equally new to the yet uncompleted tract neighborhood, were attracted by Vincent's unique nautical possession, and began spending their days at our place. Before summer vacation ended, Vincent, Steven, and three other boys began one of those eardrum puncturing contributions to our culture, a musical combo. To our boys' electric guitars the others added drums, harmonica, and a bass guitar. Bill and I hated the din, but the kids looked happy.

In his new bedroom, Vincent painted with renewed interest. Steven began working with more determination than skill on some built-in shelves he needed for his large book collection. Bill organized his study for the start of the school year.

With everyone busy, I felt free to accept temporary outside work that appealed to me -- an assignment that a respected local theatre director said could not be done. I was to write, direct, and produce an historical documentary play with a cast of 350 amateurs and professionals. It was an exhausting job that took most of my waking hours.

School opened, and with it many wounds I thought had healed. Both boys felt uneasy. Steven, at least, had the other boys from the combo to walk to high school with, but Vincent, only in seventh grade, had no one.

Vince pulled out his old sailor hat, long abandoned, but not discarded like his old boxes of broken toys. He walked out of the house with the swagger he put on whenever he felt particularly insecure. In the past, that attitude served as a warning to all to stay away. But at junior high school, such a tough look and sneer were interpreted as a challenge.

Vincent was on the staircase, on the way to his first class, when a dark haired boy, much taller than he, approached. He blocked the stairway. Children in the vicinity froze where they stood to watch.

"Excuse me," Vince said, with just a touch of sarcasm.

"You haven't done anything yet," the stranger replied.

The other boys and girls laughed.

"I gotta get to my class," Vince tried. "The bell's going to ring in a minute."

"You don't say. Why don't you just go on ahead if you're so worried?" he mocked.

Vince sighed. "Look, I don't want to hit you. I just want to get to class." His sneer faded into earnestness.

"Go ahead," the bigger boy said as he squared his stance on the stairway.

Vincent stood quietly for a moment, then lunged forward, pushing his head into the obstancle's stomach. The obstacle caught himself just in time to prevent falling, then began pounding fists into Vincent. Vince, furious now, pounded back, hard, fast, in the chest, torso, finally on the jaw. The challenger fell with his back on the stairs, crying.

The staircase was jammed now with spectators, many of them shouting encouragement to the little drama livening up their day. The hubbub attracted the power structure in the form of a balding, male teacher. He took both boys by their collars and hustled them to the office of the principal.

Although Vincent was unscratched and the other boy was crying and clutching an elbow, the principal addressed his exasperation only against the tall challenger. "Are you going to start another year like that, Ollie? Now see here. I've had about all the fighting I'm going to put up with from you and that's final. You are to be suspended until next week, at which time I want one of your parents to come with you to see me."

He then turned to Vince. "Give me your phone number. I suppose I'll have to see your mother, too."

Word was around the school before the day was over. Someone had beaten up Ollie. Vincent was a hero, and, as such, attracted all the wrong people as friends -including, eventually, Ollie.

Vincent hated his new school. There were no art classes of any kind. The teachers, seeing what kind of boys he teamed with, decided at once that this was a kid to teach respect for authority.

Vince came home every day alone and went straight

to his room to play the guitar or paint. He grew more withdrawn and silent.

I wasn't very sympathetic. There was work to be done. I shut myself up in the study when anyone was home, and, feeling mildly sorry for myself for not being able to tackle the new landscaping, I went through one resource book after another and wrote. I searched for quotations that I could use, poetry, old letters, music, anything to keep the two hour drama from getting heavy handed or dull.

Sometimes, while I was in the middle of an important bit of dialogue reorganization, Bill would stick his head in through the door and say, "Hey, honey. You've worked long enough. How about a game of cribbage?"

Or Steven would burst in to ask the whereabouts of a favorite shirt, or to borrow my dictionary.

Vince crashed in frequently with something like, "Hey, Mom! Listen to this great new piece I just composed!" Or to display his latest painting. "Don't touch it! It's still wet!"

To each of these interruptions I would either plead to be let alone to work in peace, or, if it came at a particularly bad time, I would get angry. It took many weeks, but I eventually had everyone trained to tiptoe around when Mom was in the sweat shop.

I needed music for my show. The leading man was a folksinger, well known locally, and it seemed natural to let him sing as much of his part as possible. One of the leading women also had a pleasant singing voice. There was some historical music I could use, but I wanted original songs, too.

"Why don't you go see Malvina Reynolds?" my boss suggested. Malvina's "Turn Around" and "Little Boxes on the Hillside" continued to be popular in our area long after they were no longer heard on radio and television, making her something of a celebrity.

Malvina Reynolds lived with her husband in an old, brown shingled house. The shingles needed paint; the yard needed love. I was welcomed warmly at the door by the lady herself, and ushered through a living room that was full of paper and record albums. Pleasantly, this white haired, cotton dressed grandmother offered me a chair at the dining table.

There was no glamor about Malvina Reynolds or her

home. She looked like the head of a church ladies' auxiliary. Her husband, retired and wasted in body from long months of illness, did his best to be helpful, clearing away some of the clutter from the table where we sat, then bringing in cups of coffee. The room looked like exactly what it was: the work place of a serious composer --nothing more.

"I'm so glad you came," Malvina Reynolds told me. "There's a Mothers' March Against Nuclear Weapons today and I simply did not feel up to taking part. I've been a little under the weather lately, but that's no excuse. I feel so guilty when I don't take part in things like that."

I wondered uneasily if she might be implying that that's where I belonged, too. She probably was not requiring it of me, but I felt the need to explain myself.

"Yes, I know what you mean," I told her. "I'm a mother, too. But, you see, this job of mine takes every waking moment I have right now."

"How is that?" she asked me. Her eyes searching my face showed that she was asking a serious question, not making small talk. I found myself telling her about my husband and our two boys. Her eyes never left my face; encouraged, I talked on and on.

Malvina Reynolds smiled knowingly when I told her how my family got into my hair whenever I tried to do serious work at the typewriter and how frustrated that made me feel. "Do you have that problem?" I asked.

"No," she replied. "My only daughter is married and has a family of her own." She did not seem to want to pursue the subject. She said, "Tell me about this show you're writing."

I explained the vast historical perspective of the undertaking. "But I don't want it to sound pedantic," I told her. "I need some songs with personal feelings so that the audience can become involved. Have you written any songs that I might use?"

Malvina Reynolds was too good a poet to waste words. She sat for a few minutes, thinking. Then she reached for an uncased guitar on a side table. She began to sing.

I was warmed by the wonder of her sweet untrained voice doing a personal concert for me. She sang of the pain of the persecuted, of the wrongness of war, of the murders of young idealists, of the guilt of "The Bloody

Neat" who, through noninvolvement, become accessories to the crimes of their society. She sang of the frustrations of being unable to solve so many of the world's ancient problems: "Too much needs doing here / That I can't do."

Then the compassionate face etched with two deep lines between its eyebrows looked up at me, smiling suddenly. "Now here's one," she said. "It's not a song for your show, but maybe it's a good one for you."

She looked directly at me as she sang:

I wish you were here to get under foot,
I wish you were here to get in my way;
To call me from work, to call me to play.
I wish you were here again.

Oh, what did I do that had to be done
And what did I read that had to be read,
When I might have turned to watch you instead;
I wish you were here again.

The monuments rise; the monuments fall;
The papers are signed and turn into chaff;
But I can recall the sound of your laugh.
I wish you were here again.

I wish you were here to get under foot,
I wish you were here to get in my way;
To call me from work, to call me to play.
I wish you were here again.

I thanked Malvina Reynolds, left, drove to the nearest telephone booth and canceled the other appointments I had for that day.

Then I went home to my family.

December 8, 1978

Dear Ms. Brown,

The Christmas Thing has come up again. Vincent's mother has instructed him to call you regarding arrangements for special visiting privileges. I expect you'll be hearing from Papa soon, too. So far, I have not.

So, Vince has asked me to ask you to call him after

four o'clock to discuss Mom and Christmas visiting.

I would appreciate it if it could be arranged so Vince would be here on the morning of the 24th because he has a dental appointment on that day which I made two months ago.

These Sundays twice a month, and all day long, are simply hell. Vince dreads them and comes home a nervous wreck. His mother is often late both arriving and bringing Vince home. Last Sunday she arrived at nine a.m. and, I believe, she had already begun drinking. (Or, perhaps she was quite ill.)

Well, anyhow, please call soon.

Cordially

The thought of Christmas again without Vince dampened Bill's and my holiday anticipation. When kids get beyond the Santa Claus stage, the main joy of Christmas lies in having loved ones around, opening gifts, reveling in everyone's fun and pleasure. The emphasis, though, shifts from things to people. Those who are absent are noticed, and in that way, seem even more present.

But we were prepared. We planned weeks before how we would keep busy all that Christmas day. While Vince spent the holiday with his sister, the three of us at home would work together to create the one perfect gift for a boy like Vincent.

First we cleared a large corner of the garage close to its only window. Then, using masking tape to give a clear line of demarcation, we painted the walls stark white. To further emphasize the area and to prevent the kind of accidents that were happening regularly to the carpet in Vincent's room, we laid a large piece of multi-colored vinyl flooring. Once the paint was dry enough, we lined one wall with shelves. Then, in Vincent's corner, we put an old lamp equipped with high wattage lights, an electric heater, a new easel set up with stretched canvas, and a palette that was actually a large scrap of formica nailed to an ancient record cabinet. On the shelves we placed a roll of artists' canvas, stretcher boards, a staple gun, oil paints, a set of good brushes, and a palette knife.

When Vincent came home late on Christmas night, Bill, Steven and I met the weary boy at the door. Our enthusiastic welcome made him brighten a bit. He smiled his appreciation.

"Do you want to see what I got?" he asked. On the couch he spread out a model boat kit from his sister and from his mother some shirts, two sizes too big.

We hardly looked at his presents. Soon, unable to restrain himself further, Steven said, "Here's a Christmas card for you from us, Vince."

Probably expecting money, Vincent opened the envelope. It was, in fact, a Christmas card with no signatures -- just the words added, "Look in the entry hall closet."

With natural politeness more than interest, Vincent did as he was bid. In the closet he found nothing unusual except for another note. This one directed him to look under the new television set, where, of course, there was one more.

The corny joke revived Vincent. With a smile that grew to a grin and finally outright laughter, he followed the "clues" all through the house, back and forth from room to room. After about a dozen such messages, he was led into the garage with Bill, Steven, and me following behind him, trying to conceal our anticipation.

When Vince turned on the garage light, he stopped short. His jaw dropped slightly; his eyes grew wide. He stood still for a moment, then said, "You guys shouldn't have done that."

He looked around his makeshift studio, first taking in its entirety, then carefully examining each part of it. Finally, he turned to us, his face shining.

"Can I use it? Now?"

"Oh, honey," I said. "It's after midnight."

"Don't be so uptight, Grace!" The remark, so unlike him, came from Bill.

I didn't say any more. Vince, his jacket dropped to the floor together with the last clue note, was already mixing oil paints on his palette.

He did not get to bed until dawn.

Steven's new high school was small, but there was more than enough to keep him busy there. His activities left him little time for Vincent, and friction developed. Arguments became louder and more frequent between the two boys. Vincent picked up several irritating techniques from his new friends at school, like putting his fingers in his ears and singing loudly when Steven tried to talk to him.

My documentary play came and went. It was quite successful in a local way, and something happened to me that had not happened when I did shows before. I fell in love with all the major actors and actresses in my cast.

Love has a way of surprising me. I didn't know very much about it until I met Bill, but loving him seemed to open up the door for more and more love, and I was unprepared for it.

The love I felt for my cast was like a physical joy when I was with them. It was all laced with getting to know each other at far deeper levels and then working terribly hard, at no small personal inconvenience, toward one mutual goal. Maybe it was the sort of things writers say happens to men in battle. I found it just a little bit frightening. The end of the show left me feeling much like I did when I lost Rena.

I couldn't tell Bill how I felt. He understands me better than any other human being, but I didn't know how he would react to my telling him I had fallen in love with an entire group of adults and children, male and female. It seemed kind of immoral to me.

But I wanted to understand, if only to prove to myself that I wasn't odd. I brought up the matter with Jo Anne, an actress who lived in my new town. We had been friends since the earliest days of the Jefferson Players.

We were sitting on my patio, trying to coax a shy, green headed mallard duck to take bread from our hands. I asked her, "Do you ever feel a sense of loss once a show is all over?"

"Oh, I should say," Jo Anne replied. "And the longer a show runs, the deeper the feeling of loss. I think it's something like post partum blues."

"How do you mean?" I encouraged.

"Well, when you're going to have a baby, you put an awful lot of yourself into it, physically, emotionally, other ways we don't understand. Then, once that baby is finally born, there's all that energy with no place left to go. It leaves you acting very strangely when you should, by all rights, be glad it's over."

I felt better already. Putting down my piece of bread, I asked, "And how do you feel about the cast of a show that's over?"

"If I'm not going to see them again I feel like someone very dear to me has died. I think that's the hardest part."

"Why is that?"

"Because we've fallen in love with each other."

"Isn't that -- well, dangerous?"

"Dangerous!" Jo Anne laughed a kind of snort. "What a world we live in! Do you realize how severely we try to restrict whom we may or may not love? It's 'normal' to love one's own spouse, but not someone else's. It's O.K. to love your baby, but 'sick' to love your teenager as anything more than a platonic friend. Several plays have been written on that little doctrine!"

"I see what you mean," I replied, relieved. "One may love an animal or a sibling of one's own sex but not a sibling of the opposite sex."

"Sometimes," Jo Anne said. "Only sometimes. There are also rules about which parent you may love and under what circumstances. I have a sister-in-law who won't rent an apartment in her building to any two men for fear they may be gay," she said, making a little swishing movement with her hand.

"And you don't agree with these rules."

"I certainly do not!" Jo Anne pronounced in her best stage voice. "I tell everybody that I am absolutely crazy about my son, and let them think what they will. Now, if I said I couldn't stand him, no one would lift an eyebrow."

"Sure," I agreed. "You see articles about the importance of 'letting off your hostilities,' 'working out your aggressions,' and such. Then there are those places that teach boys how to 'take care of themselves' -- in other words, to fight. All these forms of violence are to be coped with, but they're considered perfectly normal."

Jo Anne nodded. "Even prejudice is considered 'unfortunate but normal' while it obviously runs in epidemics like measles."

We sat quietly for a few minutes, enjoying our silence as only old friends can. Then Jo Anne said softly, "You know, it wasn't always llike that. In the Bible David loved Jonathan, Jesus loved his youngest disciple, and no one made sarcastic remarks. You've probably read enough anthropology to know that many cultures, some of them still around, take entirely different outlooks -- even considering hatred, anger, and competitiveness as illnesses."

"Then *why* are we so afraid of love in all its various faces?" I asked myself more than I asked my friend.

"We're the aspirin economy, remember?" Jo Anne answered. "Love can cause hurt, particularly when it's mixed with liberal dashes of something else like power, lust, or possessiveness. Why do you suppose you and Bill are the only foster parents you personally know? Because people don't have room in their homes? Bosh. It's because from babyhood on, most of the people you and I know have been taught to avoid pain at any cost."

"Don't you?"

"I used to," she replied. "Then, finally, it occurred to me that everything I'm really proud of cost me a lot of pain, especially in the early stages -- having a baby, my college degree, every dramatic role I ever attempted, even my marriage. But, if I had tried to avoid pain, I'd have none of these now. Maybe the pain helped me to appreciate them."

"And to appreciate life," I added.

"And to *love* life," Jo Anne corrected.

"No wonder you're such a terrific actress," I told her.

May 6, 1979

Dear Ms. Brown,

You must be getting awfully tired of hearing from us. I'm sorry. But things are bad, and I feel they're getting worse.

Two weeks ago, Vincent was brought home at 11:25 p.m. Tonight he arrived at 11:45. Both times we were notified at 9:30 p.m. that he would be late. The arrangement is that he is supposed to be here by nine. Both times we were told long, involved stories about the trials and tribulations of the long trip back and all the good reasons he should not have to come home early. Last time, as I believe I told you, Vincent's mother was angry that I would not permit her to keep him overnight.

We feel that something devastating and definitive has got to be done about all this visiting business. Bill has some ideas and suggestions on the subject. Please phone and talk to him about it.

As always, many thanks.

Cordially

Ms. Brown did not call. We needed her help desperately at that time, not for any big problems, but for the multitude of small ones that were growing, by the weight of their numbers, harder and harder to cope with.

I was at the school more often now to talk to teachers who did not like Vincent at all. The English teacher complained about his handwriting. The social studies teacher complained about his attention span. The math teacher was tired of late papers. Every teacher and the principal warned me about the bad company Vince was keeping. Vince was evasive when we tried to talk to him about these matters. We never met any of his new friends. Perhaps he knew we would not approve of them; or maybe he did not want those boys to know of his love for art and music. These could not fit in very well with his "kid that beat up Ollie" image.

At home Vincent was restless. He filled his after school and weekend hours with painting, singing to his guitar, and picking fights with Steven.

His bicycle gathered dust in the garage. The kids in our neighborhood laughed at others who rode bikes, calling them babies. Boys of junior high school age either thumbed rides or walked, so that erstwhile pleasure was abandoned.

One day, Vince left his wallet in the pants that he threw into the laundry. When I removed the wallet, a letter fell out. It was from Vincent's father. To my knowledge he had never written to Vince before. Perhaps this letter was in the box with a watch he sent Vince for his birthday. "Dear Son Vincent," it began.

"I hope you like the watch. It is made by the Bulova watch company, even though it has a different name. It should be good. I'm sorry I am getting it to you so long after your birthday.

"I am going to talk to the social worker people tomorrow about getting you. I think it's time you lived with your own father, and we can make room.

"Love, Dad"

I don't know how long Vincent carried around that letter. I had heard nothing about custody proceedings, so I assumed that this was one of the thousands of unfulfilled promises his parents had made to Vincent since the day he was born. What did surprise me, however, was that Vincent carried the letter with him. To us, he was our son. But perhaps, very deeply, he really longed to live with people of his own blood; people who bore his own last name.

When Bill and I talked about the letter that evening, Bill made a point that had not occurred to me.

"Well, the fact is, Vincent is ready to take on that family," he said. "Of course he isn't 'perfect,' whatever that means, but Vincent is the first foster child we've ever had that we were able to 'finish.'"

Perhaps that was true. Vincent now appeared able to cope with anything except his mother's drinking. When he visited her apartment, he came home torn between love and disgust. The strength he had been accumulating over the five and a half years he had been with us seemed depleted after each Sunday spent in his mother's apartment.

June 28, 1979

Dear Ms. Brown,

Vince is really suffering. His nightmares have returned, and last night for the first time that I know of, he was sleepwalking. (We had one other foster child who used to do that often.) I had a hard time getting Vincent back to bed, and when I did, he clung to me and did not want me to leave the room.

I feel that his mother could quite easily undo everything we've tried to do for Vince. We take him to Meeting; his mother tells him it's a bad church -- just a bunch of kooks and hippies. He was getting somewhere with his painting until his mother told him that he was a genius and needed no training or guidance. Adding to the point, she took home all of his water colors for herself, maintaining that any talent he had came from herself, so he owed the paints to her. She has told him that we and our friends are Communists. It goes on and on.

I really wish you would do something about curtailing this destructive influence. Otherwise, I can only foresee Vince following along puppy-like in his mother's footsteps no matter what you, Bill or I try to do. I believe that a few hours once a month of that woman are about all Vincent's health (and our patience) can take.

I appreciate your interest in Vince and his welfare, and I also appreciate that I can write to you this honestly.

Cordially

I was mistaken about Vincent's father. His own alcoholism well under control, he went to court and asked to have the boy placed in his custody. The judge lectured him on the necessity of "regularizing his relationship" with the woman he had lived with for seven years and who had borne him two other sons. The father tried to explain that the financial burden of winning two divorces from uncooperative spouses, his and Carolyn's, would bankrupt him. The judge was unmoved on the matter of legal expenses, but assigned Vincent to his father "on a temporary basis" nevertheless. Predictably, "temporary" proved to mean "permanent."

I don't know why Vincent's mother did not fight the ruling. She must have realized that she would probably never see her only son again until he was full grown and on his own. Perhaps our family seemed to her the greater threat to Vince, whom she, too, loved.

It was love that enabled Bill, Steven, and me to agree with the judge and with Vincent, himself, that the father who wanted to make a home for his son should be allowed to do so.

The four of us, foster family as well as natural mother, loved enough to let go.

There is a sound the heart makes. You can hear it if you will only bother to tune in to those communications that come from beyond words. It can come from people of both sexes and all ages; from people close to you and people you hardly know. It may come through the eyes, or perhaps through some part of us we don't yet know. It can be a cry for help that is inexpressible in words, because the kind of help needed is not fully understood. Or it can be a high pitched "Understand me! Please, just understand me! I don't even understand myself!" Sometimes the heart asks only that you notice it is there, so that the owner may be sure he truly exists.

* * * * *

Symbolically, as well as actually, Vincent threw away almost everything he owned. He kept a few favorite clothes, all of his art supplies, and his guitar. We insisted he also should keep his bicycle.

Vincent's short, balding father did not want to talk to us. He came to get his son in a small Volkswagen. It was necessary for Bill to drive to a hardware store to find a piece of rope for tying the guitar on top. The rest, except for the bicycle which was to be sent up later, miraculously fit inside, still leaving room for the long haired, green eyed boy, with the fine, straight posture.

Vincent shook hands in a slightly embarrassed but manly way with Bill and Steven; then he hugged me hard, looked into my filling eyes with his own wet ones, smiled slightly, and was gone.

Bill turned to me with overstated cheerfulness and said, "Let's take a long drive. Somewhere up in the hills where we've never been before. Then we might try some new restaurant."

It was a lovely ride. I tried to look at the plants, at the buildings, at the way the sun did things to colors, the way Vince had taught me to look at them. I only wept a little. I don't think Bill knew that I wept at all. But Steven knew. Several times he reached over and touched my hand or my shoulder just slightly, with a warm message in his touch.

About a month after Vincent had left us, Steven came to me and asked, "Mom, when are we going to get some more kids?"

"What's the matter, honey? Do you miss Vince?"

"No. Not really. I thought I would, but I don't."

"Are you lonely?"

"No."

"Then, what is it?"

"Well, Mom . . . it's just that we have this big house . . . and the bay . . . and so much. You know. It just feels right that we should have more kids living here."